BETWEEN KINGS

The City Between: Book Ten

W.R. GINGELL

For more information on the *City Between* series (and the two other series set in the Between world) you can sign up to:

The WR(ite) Newsletter!

This is where you'll hear about all new publications, serial WIPs (with access to read as they are written), and specials on my backlist. You'll also get to hear more about Australia, including why I like to write what my friends affectionately call "crikeycore".

CHAPTER ONE

THERE ARE SOME THINGS IN LIFE THAT YOU HAVE TO LEARN FOR
yourself. You know: how to make the perfect cup of coffee; how
to step between the layers of the worlds without getting stuck
somewhere you don't want to be; who you should trust and who
you definitely shouldn't. That sort of thing.

Then there are the things that should go without saying.
Throw away the milk after it's chunky and smelly; run when
something with teeth bigger than your forearms looks at you the
wrong way. Maybe don't keep a serial killer locked up in your
parents' bedroom.

G'day. I'm not really Pet anymore—don't actually know who I
am—but you might as well keep calling me Pet for the sake of
consistency. Life's confusing enough already, and there are a few
too many people out there who know my name. Better not to
spread it around any more.

Like ogres, the world has layers. The human world is on top,
with another world Behind—full of fae, vampires, and stuff that
goes *bump, scream, burp* in the night—hiding just beyond what you
can see. Then there's Between, the sticky middle, where you
might run into something human or something Other, depending

on how you see the world. Between, that world of possibilities that might include wonders and definitely includes death, a place where the cricket bat you're carrying can be convinced that it's a sword just in time to help you fight off the troll you're certain was a fire hydrant two seconds ago.

You might think that the human world is the most important and powerful, being on top—and that's an opinion, I suppose. You're pretty quickly told otherwise when you deal with behindkind, though, and given the fact that humans on the whole are pretty easily killed compared with most behindkind, you'd probably have to admit that we're not the most powerful.

I can admit it. The thing I can't admit to is that humans are less intelligent, important, or valuable than behindkind because they aren't as physically powerful.

We have to work harder to stay alive, that's all. And when your world includes vampires, werewolves, fae, and trolls, you have to be informed, as well. Not many behindkind are willing to talk to humans, let alone tell them stuff—ask me how I know! And most of those behindkind are pretty willing to betray, trick, or otherwise dispose of any humans who happen to be in their way.

Which brings us to now. The now where I'm being squashed in the arms of a terrified vampire who has gone protective-mode and is snarling over my shoulder at anyone who gets too close even though there aren't too many people left to get too close because about half the people who *were* in the house have now disappeared.

The now where I've got a serial killer locked up in my parents' room.

It's not a random serial killer, mind you. It's one of the ones we know—the one we've been looking for over the last year. The one who was one of us.

"You better start making some sense, or I'm going to reach into your head and start pulling out answers," I said to our resident serial killer. We'd just got out of the Heirling Trials—all of us still alive, for a wonder—and now Zero, Morgana, Ralph, and Sarah had disappeared, and I wanted to know why.

"Shall you?" said Athelas. I thought he went a shade paler, but he only smiled at me.

It was familiar, that smile—he had smiled at me the same way nearly every day for something like a year.

I said shortly, "Yeah. And if you think I can't do it, you've got another think coming."

Our lycanthrope, Daniel, all sharp and furious, asked, "Did he do this, Pet? Did he make the heirlings disappear?"

That question appeared to amuse Athelas. "Only in a manner of speaking," he said. "And if one considers cause and effect. If one is going to do so, one could also suggest that the Pet is responsible for this situation, given that it happened as a direct result of shutting down the Heirling Trials before a true choice had been made."

"The old man is trying to pick a fight," Jin Yeong said warningly. He snarled slightly at Daniel, who was also pretty close to snarling.

"Look at you, being all emotionally mature and stuff," I said, looking up at him rather blindly. "Daniel, don't let Athelas bait you. He's really good at telling lies when he tells the truth."

"You are safe, and I do not care very much about the wolf," Jin Yeong said with devastating honesty, while Athelas murmured, "What a delightful compliment!"

I said directly to Athelas, "You said that the king has our friends. What did you mean by that?"

"He stole them away by Name," said Athelas. "I expected him to make his move somewhat more quickly, I must admit, but it would seem that all has turned out for the best."

"The best for *who*, exactly?" I demanded, cold right to my toes. "And how can he have them? We just got out of the Trials!"

"Triumphantly, in fact," Athelas said, nodding. He didn't look as deathly injured as he had looked half an hour ago—he must be healing now that we had him out of the prison we'd found him in —but there was still the same desperate tiredness to his eyes that gave me a pang to see, overlaid by a thin veneer of his usual calm amusement that seemed as though it would only take a slight blow to shatter.

It hurt in a still-broken part of myself that I could feel sorry for him, even now. I said harshly, "We're not talking about the Trials. I want to know what you meant before when you said that it's all up to Zero now."

"The king has them all—all the heirlings whose names he knew. He's started a Challenge."

"He doesn't have me," I pointed out.

"He does not. It's very interesting."

"Challenge is very Not Good," said Jin Yeong, somewhere around my ear. His arms had stiffened around me, too.

From the curious, thinly amused look on Athelas' face, Jin Yeong must not have been translating for him any longer. Serve him right. Sometimes it's obvious that Jin Yeong is exactly as petty as I am; refusing to translate his Korean to English for people he didn't want to understand him was also something I would have done.

I stifled the desire to kick an answer out of Athelas, and asked shortly, "What's a Challenge? We just had a Trial."

"The Heirling Trial is what happens when a critical mass of heirlings begin to become obvious—the world Behind itself takes in as many as are officially within the parameters of what it means to be an heirling. A Challenge is a direct call by name from one heirling to another—or the king to multiple heirlings—to come and fight to the death."

"How does the king have everyone else if he doesn't have me? He knows my name."

"Yes, it's very curious," said Athelas. "One might almost presume that he finds you too inconvenient to deal with at close quarters."

"I don't care what he thinks," said Daniel, from beside me. "He's not pinning Morgana into another arena and killing her. I don't care if he's king, and I don't care what the laws say—I'm getting her out of there."

"Of course we're getting her out of there," I said impatiently. The impatience was probably a result of the vampire spit still circling around in my blood from the last couple of days, and I knew it was a ridiculous thing to say.

I didn't need Jin Yeong's murmured, "Yes, but how?" to know that it was an impossible task.

I mean, technically speaking, we'd just got back from finishing an impossible task. Maybe that was why it felt so breathtakingly *unfair*. We'd *done* the thing. We'd beaten the impossible. We'd escaped the inescapable. And now some fae with overgrown limbs and a bad haircut had put us back at square one.

Back to impossible.

"You'll find it somewhat difficult to get into this arena," Athelas said. "More than getting out of the Trials, I should think. Your energy would be better spent elsewhere. Your friends are gone, and there's nothing you can do about that."

"You blokes keep saying stuff like that," I said, though it felt hollow. "And every time you do, there's always something I can do about it."

There had to be something I could do about it, because there was no way I was going to find out that Zero was my (great great) uncle and then lose him to the King of Behind for a stupid fight that none of us ever wanted to join in the first place. He was the last of the family that I had—real, blood family, anyway—and I had already lost too many people.

Athelas' head rolled against the back of the chair, and I saw the shadows in his grey eyes. "So you say," he said. "But in this case, I think you may very well end up helping only the king."

He was playing games again. I knew that. And I knew the way he was using his words: Athelas expected me to help Zero, and in helping, to have no option but to make him the next king of Behind. That had probably been his plan all along—it had been Lord Sero's, after all, and the two of them were connected indissolubly. And now he said that in the plainest of ways, by talking about the king—not the king now, but the king he had in mind.

"Don't think that I don't know you're trying to manipulate me," I said to him. "I know how this bit goes: you blokes all tell me that something won't work and can't be done, then I go and do it because you keep underestimating humans. I'm going to find Zero and the others, but I'm not going to help him become king, so you can stop pretending to disapprove."

"Happily for the fate of the worlds, I should very much doubt your wishes have anything to do with it," Athelas murmured. "Should you find my lord, you'll no doubt be pulled into the succession whether you will or no."

"Yeah, we'll see about that," I said.

"The old man never stops his tricks," Jin Yeong said. He had loosened his hold on me enough to let me wriggle free, but there was a wary look to his eyes. "And now that *Hyeong* is gone, how will we keep him under control?"

"I'll see about that, too," I told him, feeling the tenseness in my jaw. I was probably looking pretty mulish, because I saw the sharp grin come and go on Jin Yeong's face.

"Talk so that everyone can understand," Daniel said.

Stroppy little wolf.

I jerked my chin at Athelas. "Really? You want him to understand what we're talking about?"

"I suppose not," he said grumpily. "What are we supposed to do now, Pet? You're the one with the ideas."

"First of all, we're not gunna kill the king in the Challenge arena."

"I'm happy to kill the king," Daniel said flatly.

"Me too, but I'm not going to do it as part of anyone's plan—

and I'm definitely not going to do it somewhere that it'll make me king if I do. I wouldn't give him the satisfaction. Or Athelas."

"Speaking of..." said Daniel significantly. "Maybe we'd better go back downstairs where he can't hear anything he shouldn't hear."

"It would be safer to kill that one," Jin Yeong said.

Athelas may not have been able to understand the words, but I was pretty sure he understood the underlying threat to them.

"Yeah," I said. "But I have a lot of questions and that's not how I do things."

"*Arra*," Jin Yeong said, nodding. "So I did not say we should, even if it is more wise."

Daniel, with a touch of impatience, asked, "Coming?"

"You lot go ahead and start without me," I said. I had a few things to see to before I went downstairs—first and foremost of those being to make sure Athelas wasn't going to be able to get away from whatever Zero had done to the room to keep him in there. Even if Athelas wasn't fully healed yet, I didn't trust him not to make a break for it—nor did I think it would be easy to keep him imprisoned if he really tried to get away.

"I will stay," said Jin Yeong, his nose lifting very slightly as Daniel left the room. To Athelas, he said coldly, "Old man, if you try to injure her, I will *bite* you."

"Is that what happened to my lord's father?" inquired Athelas. "I'm quite certain I would not be here if he were still alive, and I heard a murmur a little while ago that there had been a bite of some sort."

"I bit him," I said. "He's as dead as a doornail. I don't know why you're concerned about that—he had you nearly killed and locked up. You didn't still think you were going to get a reward from him, did you?"

"Then my agreement with Lord Sero senior appears to have run its course," Athelas said, as if to himself. "Either his death or mine ended it, of course, but how delightful to be the surviving party!"

It should have sounded triumphant, but it had that same weary, grey sound to it that Athelas had had to his voice for quite some time now. That sound prodded at the small, wobbly part of myself that had trusted and even loved Athelas.

"Yeah, you're all about surviving, aren't you?" I said. "You stayed with us until you thought it was safe to go back to Zero's dad, and then found out you were wrong. Maybe you should have tried harder to kill me before you went back."

"I tried...exceedingly hard," he said. "It would seem as though the contract we had between us had something to say about that. After all, we can't all be as wildly and dangerously careless of our lives as you are, Pet. Some of us don't have the might of an involved fae lord behind us no matter what we do."

"You don't get to try and make me feel sorry for you," I said. "You lost that right when you killed my human friends."

"Not when I killed your parents? Goodness, that is a surprise!"

"You should stop talking, old man," Jin Yeong said, silky soft.

Athelas' eyes glittered with something very close to malicious amusement. "Why? Will you stand by and watch her kill me?"

Jin Yeong said even more softly, "No. I will bite you and watch you fall to pieces before she can touch you. You will not have the chance to corrupt anything else."

Athelas shrugged one shoulder, the amusement in his eyes more pronounced. "I suppose *corruption* is one word for it. The world is falling to pieces, so why should not I?"

"I didn't say I could forgive you for killing my parents," I told him. "But I know you were with Lord Sero then, and—"

"Then, after, and now," he said, shifting in his seat. "There's no difference. If you think to pull me back from corruption—"

"I'm not doing anything with you except holding onto you until we can get some information," I said flatly. "And making sure you're still around to get whatever justice your messed up world will give."

"I shouldn't depend on that too much if I were you, Pet," he said. "If you should be successful in all of your endeavours, anyone wishing me dead bar yourself will already be dead."

"Yeah?" I said. "'Cos if everything you planned to happen actually happens, Zero's gunna be the next king, and I'm pretty sure he'll be wishing you dead."

"But then, Behind politics are so convoluted," Athelas reminded me. "The chasm between what one wishes to do and what is expedient to do is often so vast, after all!"

"*Hyeong* is not the only heirling," Jin Yeong said, this time for Athelas to understand, too. "There is also the zombie and the revenant, and the little girl who has the North Wind wrapped around her finger."

"Behind is so prejudiced toward the living! One of them might survive the crowning, but would they survive subsequent challenges to the throne?"

"I'm still very much alive," I said, without tackling the question of how to survive taking the throne. I hadn't actually thought about that before, and it was just one more reason to be glad I was in no position to be a real contender for the throne. "And I'm not the only human kid you left alive, either. There's that other one—he's the one in Queensland, isn't he? The one whose file you kept to yourself."

Athelas' eyes roamed my face. "Still so terrier-like!" he said wonderingly. "It's most likely that he was in the Trials with you. One doubts that he's still alive by now."

I mean, I didn't think he was going to answer the question properly anyway—and that was all right. There would be time for getting answers later. Right now, I only wanted to ask one more question.

"You could have killed everyone, right from the start," I said. "Why play with people like that? Why risk someone like me surviving it—why risk Morgana and Ralph leaving their houses, even if they are dead? You must have known that Lord Sero would be pretty angry about it."

"One should enjoy one's work," Athelas said. "And I believe it's tradition to offer a bargain to one's playthings, after all. Even Lord Sero senior couldn't have denied as much if he'd known of it earlier."

"So playing was what you were doing?" I asked slowly.

I could feel the stirring of Between around him, but it wasn't Athelas trying to do anything; I had opened myself up more to every connection there was to see—even the ones that weren't out in the real world. Around Athelas' brown curls, memories swirled, big and bloody, inviting me in to catch them and see in first person the answers I would desperately like to know.

It wasn't exactly that they were *actually* swirling around his head—they were stuck inside, safe and squashed down so that no one could get to them, least of all Athelas, I suspected—but with my way of seeing the world, they were pretty obvious. Maybe I should say that the way they interacted with the world was what was visible. A kind of magical version of the chemical reactions you can make in the human world just by existing in it and interacting in it.

He barely shrugged, suffocated in the pollution of those memories. "One can't exist always performing merely the letter of the law, after all. To what do these questions tend, Pet? I should have thought you'd be eager to get your revenge—or are you planning on keeping that until after you find my lord?"

"No one's getting revenge," I said. "Not right now, anyway: I'm looking for a memory. I'm looking for a few, actually, so you'd better get ready."

"One should never give warning when one is about to do something unpleasant unless one is trying to incorporate the knowledge of coming pain into one's torture."

"Suppose it's a good thing I'm not trying to torture you, then," I said, and slipped right into his memories.

It's funny how stuff gets easier with practise. Your brain knows the right pathways and does what it needs to do to get you where you need to go, even if that stuff is magic and the right pathways involve seeing the world in just the right way to be able to get hold of everything there is to get hold of instead of just the stuff that's in the human world.

Funny how even though Athelas had called it torture to have memories extracted, he didn't seem to be trying to keep many of them from surfacing. There were one or two that he was making a decent effort to keep down, of course, but the rest were just sort of floating around, ready to be seized and seen.

The ones he was—carefully?—suppressing might have been interesting to me if I had really been here to get my questions answered, but I wasn't. I stored away the realisation that Athelas was probably trying to tempt me into going after the carefully suppressed memories instead of the ones that he was allowing to float free, and dipped into a nearby memory at random, taking Athelas with me. I'd known he would come with me, because if he was in here experiencing a memory, he wouldn't be lost in the depths of his mind, trying not to think of things he really didn't want me to see.

Funny how deceiving people gets easier when you know them very well, too.

The memory flowed around me, making me a disembodied Athelas who wasn't quite connected with the body or the memory, limited in what I could sense and feel. I could have let myself sink further in, but I didn't because I was here to do something else. There would be enough time to be going over Athelas' memories later, when there was some consensus about what we were going to do—right now I wasn't here to see them, I was here to trap Athelas within them. I didn't have time to be making sure that he couldn't escape while we were busy, and it was the one fitting prison in which I could think of keeping him.

The memory came to me easily, but not so easily that it was suspicious. Used to dealing with Athelas, I found that suspicious. There were other memories I could have fought for, but I had chosen this one at random and I wanted to follow it to the end. If I'd been trying to make sure I found memories he didn't want me to find, it was probably the method I would have used. I wasn't, but despite that, the memory I was following was one I was quite sure Athelas didn't want me to see. He wouldn't be so clumsy as to make it too hard to get into, either, though, so I wasn't worried about not being able to do what I'd come here to do.

Caught up in the memory, I found myself striding away from my house—from the Pet's house. The head I was in knew that it was the Pet's house and not its own. It had brief, fluttering thoughts that made up a whole but didn't connect anywhere that I could see; I caught a glimpse of a few of them. There was one that just said *ticket of return: death of a pet* that trailed back through his mind, tumbling past another that suggested quietly a similar thought: *ticket of return: clean up human risk factors.*

Maybe I muttered it aloud. I certainly thought it. "Can't even think in a straight line. You gotta corkscrew everything."

It was hard to keep hold of any of those fluttering thoughts: they didn't sit still long enough to be able to be fully read, and I wasn't sure it would have helped me too much if I had been able to read them. I had a feeling that it wasn't the thoughts themselves, but the tenuous, momentary connections they made with the thoughts around them that was the important thing.

I couldn't fathom thinking in this way—not inside my own head —and it made me wonder suddenly how Athelas existed like this. His mind divided, his loyalties even more so, and no way of being able to settle back to consider his own self or goals to gain any perspective.

It would have been hard to figure out exactly what was going on in the memory if I hadn't matched up the two flittering thoughts with the part of town I was rapidly approaching in Athelas' body. He hadn't travelled by bus or taxi; he'd moved so swiftly and seamlessly Between that I only noticed him coming out when I recognised the street he was walking down.

And he apparently knew the street very well, too: he didn't even hesitate at the gate, though he must have known he set off every fae-tripped sensor in the place.

Athelas had arrived at the headquarters of the human group, and uppermost in his mind was the curly-edged thought of *ticket of return: clean up human risk factors*. That thought stayed close, wafted around by the turmoil of Athelas' mind, and at last I understood why the scrap of thought that was *ticket of return: death of the pet* was so nearby and buffeted against the first thought so often.

This was the day. This was the day that Athelas had tried to kill me, and then had gone out to murder all of our human friends to assure his return in safety to Zero's dad.

I wasn't here to observe memories or try to find out why he had done what he had done, but I couldn't help paying closer attention to what was going on in the mind around me anyway. If I had expected to feel even a faint sense of sorrow or shame from him, I was disappointed. I wasn't connected enough to feel things easily, but I could feel the emotions nearest to Athelas' mind, and there was nothing there but a certain cool determination to get the job over and done with. He must have been just coming away from trying to kill me in my room, and there was nothing there to show for it: no regret, no shame, no sorrow at having to do something that he hadn't wanted to do.

All I could sense was the urge to get on with the job quickly and so completely that there would be no doubt at all about the fact of the death of the humans. I followed that urge, that determination, to see if it was attached to an order from Lord Sero—

an inviolable order that he couldn't help but perform—and found exactly what I'd dreaded.

It wasn't direct orders. It wasn't even something that Lord Sero had known about, let alone given contingent orders about. It was Athelas' own thought that it would be much easier to return to the older Lord Sero with the death of the Pet and the deaths of the humans as a sign of good faith. It would be something that would cover any possible slips in the past.

I let the idea of possible slips in the past flow over me without following that thread. It was stupid to have had hope or dread when it came to Athelas and his motivations.

Why should I have dreaded confirming the exact answer that had been most likely? Why should I have expected anything else of the fae who had killed my parents, my friends, and nearly everyone around me? Why had I allowed a small, sick little hope that Athelas hadn't been able to do anything but what he was ordered to do grow in my heart when I should be hating him, pushing him out of my mind, and concentrating on the friends who were still alive?

Athelas should be nothing to me, because I had been absolutely nothing to him. Worse than nothing—I'd been a momentary stop and a momentary alliance that was built on lies to tide him over until he could return to his own place. And the deaths of my human friends had been nothing but a tidying up of loose ends that would make things easier for Athelas when he returned to Lord Sero senior.

Smoothing the road was the faint thought I caught from somewhere, and it made me so tired and miserable that I must have made some sort of movement out in the physical world. I felt a warmth around my left hand and took a moment to let it sink in before I distanced myself from my own body and drew myself and Athelas deeper into the memory.

He had to be fully immersed in the experience if what I was trying to do was going to work. I felt a brief sensation of minds merging and relaxed a bit. Athelas had sunk deep into the memory, and he wouldn't easily come out.

Still, for safety's sake, I let the memory play a little longer.

"It's the old man!" said someone's voice, cheerfully disagreeable. Ezri, grinning, and with a cricket bat on her shoulder, approached.

There was a familiar echo to the sound of it, and it took me a few frozen moments to remember that I had heard Ezri say the same—or something very similar—just a few days ago through the closed network we'd used to stay in touch while hunting sirens. A ghost in the network was what we'd thought it was, and we had been right.

My stomach lurched. It really was that night.

I missed the next few words, and even some of the movements, caught in the horror of that thought and by the familiarity of their faces. It wasn't fair for me to take comfort in seeing their faces through the eyes of their murderer, but it was the only closure I had.

"I don't think he's here to talk, Ezri," said Abigail, her eyes watchful and hard, and I knew then that I would have to leave the memory soon if I wanted to avoid seeing anything that I didn't want to see.

"You are, as usual, inconveniently perspicacious," Athelas said, and I felt the vibration of it as though I had said it.

I would have closed my eyes if I could have, but my eyes weren't my own. I had a few moments of blind, awful sickness, and when I came out of that unseeing and momentary panic, the first thing I heard was Athelas once again.

"There's really nothing you can offer me, I'm afraid," he said, and as he said it, I felt my own body moving as if it were his. Two swords slicked out of his sheaths at once, swift and liquid in the draw, and his stride lengthened and grew light.

I let myself drift gently up and out, sealing the memory behind me quietly as I left him there in his own memory, caught in the same night over and over again. I didn't want to see what would come after this. I had already heard the voices of my dead human friends, caught in a loop that played their last words over and over again and I didn't want to wait and see the visual representation of it. I didn't think I could bear it.

I took my time slipping from Athelas' mind, with the steadily increasing warmth around my left hand guiding me on my way out, wary of leaving any trail by which Athelas could possibly follow me out. But all was quiet as I woke in the physical world, memory-Athelas and metaphysical-Athelas one and the same for as long as I chose to leave him there.

When I opened my eyes again, the physical Athelas I saw might well have been Athelas from a few weeks ago: pensive, lost in thought, and gently sorrowful. He looked as though he could glance up any minute and catch me watching him, but I knew otherwise.

I didn't have to speak in a softer voice, but I found myself doing it by instinct, as if Athelas could wake up if we were too rowdy. I said, "We can go now," and headed for the door.

There was a soft resistance at my fingertips—Jin Yeong, who couldn't see what I'd just done, clinging to my fingers and pulling me back with an inquisitive look.

I stopped long enough to explain, "I've looped him up in a memory. He won't come out of it unless one of us touches him, and there's already some sort of Between magic coating the room. Reckon Zero got that done before the king called him away."

"Will it be enough?" he asked, allowing himself to be drawn toward the door.

"Dunno," I said, more from habit than conviction. I was as sure as I could be when it came to something I'd done using Between tools. "But it'll have to do, because I don't have anything else. Even if he figures out that he's trapped in his own memory and wakes up, I don't reckon he'll be able to get out of the room without one of us letting him out—don't reckon any fae that might want him will be able to get him out, either."

"It would be better if he were dead," JinYeong said darkly, exiting the room after me.

"That's rich," I said, with a surprised snuff of laughter. "You were just advising me not to kill him."

JinYeong shrugged one shoulder and drew even with me on the stairs. "It is different."

"What, him being dead and me being the one to do it?"

"Yess," said JinYeong through sharp teeth, sibilantly thoughtful. He said it in English, too, which was surprising. "I am already a monster: even if I kill him, I can live happily. I think you can't."

He moved ahead as I stopped on the stairs to contemplate the odd warmth of feeling that had so suddenly spread over me. Then, as he turned back with an enquiring look, a step below me, I leaned forward and kissed him on the cheek.

"Thanks," I said.

I probably should have expected him to step swiftly forward and nudge me into the bannisters to kiss me properly, but it still took me by surprise. He had his arms around me before I was prepared for it, but the kiss was soft enough that I could have pulled away from it if I'd wanted to.

I didn't pull away. I tilted my head back a bit and pressed up instead, and although I didn't remember reaching out, my left hand was curled around the right side of JinYeong's collar a moment later.

He pressed tighter, closer, and suddenly it was too much. Too much heartbeat in my ears. Too much breathlessness and confusion and warmth. I pushed JinYeong away, and he let me do it with a warm reluctance that confined itself to my fingertips, which he still held.

"You did it first," he said, and he sounded about as unsteady as I felt.

I tried to say, "That's fair," but I didn't seem to have the breath to do it. Then a voice from around my ankles said explosively, "Lady! There are no *spoons* left."

"Heck!" I said, jumping. The old mad bloke clung to two of the bannisters behind me, his head poking as far through them as it could get, looking up at me with slightly wild eyes. I complained, "Do you have to do that *right behind me*? Hang on—you were the one who pinched all the spoons in the first place! If there are none left, that's your fault!"

"We don't need to be talking about spoons right now," Daniel said from the living room, on a growl.

I had to bite back an irritated reply, because Jin Yeong had already continued down the stairs, though he lingered at the bottom. I would have preferred to have had a moment or two longer to say something to him, even if I didn't know what it was that I wanted to say. Instead, I had to go down to the living room and join everyone else because Les liked to hang onto the banisters and burble about spoons.

Les was pulling at my sleeve and still protesting the lack of spoons by the time I got to my seat in the living room. You could say that the living room is our council of war chamber these days. Normally, I'd go and get everyone coffee, but out of the everyone I'd usually get coffee for, one was a serial killer and another had now been snatched away by magic to fight or die. The third was already sucking on a blood-bag—and he'd gotten that himself while Les was still complaining about spoons.

I might have tried to make coffee anyway, but one of the lycanthropes was doing it by then. Maybe Daniel had told them to—he was waiting in the living room, arms crossed, and I knew that he still had a lot to say.

Before I could sit down, someone knocked on the door. Luckily for me, it was the outside door instead of the linen closet door. I didn't trust the linen closet door too much these days. It could be Palomena, our friend and ally, or it could be another member of the King's Enforcers, who definitely weren't friends or allies, in so many different ways.

I went to get the door before one of the lycanthropes could get there and found Detective Tuatu standing outside.

"What's wrong?" was the first thing he asked me, looking narrowly at my face as he stepped into the house.

"Funny business," I said shortly, as the North Wind also swept through the door in a furious gale behind him.

"*Where is Sarah?*" she demanded.

She had probably felt the lack of Sarah in the house as soon as she got through the gate and into the yard.

"King's got her," I said. "That's the funny business. Her and all the other heirlings in the house except for me. We've still got the Harbinger, though."

Tuatu went faintly ashy grey. "We told her parents she was safe!"

"She was, until about twenty minutes ago."

North, her delicate, vivacious face alert, said, "Sarah's in a Challenge? All of them are?"

"That's what Athelas reckons."

This time Tuatu went wholly grey. "You've got the psycho one here?"

I couldn't help saying, "There are two psychos here," but it left me with a bit of a wobble in my chin.

JinYeong, looking pleased with himself, purred, "*Ne,*" at Tuatu and put his arm around my waist, still sucking on his blood bag.

Tuatu's eyes flicked down to that arm, then to my face. "Is he allowed to do that?"

That did away with the wobble in my chin; I grinned, warmth in my chest. "S'pose," I said. "I told him I'd date him, and I'm the one who kissed him, so—"

"You're mad," said Tuatu, but the frown went away from between his brows. "I hope you know what you're doing."

"Me too," I said. "You better come into the living room and sit down. We've got a lot to talk about."

"I don't feel comfortable being in the same house as the creepy tea drinker," Tuatu said. "Please tell me you've at least got him locked up in whatever the fae version of irons is?"

"The fae version of irons is irons," Daniel told him. "Pet did something tricky upstairs—I don't think he'll be able to get out. She's got him locked in the master bedroom."

Tuatu stared at me. "You've got him *locked* in your *parents' room?*"

"We're not going to give him the run of the place," I said, hunching my shoulders. Someone pressed a cup of coffee into my hands and I took it. Since no one seemed to be moving toward the living room on their own, I moved that way myself; the rest of them followed from the hall and the kitchen to gather around the coffee table.

"Yes, but—"

"I know," I answered Tuatu. "He killed my parents. But it's still the best place for him right now."

"Are you sure he can't get out?"

"Yeah," I said, committing myself without hesitation this time.

I might have found it hard to recall the past of how I lived my life for the years before I met the psychos, but Athelas wouldn't be able to escape the cage of his memories once he was in there. It was why he kept them so divided and piecemeal. No doubt there was a desire to avoid punishment if Lord Sero senior found anything there he shouldn't find, too, but I also didn't doubt that Athelas, once caught in his own memories, would not be able to escape.

"All right," said the detective, sitting down. "Then what's the plan?"

"I won't let Sarah be killed," North said, fluttering to a

susurrating stop behind Tuatu's seat without actually ceasing to move. "Add that to your plan."

"I'm not letting anyone get killed," I told her. "Not a single person more."

"If you're planning on getting in there to help them fight against the king, I'm in," said Daniel. "I'm staying here until then."

"Nope," I said. That was the tricky part—or at least, the tricky part to get everyone to agree to. "We're gunna have to trust Zero to keep the lot of them safe until we can get 'em out. That's not what I'm planning on."

Daniel stared at me, his brown eyes glittery and his chin mulish. "You're trusting *Zero* to do that? No offense, Pet, but he doesn't really care about any humans apart from you. I'm not going to trust him to keep Morgana alive."

"First of all, Morgana is already dead. Second of all, Zero does care about humans other than me—it's just that it got sorta smacked out of him and he's learning how to do it again."

Despite that, I could understand Daniel's reluctance: if it wasn't for a conversation that I'd had with Zero not many nights ago, I might have been worried myself. I mean, I was still a bit worried, because there was a very slight chance that Zero could decide to simplify the process and go ahead and try to kill the king instead of protecting the others as his first priority. It would make sense to that part of him that wanted to help as well as the part of him that just wanted to get down to business—killing the current king would do away with any danger that he posed, even if it gave him a chance to kill more heirlings in the meantime.

But a few nights ago, I'd seen a Zero who was still wracked with guilt about a human friend he'd seen die because that friend couldn't trust him, and I had a feeling that this version of Zero— this Zero who had slowly grown different since I'd known him— would choose to protect the other heirlings. Our friends.

And I had to trust him because there was nothing else I could do.

To Daniel, I said, "Trust Zero. Or if you don't trust him, trust me. He'll look after the others—especially in this situation, he'll look after them. I don't think he'll be able to help himself."

"What are you planning on?" he asked me, without making any promises.

I didn't blame him. I probably wouldn't have in his position, either.

"I'm going to stop the Challenge," I said. "But I need more information before I can figure out how to do that."

I took a sip of my coffee and nearly spat it out. Across the coffee table I saw similar expressions mirrored on North and Daniel's faces and put my mug down gloomily.

Heck. Next time, I was getting the coffee, hierarchy or no hierarchy.

"It doesn't have to be the king, right?" I asked. I had a nice little nebulous idea that had been building for some time—ever since I'd been in the heirling arena, in fact. I just didn't know how I could do it without tying myself to something I didn't want to be tied to.

I was still looking across the coffee table, but I was asking Daniel and North more than I was asking Tuatu. Daniel's still a gangly not quite twenty year old and North looks like a cross between a dangerously starry blue Glinda and someone's barefoot vodka aunt, but even though Tuatu looks put together and competent, he's still only human, like me. We learn fast, but North and Daniel were behindkind and were supposed to know stuff we didn't.

"What doesn't have to be the king?" asked Daniel. There was a deep frown between his eyebrows that hadn't gone away since he came tearing up the stairs to tell me that all the other heirlings in the house had disappeared.

"The challenging—" I started, and someone knocked at the linen closet door.

"If it's not Palomena, kick 'em out!" I called out to Darren and Dylan, who were both going to answer it. "She's the one with the black braids and a viking look."

Luckily for my newly fixed house, it was Palomena. I saw her stride out of the back of the house to join us in the living room and felt a cool rush of relief that I hadn't expected. So she was still alive and healthy now that Lord Sero senior was dead. That was a relief. It probably was for her, too, come to think of it.

"Congrats," I told her, hoping to surprise a smile out of her.

She gave a short *tsk* of a laugh that was unnervingly similar to Zero's usual dry laugh, and settled herself in Athelas' chair, fore-arms resting on her knees.

"I won't pretend not to understand that," she said. "I'd say my thanks but I don't fancy being in debt, even to you."

"Fair enough," I said. "Oi, what's the go with Challenges? Who can call them?"

She froze slightly. "I came to congratulate you, but if you're talking about Challenges it sounds like you're already over-confident."

"Boot's on the other foot," I said. "The king called a Challenge and snatched Zero and the others."

Palomena let out a breath, slow and thoughtful. "So we're to have the new Lord Sero as the next king, after all," she said. "That's a bit of good news—though I don't think he'll agree."

"Too flamin' right," I said. I also thought that Zero was the best option for king, but he didn't want the job any more than I did and he should have the right to refuse it. "We're trying to get them out of it before they all die."

"That will be...difficult," Palomena said. "No matter who calls the Challenge, it can't be ended until the Challenger is taken out of the equation or is successful in their enterprise."

"So heirlings can call a Challenge?" That was close to the question I'd been asking earlier, and I was asking it for the same reason.

"Only if they know the name of the person they want to call to fight," she said.

"What if you call a Challenge while another Challenge is going on?"

"Pet," said North, her eyes sparkling. "What are you planning? Are we to try and call them out by name and into our own Challenge?"

"It wouldn't work," Palomena remarked. "The only moving piece in the Challenge is the challenger; they decide the arena and call the challengees. Once they're successful or dead—"

"Dead, or just gone?" I asked.

Palomena's eyes rested on me in some amusement. "You think you can kill the king from outside the Challenge area?"

"Nah," I said. "North was close—I reckon I'm gunna call the beggar into an arena of my own choice and see how *he* likes it."

CHAPTER TWO

"Nah, I'm still working on that bit. I've got a friend or two who know the sort of thing to look for—one of them is already on the case and I'm going to see the second one today."

"That's me," said Tuatu, nodding at her. Of me, he asked, "Are you talking about the slightly criminal merman as the other friend? Because if you are, I'd like you to know that—"

"Hacked you, did he?"

Tuatu froze, then looked exasperated. "Is *that* what he did to my phone? It's been as slow as a wet week ever since he put those files on it, and I'm warning you, Ruth—"

"Nah, it's probably just all the information he had to put on there," I said. I wouldn't exactly put it past Marazul to hack an ally, but he knew that Tuatu was allied with Zero, and Zero was one person he was definitely not willing to cross. "Reckon it would have been a lot. You tried turning it on and off again?"

Tuatu shot me a nasty look. "My phone is old enough to never turn back on again if I turn it off."

I couldn't help grinning. "I bet that annoyed Marazul!"

"I don't see how you're going to get the king's name, no matter how many friends you have," Palomena interrupted, without mincing matters. "Still, as they say in the ranks, when the Pet bites—"

"They say *what* in the ranks?" I said, my eyes wide.

"Let's just say you've had a pretty big impact on our culture," she said dryly. "Especially recently. You realise I can't be involved in this in any way, don't you?"

"Yeah," I said. "So long as you don't go telling on us…"

"I'm not presently under direct supervision," Palomena said. "Nor am I subject to briefings, especially of the more invasive kind, now that Lord Sero senior is no longer…interested in proceedings."

"That's a polite way of talking about someone being dead," Daniel said bluntly.

"There are still other interested parties, but so long as they're otherwise engaged, I can't very well report to them."

"You mean that you don't have to report to the king so long as he's in the arena."

Palomena inclined her head in a nod. "So long as he's in any arena, I can't report my suspicions or knowledge to him. When he isn't otherwise engaged, it will of course be my duty to inform him that another party is trying to find his name."

Tuatu stared at her, then looked at me. "Ye gods," he said. "They're all like this?"

"That's what happens when you have a boss nobody likes," I explained. "I tried to tell you about Marazul, didn't I?"

"Yes, but—" he stopped. "This isn't getting us very far, and I don't like discussing it with someone in the room who technically isn't on our side."

"That's sensible," said Palomena agreeably. "Do you have any orders for me, Pet?"

This time I was the one who stared at her. "You want orders?"

"We've still got an agreement," she reminded me. "That wasn't done away with when my lord's father died. I'm still permitted to be useful—so if I *can* be useful, don't fail to let me know."

"I'll remember that," I said gratefully.

I would have given her some biscuits or pastries to take home with her, but we'd been trapped inside the house until today, so it wasn't like I'd been able to get to the store for baking supplies. What with the bunyip taking out half the kitchen and having to grow it back again, it wasn't like I would have had anywhere to bake until the last day or two, either.

I saw Palomena out by way of the linen closet door again instead. It was my job, after all, even if only one of my psychos was still around to appreciate it. That particular psycho was still sucking on his blood bag when I got back and plopped myself down on the couch again, but he shifted a bit to rest his arm around the back of my seat.

"I don't want to waste time chasing a name we'll probably never be able to get while Morgana's stuck in there with the king," Daniel said, as soon as I sat down. "I know you trust Zero, Pet, but do you really think you can trust him to keep anyone safe? Anyone who isn't you?"

There were still a lot of things I didn't trust Zero to do. Still a lot of things that I wanted him to be that he wasn't. But this was one thing I was certain of, right here and now.

"Yeah," I said. "And even if I wasn't, Athelas is right: there's no way into the Challenge. Reckon Lord Sero had been waiting for the last ten years for the Heirling Trials to happen; he would have had his handy little Trial doorway put into his house years ago in case he needed it to bring in reinforcements like he did. You heard North and Palomena. We'll have far better luck trying to set up our own arena and slap the king into it when we get his name."

"How are you going to stop yourself becoming king, at that rate?" asked North. "If you're successful in calling him—if you can kill him—you'll find yourself the next King Behind."

"Don't know," I said honestly. I couldn't help the feeling that there was something we were missing—some thread that hadn't quite pulled itself tight enough to be noticed. "I'm hoping there's a way we can find an heirling who does want to be king and would be a good one. If we can, I'll take them into the arena with me."

"We don't have time to wait for that," North said.

Daniel nodded and Tuatu said, "Every moment they're in there, they could be killed."

"I know," I said. "I'll see if I can get some help for finding another heirling while we're trying to find the King's name, but if we can't, I'll just have to go ahead with pulling the king out of the arena without someone as backup."

Maybe I'd be able to find a way to slip out of being king—if, as North pointed out, I actually managed to defeat the current king. It wasn't like he could be allowed to stay as king when he was still actively trying to kill people. We could sort out who was going to be king later.

"The harbinger can kill the king," said Les confidentially, from beside me.

I managed not to jump this time. I glanced over at him and said, "What, you're offering to go in with me?"

"Being king is a tricky business, lady," he said. "You should be careful. You should take many tricks with you."

"You will not go into the arena alone," Jin Yeong said, leaning forward to put his empty bloodbag on the coffee table. "*Tangyeon-haji*, many of us will go with you."

"What if one of you lot kills the king?" I asked. "Would you end up being forced to be king?"

"No," said North with a cold smile. "We'd be executed. No one is allowed to meddle with the selection process."

"Yeah, I see how well that's worked," I said sourly. "If that's the way it goes, me and Les are the only two who *can* kill the king without getting into trouble."

"Yes," she said. "There aren't many good choices for you if you don't wish to be king."

"What if the harbinger kills the king?"

"Then the harbinger selects the next king," she said.

"I'd prefer Pet as king to the bozo we've already got," Daniel said.

"Thanks a lot," I said.

"So what's the plan? I'm not promising anything—I still think we should be focusing on getting the others out—but what do you want to do?"

"Two things," I said. "We need to find the king's name, and we need to find an arena that'll give us the best advantage."

"And one more heirling," Jin Yeong said firmly.

"Yeah, but that's not a given, just a nice bonus," I said.

Slowly, Daniel said, "You need something private for the arena, right? Private but connected to Between, so that you can do your Between thing where no one else will see or get hurt."

"Or get in the way of doing what needs to be done," I agreed. I was still very much against having to kill the king and become the next king by default, but I was hoping to at least be able to capture him and see that justice—of whatever sort could be found Behind—was done.

"Why not use the Hobart Rivulet, then? The underground portion, I mean; it's under Hobart, so you shouldn't get anyone wandering in by accident, plus it's stuffed with Between. There's running water there, but probably not enough to give the king more power than he'd have anyway, and you'll be able to access every bit of Between."

"He'll also be able to use Between," I said uneasily.

I'd visited the underground part of the rivulet many times when I was a kid, and the remembrance of the quiet, peaceful power of it hit me with a sudden shock of recognition: the rivulet wasn't just Between, it was threaded with magic. I still had too many memories I was only just beginning to remember—and remembering, to understand things I hadn't while the events themselves were occurring. The rivulet was one of those things I now understood in the light of my new memories.

"Reckon he's been there before? It'd help if we know it better than he does, and I've only been down there a few times before they shut down the walking tours. I remember the magic in the walls now—don't think I knew what it was back then."

Daniel shrugged. "I wouldn't have thought the king would have been in Hobart before, let alone sitting in one of the houses here like a Uni Lit professor, but he was."

"Yeah," I said gloomily. "Don't reckon we can take anything for granted."

"We will prepare for the worst," said Jin Yeong. "And I will be there to bite him if I must."

"Getting squeamish, are you?" I asked him. "You didn't mind ripping out the golden git's throat."

"Yes, but I was *angry*," he explained. "I do not like to eat garbage."

That made me grin, loosening the knot of worry in my chest. "What, humans taste the best? How's that for irony."

"Everybody wants what they cannot have," he muttered. "Of course human blood is more sweet."

"Lucky I took a chunk out of Zero's dad instead of you doing it, then," I said. The reminder of Zero sobered me a little.

I knew he was taking care of the others—I had to trust he was taking care of them—but not being able to do anything about helping them myself was a lot harder than I'd bargained on. That discomfort kept boiling up unwelcome thoughts to the surface of my mind: unpleasant, unhappy thoughts that maybe I couldn't trust Zero as thoroughly as I'd assured the others that I could. I pushed those thoughts away because if I was wrong, a lot more than any hope of ever being able to trust Zero had gone out the window: lives would have gone out the window. Lives I cared about—lives that people I cared about cared about.

"All right," Daniel said, breaking out of his own thoughts at a surprisingly fitting time. The other lycanthropes must have been waiting for him to say something—decide something—because they all seemed to relax a little bit. "We'll trust you for now—there's nothing else I can do, anyway. Just give me something useful to do so that I can keep moving, all right?"

"Reckon you can help us scout out the rivulet," I said. "Come out with Jin Yeong and me and show us what you know. It's been a few years since I've been down there."

"We'll go first," North said, her skirts sweeping with an impatient breeze. "We have the records the humans sent to us. We can bring them to the merman and ask for assistance—you would like us to look for a human name among them?"

"Yeah," I said. "Tuatu knows; he's been looking for the same name. I want Marazul to check the human internet for the name as well, so make sure he knows to do that. There's someone else who might be able to help, but I don't want to go calling him unless I have to. I've got the feeling it's a one-and-done kinda favour, and I don't want to waste it."

Jin Yeong threw a look at me as North wafted toward the door with Tuatu in her wake: it was questioning and slightly apprehensive.

"Don't wear your best suit," I warned him, and caught the faint expression of disgruntled resignation that crossed his face. "The rivulet isn't the cleanest, and since it's closed off these days, we'll probably have to get in by the storm drains around Collins Street. It's not raining right now so it should be pretty safe, but I don't reckon it'll be real clean."

Jin Yeong muttered something about damp but didn't otherwise complain. Daniel only nodded and the lycanthropes, as if they were all on the same inaudible and invisible wavelength, started stirring around the room.

"What about the old man?" asked Jin Yeong. "Will you leave him alone? I do not trust him."

"I don't trust him either, but I don't reckon he's gunna get out of what I did to him in a hurry. Maybe Les can—heck, where's he gone *now*?"

I ducked my head into the kitchen to see if the old mad bloke had vanished in there, but was distracted by the buzz of my phone against my hip.

I pulled it out of my pocket and picked up the call to hear Detective Tuatu's voice say, as if through a saucepan, "Ruth? North says to tell you there are—sorry, did you say *brownies*?"

There was a pause that sounded like it came through a saucepan, too, before I heard his voice again.

"North says to tell you there are brownies out here watching the house: she caught sight of them as we were leaving. I hope that's useful to you."

I glanced at JinYeong, who had begun muttering to himself, bright-eyed, then at Daniel, who just looked gloomy. "Yeah, I reckon that's helpful," I said. "I dunno why, but it looks like this lot does. Oi! You got your phone working again!"

"Not for long," he said—or started to say, anyway. The call cut out before he could finish the sentence. I heard a brief shuffling noise, as if there were now a good few people in the saucepan, shoving each other, and then the dial tone.

"All right," I said to JinYeong, who was loosening his tie. "North and Tuatu saw brownies watching our house, apparently. What do you know about brownies?"

"Brownies belong to the king," Daniel said shortly. "A spy in every home, that sort of thing. Very good with cooking and cleaning and making bombs out of whatever they can scrounge from the kitchen and garden. Fantastic at listening at doors and sneaking tracker spells into your socks, and *very* good at knowing how to kill someone and clean up the scene like they were never there."

"Heck," I said, my eyes wide. "Thought brownies were meant to be helpful little home bodies."

"Very helpful," JinYeong said, stripping off his tie. "Verrry useful. I will not wear my tie; they will strangle me."

"You reckon they'll attack us if we go out?"

He shrugged. "*Kurol su isseo.* I prefer to be prepared. Perhaps they will just follow us."

"They're more likely to follow you in particular," Daniel said to me. "Looks like the king wanted to keep up with what you were doing before he decided to go with the Challenge, and didn't call off his dogs."

"We'll go out anyway," I said to Daniel. "Me and JinYeong first: they can follow us if they want."

JinYeong's brow lifted. "That will make things difficult. Shall we lure them somewhere and kill them? If they discover what we are trying to do—"

"Nah," I said, grinning. "We're not going out to look for a name and somewhere to fight; we're going out on a date."

His other brow went up. "Now? We are going on a date *now*?"

"It's a bit of a weird time to be dating," protested Daniel, quicker to catch my meaning than JinYeong. "Won't they be suspicious?"

"If there's one thing I know about the bulk of behindkind, it's that they don't tend to think about human-kind emotions much. You reckon it's going to occur to most behindkind that we're worried about our friends, or do you reckon they think we're just relieved that we're out here and safe instead of in the Challenge with the others?"

"Good point," said Daniel, after a brief moment of thought. "And they're brownies, so they'll be used to seeing humans doing human things."

"What about vampires?"

"Reckon they're used to vampires obsessing over humans," he said. "It happens all the time: a vampire catches sight of a human they like and then spends the rest of their undead life stalking the human."

"At least we do not pee on our girlfriends' houses," Jin Yeong said coldly.

"We don't bite them either, blood-breath."

Jin Yeong became faintly smugger. "You could not, even if you wanted to. You would turn your girlfriend into a dog too. I may enjoy biting if I wish, and—"

"We're not going to discuss biting!" I said hastily. "We're going to discuss brownies and how to make the best use of them following us. What do you lot reckon? Would they only follow me and Jin Yeong, or the whole lot of us?"

"Did they follow North and Tuatu?" asked Daniel, withdrawing an annoyed look from Jin Yeong's still smug face. "That should tell us. Brownies are really good at improvising when it comes to focusing on or killing their target, but they're usually blind to anything else."

"Right," I said. "Well, I'll ask the detective and you lot can get ready to go out. If me and Jin Yeong can't check out the rivulet, the lot of you are gunna have to."

Daniel only nodded, but Jin Yeong's gaze settled on me at once, eyes narrow. "You should get ready, too."

I made a beeline for the stairs with my phone to my ear, but Jin Yeong, who could obviously hear that there was no sound on the other side, wasn't fooled.

His eyes followed me through the bannisters as I went upstairs, and he said firmly, "It is a *date*."

"Okay, but I'm not wearing makeup and I don't have date clothes," I called back.

"I have already bought them for you!"

Heck, he had, too. I'd had to prevent him from stealing them outright, and I would have preferred to take them straight back to the store after our job was over, but Jin Yeong would only shrug at me whenever I asked where the receipt was, and I'd finally given up. I still had the clothes hanging at the back of my wardrobe: a pair of dark brown leather trousers, a suede jacket lined with blue silk, and a simple cowl-necked shirt in yellow satin that had each cost more than all the rest of my clothes combined. They were too nice to wear, especially the jacket and shirt, so I never had worn them.

I wasn't planning on wearing them today, either, but when I tried the leather pants on for the heck of it—they were leather and should stand up to at least as much as my jeans did, right?— they fit so well and felt so comfortingly indestructible that I tried on the satin shirt as well. That felt far less indestructible but looked much nicer than I'd expected it to look when I threw a cautious glance toward the mirror. I hesitated there in front of my reflection for a few minutes, and nearly took the whole lot off again. I didn't have nice shoes, and even if I had had nice shoes, I wouldn't have worn them: you can't fight in high heels.

Well, maybe you can. I can't. Like double-wielding, high heels are a skill that needs practise—and I had never had the opportunity to practise.

But when I pulled my battered boots on with the grim thought that they weren't likely to do the outfit a lot of justice, the dark, fashionably-worn brown of the leather trousers blended right down into the battle-worn faded black of my boots, seamlessly matching.

I looked at myself doubtfully in the mirror, very aware of the elegance of the silk shirt that was tucked into the waist of my trousers, which were far more aligned with what I was used to wearing.

It looked good. It also looked perilous, as if a single cut with a blade anywhere around my midsection would see me dead in a moment. This was absolutely not the shirt to be wearing outside if I was preparing to fight someone.

On the other hand...

"Heck," I muttered, for once in my life taking the time just to look at myself. If brownie-battering-chic wasn't a thing, I was going to make it one, because the yellow silk suited me like I would never have expected it to do if I was the sort of person who could look at clothing and tell if it was going to suit or not.

Even if I wasn't going to wear it out, it would be nice to show JinYeong how good his taste was. Maybe even to see how he liked it.

I tried to call Tuatu as I checked on Athelas on my way out—then called North instead when the call didn't go through. She answered at once and I was able to comfort myself with the information that neither of them was being followed.

Looked like the brownies were waiting just for me and JinYeong.

Athelas was just as unmoving and unnaturally still as he had been earlier when I hung up on North and left the room. Still, when I got back downstairs it was a relief to see Chantelle sitting on the couch looking very human, while the rest of the lycanthropes were in their wolf forms.

"If the old tea-drinker comes down the stairs, I'm running for it," she warned me.

"Good," I said. "It's no good trying to fight him, anyway. Are you staying alone?"

"That's what the boss says," she said, but she didn't seem bothered.

The lycanthropes left as JinYeong was still fiddling with his top button—trying to decide whether or not to button it, by the looks. He caught sight of me in the mirror, then left his button alone to turn and look at me properly.

"Ah," he said, the sound of it deep with satisfaction. "I knew that would be best."

"It's too nice to wear out," I said, startled and very slightly breathless at that satisfaction.

I was already rocking back on my right foot, and I turned as I spoke, but JinYeong caught my hand and tugged me toward the door.

"No changing," he said firmly. "We will go now, and we will date."

"All right, but if I get stabbed because there isn't enough protection in this, I'm gunna kick you in the shins."

"I will not let anyone stab you," he said, releasing my hand outside on the front patio. "And if it is ruined, I will buy more clothing."

"Thanks a lot," I grumbled below my breath, and we took to the streets.

We got to the end of the street before we saw the brownies. If I hadn't been able to sense the clustering disturbance of Between they made, I wouldn't have been able to tell they were there; the façade of school-children they were currently wearing was as dense as it was well done. I didn't think it was a fae-type glamour, because I was pretty familiar with them by now, and that thought left me with the further, unpleasant one that there was probably about as much variation in spells and magic as there was in dialect. I had as yet still only experienced a very small selection of that variety.

"Can you see 'em?" I asked Jin Yeong, beneath my breath. "The sneaky little beggars are good at this."

"Mm," murmured Jin Yeong; an affirmative. "I smell them. There are many—perhaps twenty."

"So long as we stay to public areas, we'll be fine, right?"

"They like to do their work inside where it is quiet," he said. "Shall we lose them in the crowd when we enter the mall?"

"Nah," I said. "I don't want them to know we're onto them too soon—not until we really need to get away. Let 'em follow us and think we're just dating. All we need to do today is make the brownies think we're not up to anything much and maybe visit the library. We'll head down to the rivulet if we get the chance."

"What is at the library?"

"Old newspapers, for a start," I said. "Stuff that isn't on the computers. We can have a bit of a squiz at 'em and see if there's anything there to help us out."

"That is not a word," said Jin Yeong in disfavour. He repeated it as though he was saying *rotten egg:* "*Squiz.*"

"We probably shouldn't go Between right now, either," I said gloomily, ignoring him. It would take longer to get into the heart of Hobart if we walked or took the bus—I'd gotten used to the ease of stepping Between and shortening distances, even if it did leave you more open to weird and non-human threats.

"We will take the bus," Jin Yeong said grandly, and then refused to jog for the bus that was just pulling up at the stop thirty metres or so away.

Instead, he sauntered up, holding the bus driver's eyes the whole time, and stepped aboard in a kingly fashion without so much as a thank you.

"Thanks," I said hurriedly to the bus driver, but he didn't seem to hear me.

I'm not sure he even asked the rowdy bundle of fake schoolkids if they had tickets—he certainly didn't warn them that they should be in school, and that was out of character for most of the drivers along this route.

Luckily, the driver's momentary vampire haze didn't seem to make it hard for him to actually drive, because we were on our way again in a moment, juddering down toward the city centre and trying not to slip out of the vinyl seats with every bump. Jin Yeong, at least, seemed to be having difficulties with the seat— my leather trousers had far better grip, and I was at leisure to grin at him doing his best to sit primly in his seat while the bus bounced us around.

He looked far less kingly and more irritated by the time he slid out of his seat for the last time and stalked toward the front of the bus. I followed him, openly grinning, and we found ourselves between the Chinese restaurant and the bakery along Elizabeth Street, looking down toward the mall.

Behind us, the group of brownies tumbled off the bus, shoving each other and giving a good enough impression of schoolkids to make the Chinese man leaning through the restaurant window grin.

"Reckon we better keep moving," I said quietly to Jin Yeong. There weren't too many people on the street here, and I didn't like the idea of brownies crowding around us as we walked down the road, given Daniel's characterisation of them as innovative killers.

They didn't crowd us, though; they just followed along behind, nice and natural, believably obnoxious without being unpleasant.

"I think they are going to follow us very closely," Jin Yeong said.

"I reckon," I said, my eyes on the mall, which was now just across the street. "What'll they do if we go out of the mall, though? A bunch of schoolkids following two people around is going to be noticed, and I don't reckon they want to be noticed."

"They will follow—but perhaps not all of them."

"Library first, then," I said. "It doesn't open until eleven though."

"Very well," he said, throwing a quick look around the mall. "Then what shall we do until then? What is first on a date?"

"*I* dunno," I said, staring at him. "I thought you knew! I haven't dated anyone before!"

"I have not dated either," he said, putting his nose in the air.

"Yeah, but you've been out with women before, so—"

I stopped, because he was gazing at me in what looked like absolute perplexity.

"That was for *eating*," he said. "All that was needed was a quiet place with not too much light."

"Heck," I said. "I should have done some research before we

came out. Reckon I'm supposed to be holding your hand, for starters—that's a normal thing, right?"

I slid my hand into his as I said it, entwining our fingers. At first cool and loose, his hand tightened around mine and grew warm between one breath and the next.

"I like this," Jin Yeong said. "We will walk until we know what to do. I think there are no rules."

"All right," I said. "Well, that means we can do what we want, right?"

Jin Yeong considered it, then nodded precisely. "I wish to kiss you beneath the trees over there."

"Pretty sure that's the sort of thing that'll get lots of people looking at us, and not just brownies," I said, trying to be cooler than I felt. "We'll get a drink somewhere and walk in the sunshine or something."

It felt about as perilous as the silk shirt had felt when I put it on, this moment of just walking around with Jin Yeong, hand in hand and feeling the sunshine on my shoulders. I would have thought that he didn't feel the precariousness of the situation when I looked up to see the sublime smugness of his face, if I hadn't also seen the way his eyes flicked this way and that beneath his lashes. Jin Yeong, while evidently enjoying himself, was also very much aware of the world around us.

He also seemed to be very well aware of pancakes, because when we passed the pretty little pancake shop along Collins Street he darted straight into it, pulling me behind him. I mean, it wasn't as though I had to be dragged, either.

We sat at the outside tables to enjoy the sunshine a bit longer and make it easier for the brownies to see us. If we weren't going to get the chance to do anything but go to the library, I wanted to at least get a chance to figure out how the brownies were messing with Between so effectively that I still hadn't been able to see their proper forms.

So we ate pancakes while Jin Yeong basked in the sunshine and admiring gazes alike, and I let myself float in a pancake-warmed haze so I could focus my attention on the brownies. There wasn't much for me to see, and it took a while to realise that I couldn't see much because the brownies had taken and woven Between into such a filigree of magic that their appearance almost seamlessly passed from human world to Behind world.

"Flamin' heck!" I murmured, and took another bite of pancake. "Might as well have pushed their faces into enchanted clingwrap!"

"I do not know what that means," Jin Yeong said.

"I mean that I gotta learn how to do that," I said, settling back against the back of my chair and leaning into his arm as if we really were on a date. It was comfortable, and he must have been making himself a bit warmer than usual for me, because despite the danger in the juice bar across from us, I almost felt sleepy.

I used that sleepiness as an excuse to rest my head against Jin Yeong's shoulder, and opened my gaze to the elements of Between that I'd been studying—that filigree of Between that was finer than anything I'd seen before, and that had teased magic all around it into weaving together until it made itself into something else entirely.

Just like with other things hidden Between, once I could see the fact that something was being hidden, and what it was hidden by, I started to be able to see the brownies. For a brief moment, I actually began to have an idea of what they might really look like.

First, I saw the long, clever fingers that were wide and padded at the ends, then the sunken, watchful eyes and the drooping mouths that each looked as though they were ready to make a complaint to the school principal about something that they found unacceptable for little Johnny. If I'd wanted a single word to describe the feeling I got when I looked at them, it would have been *discontent*.

I pressed a little closer to the web of Between they had woven around themselves, hoping to see exactly what they'd done to hide themselves, then Jin Yeong's fingers closed warningly around mine. "They are uncomfortable," I heard his voice say, and I drew back carefully and quietly.

"Suspicious little galahs, aren't they," I said below my breath.

"What did you do?"

"I was poking around what they've done with Between," I said. "They don't use Between like behindkind usually do—they use it a bit more like...I dunno, like I do? It's really hard to see, but I reckon I can figure out how they do it."

"Why do you wish to know that?"

"So I can do it too, of course," I said, looking up at him. "Sometimes it's good to be able to sneak into places and hide without having to stride in, grinning at everyone with your sharp vampire teeth to warn 'em not to attack."

"It is more fun to smile at people," Jin Yeong said, sniffing. "You—you are too clever."

"No, I just like knowing how stuff works," I said. "You never know when it'll come in handy. I s'pose predators don't need it as much, but—"

He surprised me by shrugging. "Even predators can die," he said. "We die because we trust our own strength and ferocity. Or we die because our anger or hunger overcomes our reason."

"That's the cool thing about vampires," I said, grinning up at him. "You're always angry or hungry or in love, and it's always one hundred percent *on*, no matter what it is. You're big, messy balls of emotion, but you don't try to pretend that it's someone else's problem."

"I am very tidy," said Jin Yeong coldly, but I saw the darkening of amusement in his eyes before he looked away. I had the impression that he was pretty pleased. "We will go to the library now."

So we took the brownies to the library with us. It wasn't like they knew what we were looking at—heck, it wasn't like *we* knew exactly what we were looking for, if it came to that. I had a good timeline, thanks to Tuatu's early investigation, but even that timeline was going to take a while to look through: the library's collection of the local newspaper was extensive, and very small when it came to print size.

We took up one table and the brownies all crowded around another one at the other end of the second floor of the library. I don't know if they were copying us or just had an inkling of what to do when you were supposed to be studying at a library, but they spread a few open books around the table and then mostly threw paperclips and pens at each other.

Just like they had done following us down the street, they were wild enough to be believable but not disruptive enough to get more than a few warning looks from the librarians. They were *very* good at what they did.

Good enough that I nearly forgot they were there while I was paging through old newspapers. And by the time we were ready to go home, with very little to show for our three hours leafing through old newspapers, I was almost shocked to find them crowding down the stairs after us, just far enough back to be unobtrusive.

"Should be fun to see what they come up with tomorrow," I said to Jin Yeong.

In the meantime, we could waste a bit more of their time by stopping for bubble tea on the way home.

CHAPTER THREE

I dreamed about Zero that night. I didn't remember much about the dream when I woke; just a snatch or two of conversation in the dark: Zero, blunt but not exactly cold, saying, "No. You already have a job."

"I can do *both*," said a voice I knew as Morgana's.

"It's too dangerous."

"I'm already dead."

"That's what makes it possible for you to do the job I need you to do," said Zero's voice, familiar in its exasperation, and the rest of the dream sank away from me because Ezri was talking instead.

I might have had the brief hope that she was alive as well, and somehow in the same place as Zero and the others, but her voice sounded so very different. So very mechanical and computerised.

"Being dead isn't as bad as people say it is," she said. "I've even got all of my fingers back!"

"Swings and roundabouts," said Abigail's voice. "And the roundabout is probably going to be a doozy."

I woke up with her voice still in my ears and Jin Yeong beside me. Waking up with a warm vampire next to me was starting to be a habit at this point, but since we were all sleeping in the living room these days it didn't seem as scandalous—or as dangerous—as it might have seemed otherwise. I mean, you can't get too romantic when there are three lycanthropes snoring around you and one dream-yipping with his paws twitching.

I could sympathise with the dream-yipping. I'd probably been doing something similar myself before I woke up. My shifting dreams left me uncertain and uncomfortable, and wanting to listen again to the recording of the human group that we'd heard through our private network. I'd assumed it was the last moments of my human friends' lives, and I'd been trying pretty hard not to hear what was happening at the time, but now that I came to think of it, I wasn't sure it matched with what I'd seen and heard in Athelas' memory.

It was probably just the combination of me blocking things out and that weird set of dreams, and there was no real reason to check through dreams again, but now that the thought was in my head, it was hard to dislodge. Since I was stirring, JinYeong seemed eager to be up and about too. I left him to monopolise the bathroom before the lycanthropes could get themselves out of the yawning and stretching stage, and headed upstairs before they could wake up enough to ask me what I was up to. I didn't even make myself coffee first: that's dedication.

Instead, I went and found the network chip that had been with Athelas' things and put it close enough to the couch I had sunk into that I could connect to the private network while still being far enough away that I could get out of range quickly if I needed to. Then I called the detective's number.

As I'd half suspected it would, the phone rang once or twice and then dropped to the incongruous sound of an internet dial tone—something I hadn't heard since I was a toddler.

"Heck," I muttered, and called North instead.

To my deep delight, it was Tuatu who answered. "What do you want?"

"Answering each other's phones now, are ya? That's a big step!"

I could almost see his lips pinch together and roll back out. "What do you want?"

"Thought I'd check up on you and see how you went with Marazul yesterday," I said, still ridiculously happy. "And I'm doing a bit of a test with our private network gadget."

"That reminds me," he said. "Marazul asked for mine back, and he seemed to be pretty anxious to get back the one you've still got, too. Can you take it to him when you're done?"

"Yeah, no worries," I said. "What's the word about the name?"

"He'll get back to us," Tuatu said. "He's searching the internet —the human one—but he suggested that your leprechaun friend would be better with the books and records on my phone. Something about them being arranged in a more Behind-style filing system than the human internet—he said your leprechaun can link them up to some sort of portal and do wide-ranging searches that you can't do as just a person who wants to look for something in the records. He also said that he's better with human technology."

"If we can get a portal for Five, he'll be over the moon," I said. It wasn't like Five could get to his usual portal while he was stuck in the human world, and he was blackballed from Behind for the crime of not killing me. That meant it was up to me—well, me and Jin Yeong—to get him a portal.

That would be interesting while we were being followed by a group of brownies.

"So long as you get me my phone back in working order once this is all over, I don't mind what I have to do. Just tell me what you need."

"All right," I said. "But you oughta stop saying stuff like that— that's how you end up owing Favours to fae."

"Don't I know it!" he said fervently. "We'll come past tomorrow if we have any news."

"Tomorrow," I agreed, and waited for him to hang up.

I could have done it myself, but I had the feeling that this was a better way to get the result I was after. Sure enough, after the call dropped there came the distinct sound of voices—at first distant and then clearer as I moved closer to the network badge.

"It's started again," said Ezri. Her voice sounded gleeful and more than slightly mischievous. "Wonder what's coming now?"

"No one is coming," said Abigail's voice impatiently. "Concentrate on connecting that line to the right place and stop sticking your nose where it doesn't belong before you get it cut off."

"I might as well stick it where it doesn't belong," Ezri said bluntly. "It'll grow back, anyway."

"It won't grow back," Abigail said, on a very deep sigh. It sounded like she'd said the same thing quite a few times now. "And if you—"

"Hang on! Is that the old man?

"Ezri! Get that *away* from the line!" Abigail said sharply, and static screamed and roared.

I don't think it was just the static screaming, but maybe that was just because I remembered the screams that had rung in my ears last time I heard these particular voices. I stepped away from the badge and the sound of static faded into a soft, intermittent clicking before ceasing altogether.

It left me feeling as if the world wasn't quite sitting right, and I wasn't sure why. There was something not-quite-right and ill-fitting about what I'd just heard, and I didn't think it was because I was listening once again to the prelude of the death of my friends that I'd avoided in Athelas' memory yesterday. Was it the words, which didn't seem to quite match my memory of last time I'd heard them?

What could do that? I wondered. Could the words, floating around in the closed network like a dvd screensaver, have changed bit by bit until they weren't exactly what had originally been said? Or was there some kind of degradation or corruption in the closed system? I would have to ask Marazul about that: he was the one who'd made the system in the first place, and he was the only one who would know.

Or, I wondered, now very wide awake despite my lack of coffee, was it possible that the memory in Athelas' mind was the incorrect one? He was still in Mum and Dad's room, caught in his own memory; downstairs, Jin Yeong had only just turned off the shower and would probably get himself a blood bag before anything else. I had the time to take another peek in Athelas' mind.

Of course, if I did, I would run the risk of jostling him free from the memory he was trapped within, but I was sick at heart and I thought—I wanted—I'm not sure what I wanted. Did I want to find something that might excuse Athelas for killing the human group? Was it possible to find any such thing?

No. There was nothing that could excuse killing the humans. Nothing that could excuse killing my parents.

But I knew that I was going to go back into Athelas' memories again despite that. Whether it was my heart clinging to the ridiculous hope that there was more than just calculation or blind, servile obedience to Zero's dad behind Athelas' actions, or whether it was a determination just to *know* everything, I wanted to find out. I wanted to find out *now*.

I entered the room softly, as if it was possible to wake Athelas from the state of fugue I'd trapped him in—or maybe I was just worried that Jin Yeong would hear my footsteps and wonder what I was doing with Athelas and come to stop me. I settled myself comfortably on the carpet with my back against the wall without hurrying myself despite that: it was no good hurrying and making mistakes. Pressing my shoulders against the coolness of the wall, I let them drop a little to ease the tension. I wouldn't have much fun fighting later if I let myself get too stiff. That was the quickest way to stupid injuries.

Once my shoulders were loose and the backs of my hands rested against my legs, I let my eyes dwell on Athelas and took in all of the Between and memory that made a turmoil around his head.

I didn't get the chance to try and find him in the memory I'd trapped him in, which was a shame. It would have made life much easier. But the act of me entering into his memories again broke him free from the web of Between that I'd woven around him and the memory, and I felt the sharpness of his eyes on me straight away—or would have, if he'd *had* eyes in here.

Pet, his voice seemed to sigh. *I might have known. How long have I been here?*

"Not telling you that," I said aloud, and I knew he heard it just as I could hear his voice.

"Have you become cautious at last?"

"Nah," I said, watching the play of memories and thoughts that shifted and slipped away and turned translucent against the blood-red background of Athelas' mind. "If I had, I wouldn't be here. I need a question answered."

"I wonder why you expect me to answer questions."

"I don't," I told him. "I'm not here to ask questions—I'm here to get answers."

I thought I heard a faint laugh from him. Ignoring it, and him, I let myself wander through the now gently snowing landscape of his mind. Today he didn't seem to be trying to keep it empty and innocuous; he seemed to be trying to overwhelm me for choice. I wafted through the drifting memories regardless, looking for the particular memory I had trapped him inside and touching memories at random with insubstantial fingers that weren't really fingers.

I don't know how long I wandered through Athelas' mind. He didn't try to stop me by any method I could see; the only effort he put forward was to keep the memories so plenteous and shifting that it was hard to keep one in sight for more than a moment. It took me a while to sift through what I was seeing around me, and a little bit longer to begin to tell the memories and fragments of thought apart from each other. They might drift and float, but the more important memories always had smaller, cascading ones attached; I don't think even Athelas could do anything about that—not when he probably didn't even know where and how some of them sprang from each other. They bubbled from each other, vast, interconnected clouds of memory that linked through some internal logic of their own.

The biggest one floated along nearly behind me, toward my right side. Vast and convoluted, with smaller memories burbling in and out of it and trailing away into the shifting mass of other groups, it connected to memories here and there so far away that I couldn't follow it with my eyes or even measure how big it really was.

Heck. Whatever Athelas had done in that memory, it had had a cascading effect, and every memory after that had been either tainted by or affected by it. I kept it in my peripheral, wondering, even if it wasn't the memory I was after. None of the others were anything like as big.

Once I knew that there were links between the memories, it was easier to work with what there was around me. Maybe it was just a matter of doing what Five and Marazul did: finding a keyword or key theme and following the connection of that word or theme back through all the memories that held it.

What keyword, though?

Human, said my mind, and as it did, a vast amount of the memories around me grew more luminous. And as they grew more luminous, the part of Athelas that was most aware sharpened his focus on me.

"Oh, I don't think so, Pet!" he said.

I felt rather than smelt the scent of Jin Yeong, and a vague warmth beside my physical body; in the real world, a freshly-showered and scented vampire had just sat down next to me and put his arm around my shoulders so quietly and gently that I almost hadn't noticed.

I was grateful that he didn't try to pull me out of Athelas' mind: Zero would probably have done that, and it was hard enough to concentrate now that Athelas was effectively trying to push me from his mind.

I caught at one of the more luminous memories before that radiance could wither away at Athelas' presence; this one was attached to the vast mass that was still softly wafting along behind me and that vanished into the far distance.

"You'll do," I said.

I felt rather than heard what seemed to be a vast exasperation sighing.

"Don't you flamin' sigh at me," I said, trying to sound cold rather than needled. "You don't get to do the *tsk tsk* thing at me anymore."

I could see the bloody colour leaching from the memory and into Athelas' mind around me, and I had a feeling I knew exactly which memory I was holding. I'd found the night that the humans were murdered after all. The night Athelas had done his best to kill me and then gone to kill my friends.

"Think about this again, Pet," Athelas' voice murmured in my ear.

I didn't have an ear in here, and he didn't have a throat, but that's what it felt like. Close, personal, and dangerous—as if he could somehow manage to slide a knife into me even inside his head.

"Nothing you see here will do you any good—everything has two edges to it and can only cut you. You'd be better off trying to find my lord."

That could be true. It probably was true, in a twisted sort of way. But he was warning me again, and that could only mean that there was more to find; there was more hidden. I slipped away from the shivery feeling of Athelas' voice and deeper into his mind, and for a moment, I lost him completely.

The moment I knew he couldn't reach me, I dived into the

memory I'd brought with me before it could wriggle away or be pulled away from the mass it was a part of. I found myself in a darkness that felt and smelt familiar, but it didn't feel that way to Athelas, whose memory it was.

Heck. I'd gone into the wrong memory, hadn't I? The only question was, had I made the mistake myself, or was it something Athelas had managed to sneak past me? Only one way to find out: I would have to wait a while and experience the memory.

There was such a comfort to the familiarity of the memory that I didn't realise until it was nearly too late exactly where it was that Athelas was stepping lightly through carpet that sank only slightly beneath his shoes. Light played briefly across the hallway as someone drove along the street, and then the memory bent and flexed, sending me gently into the next memory—one that was very nearly the same as the one I'd come from, but this time the mind I was in knew it was here for a reason other than surveillance.

This heirling, in particular, needed to die. Athelas' mind knew that with sharp, absolute certainty. As he softly stepped across the hallway of my house and toward the stairs of the upper level, it was a certainty as cold and hard as crystal: the heirling needed to die so that it wouldn't have a chance to bring down the entire, intricate web of intrigue and deceit and death that had unfurled for centuries from two different directions.

He could see the threads of it filtering through the world as it was: each of them positioned in such a place and such a way that they would slice through the web in too many places to allow for it to be fixed in time.

And Athelas knew that to do what he had come to do, he would have to be very careful to do things exactly in the right time and place—to step between those sticky filaments of web without touching a single one—and that he would need to make very certain to kill tonight.

Not, said a wearily amused thought, that he had ever failed to do so. Killing was the one thing he was good at, and if he could manage this job tonight, there was no doubt that everything would fall out exactly as it needed to fall out.

Heck, I thought, impossibly cold although the body I was in was perfectly regulated, perfectly ready, perfectly deadly. Athelas was coming to kill me and my parents, and I was going to have to watch or run.

I should have run straight away, but somehow I couldn't. And when that first urge to run had left me, I even felt for a little while as though it was only right to be a witness of my parents' last hours—that time when they had played games against death and won, even though they died. Because even if they were dead, I had lived, and by hook or by crook, I was going to bring down the entire hierarchy Behind and Between, just as Athelas had known I could.

He stepped into dark, soft shadow on the top landing and heard a faint pattering of something small and particulate showering down behind him. The sound was unfamiliar to him but put him on his guard regardless, and when he tried to step right into the upper living room, he couldn't.

I felt a little fizz of hope that was as sudden as it was ridiculous. I hadn't expected Athelas to have any trouble, but I also knew it wouldn't make any difference to the end result. I was already living in a world where this memory was the past.

"Got you," said a thoughtful voice from the direction of the nearest couch. "I wondered if you'd come back tonight."

A soft glow of light illuminated the room, and it took me far too long to realise that it didn't come from any of the electric lights, because I was too busy gazing at the faces of my parents. There they stood in front of me—or at least, in front of Athelas— smaller and far more fragile than I ever remembered them being, a human shield between Athelas and the hidden door to my bedroom. Magical light glowed on my mother's face, rounding the resolute chin and livening her grey eyes; it seemed to sink into my father's beard, turning it to gold instead of the usual piebald straw and grey mix, and outlined the lines in his forehead gently.

Mum said, "We would have preferred not to hurt you, but now that you've come back, I don't think we have any other option."

In the doorway, Athelas once more tried to move his feet through to the living room and found that he couldn't.

"How interesting!" he murmured, and I felt the amused curiosity of it radiate through his chest. Here was magic, whispered a thought inside him. Magic not behindkind or faekind, nor even anything to do with Between. I felt the sudden furrow of a faint frown between his brows. He asked, "I wonder what secrets your bloodline holds, human?"

"Typical of fae," said my mother, her voice achingly familiar. "Always thinking that humans have to have fae blood or behindkind blood to do anything useful. I'm human back as far as it's possible to go, and so is my husband."

"Impossible," Athelas said, with a small, derisive smile. "The strength of your magic alone—"

"It might be useful to tell other humans that they don't have magic, but we're not suggestible enough to be weakened by it when we've been magic users our entire lives," said Dad. "We know a few tricks against fae manipulation, too."

"How did you know I'm fae?" asked Athelas.

He could feel what kept him trapped now; as he felt it, I knew what it was along with him. There were iron shavings in the carpet—no doubt that faint patter against the carpet when he had stepped across the threshold was another shower of the same, set off by a clever bit of magic and falling to close the trap.

"You left too many traces of yourself last time," my father said. Someone who didn't know him probably wouldn't have known that the cold, flat sound to his voice meant that he was too tense, too preoccupied with the present danger, to have any emotion left over to show. "You're not the first, and I suppose you won't be the last. We'll be gone by the next time one of you comes here."

"Then it seems that I have arrived just in time," Athelas said.

He didn't sound worried; he didn't seem worried here in his mind, either. The realisation of that left me cold.

"What do you want?"

"I've come for your daughter," said Athelas.

Perhaps the most terrifying thing about it all was the complete confidence he had in himself. His brain was still turning, turning, figuring out how he was going to get out of this trap—how he was going to kill.

"We don't have any children," said my mother. "You must have found that out when you sneaked in here last night. We're not entering into any bargains with the fae either, so you can forget it."

"This room is not as long as it ought to be," Athelas said softly, and his eyes dwelt on the bookcase that was the entrance to my room.

I was in there, asleep. In an hour or so I would wake up to find my parents dead, their bodies strewn in pieces around the living room, and someone light-footed and blood-stained in the house. And I would be convinced that I was going to die for several horror-drenched minutes until I would simply...forget what had happened.

My physical body must have been shaking, because I felt a warm pressure tighten around where my shoulders ought to be. Jin Yeong, making himself as unignorable as usual.

"We can't let him go," Dad said. He said it to Mum, as though he was pleading with her, but I wasn't sure if he was pleading with her to tell him he was wrong, or right.

"No," agreed my mother. "We'll have to deal with him tonight and leave tomorrow."

"I'm afraid I can't waste any more time here," Athelas said. "Nor can I afford to be killed—I have far too much work ahead of me, and there are sacrifices that must be made, after all. Your daughter will be one of them."

"It's too easy to sacrifice things that aren't yours," said my mother, shifting forward just slightly.

I don't know what she sensed or suspected, but she was getting ready to fight.

"Easy?" said Athelas, the word slipping coldly into his blood. "No, I don't think so. Easier, certainly, than sacrificing myself, however—and I was never one for self-sacrifice."

He knelt, iron shavings all around him and making painful pinpricks through the knees of his trousers, then reached behind him to scoop up a handful of the ones that had completed the circle around him. I felt the pain of them as if I were the one picking them up, burning through his palm like molten grains of sand, and wasn't quick enough to guess what he would do with them.

"We're not fae," said Dad. "It won't hurt us if you throw them at us."

"So your wife said," Athelas said, allowing himself one more moment with that excruciating handful.

Then he tipped his head back and poured it down his throat. I, too, suffered the gravelly fire as it trickled down his throat and into his stomach, setting his oesophagus ablaze as it passed through. I felt every miniscule grain of metal filing as it burned through his stomach, through his flesh, through his throat. Felt the step forward that he took, and then the next, carrying the imprisonment with him as he came, leaking blood and metal that burned where it dropped on the carpet.

Felt his body slowly begin to heal itself as each of the thousands of filings burned through him and made tiny blue pools of melted iron in the carpet as he stepped forward again.

Saw Mum and Dad through his eyes.

They just stared at him, and for a moment I saw in their faces the exact emotion that was sucking the air out of my own chest: the absolutely horrified wonder that someone could do something like that to themselves just to get out of a trap.

Then I saw the snap of realisation that they need to arm and prepare to fight. Dad pulled a sword out of thin air with barely the movement of Between to show for it to Athelas' fae eyes; my mother had throwing knives that were between her fingers in one moment, and solidly buried in Athelas' chest and shoulder the next as he dived sideways to avoid them.

Pain dug deep in his left shoulder, but nothing like the agony of iron filings still passing through his flesh. He landed lightly and drew his swords just as lightly as he rose, the one on his left bright with magic and the one on the right slick with poison.

I knew it because he knew it, but I think I would have expected it anyway.

Mum retreated to the seat of the couch with her foot braced against the arm, and Dad took the front guard position, out of her throwing lines and ready to take the first charge. Athelas' brain lost every other function but the deadly dancing chessboard of the fight, aware and alight with the knowledge that he would need to fight well.

I knew it. I knew how he killed, and I knew how well he fought. But I still hoped for the smallest moment that I would somehow see my parents defeat Athelas.

And they fought *flamin'* well.

As one unit of sword and hissing knife-point, they defended the room together until the faintest nick of Athelas' flickering left blade felled my father in a moment of bright, powerful magic. As quicksilver as his blade, Athelas followed it through without hesitation even as my father fell, and under the cover of my father's body sank the tip of his poisoned right blade precisely into my mother's shoulder.

Mum didn't fall so much as stumble down from the couch to my father's side, her left arm hanging useless and the right cradling his head as he tried vainly to hold it up himself. By the time she was beside him on the floor, I could see that her left leg wasn't obeying her either.

Their backs to the couch seat, they could only look hopelessly up at him.

"Now," said Athelas—silkily, gently. He sheathed his swords carefully, delicately. "We will play a game of choices. If you make the right choice, you can yet live. Make the wrong choice and you'll die."

"You're going to kill us anyway," said Mum. There was a deep flush to her face that I remembered seeing when I was younger, a look of mingled frustration and anger at the gut-wrenching *unfairness* of a thing.

Distantly, it seemed somehow funny that her chief emotion seemed to be the appalling unfairness of their situation.

Dad, on the other hand, breathed too quickly, and I saw the tension in his shoulders that he still didn't seem to be able to move. He was afraid—not for himself, but for Mum and the younger me.

"We have no reason to play games with you," he said. "Why should we give you a reason to distance yourself from your own sins?"

"Then perhaps I should make myself even clearer," said Athelas, his voice only a murmur of moonlight in the room. "If you make no choice—if you don't play my game—I will kill your wife, and then your child, and then you. I will do so *slowly*."

"What are the choices?" Dad's voice was flat again, but I could see that he was somehow holding Mum's hand.

Athelas saw it, too: it twisted a bitter, savage knife somewhere in his stomach, and his voice was cold as ice when he said, "Your lives or your daughter's life: choose. You can live if you give up her life. Or give up your own lives to save her."

I saw my parents' eyes meet; saw the further flush of relief as it spread over my mother's cheeks and down her neck. My father's shoulders seemed to relax just slightly.

"Are you serious?"

"As death," Athelas said.

"Kill us then," Mum said. If you didn't know her, you would have thought that the wobble in her voice was tears. It wasn't—she was laughing. "Kill us and spare our daughter. You can't go back on it now—there's some use to fae, I suppose."

I felt Athelas' mouth curve very faintly. "You must both agree."

"Kill us," said Dad, allowing his head to settle against Mum's shoulder without trying to lift it again.

I felt the soft huff of laughter that caught in Athelas' throat, though there was no sound. "Perhaps you should take some time to think about it," he suggested gently.

"Nope," my mother said. "You're not getting out of it like that: we've entered into a bargain, and you have to keep up your part of it. Kill our daughter today and your own blood will boil you alive."

"You are…very well informed," said Athelas, stepping forward lightly, mercilessly, as I tried uselessly to clutch at him and stop him. His mind was alight with too many thoughts and connections to follow, a turbulent, violent froth of wonder that was as savage as it was incomprehensible—as triumphant as it was terrible.

"That happens when enough fae try to kill your child," my mother said. "You start to learn a few things. You fae all have your games, but you're the first one who risked an entire order on it."

"My orders are my own to worry about," said Athelas. "Who will go first, I wonder?"

They didn't answer that one, and I didn't blame them. I was proud of them for ignoring it—was proud of the way that Mum turned her face away from him as if he was nothing and nuzzled a kiss into Dad's cheek since he couldn't move enough to do it himself. I was proud of the way Dad leant his head into her embrace without even looking at Athelas, citrine glowing softly against his face from Mum's ring.

For a moment, it was difficult to tell where my feelings ended and Athelas' began. Then he took a single, soft step forward across the carpet, drawing a bone knife I had seen before, but only in other memories that weren't mine.

"I won't make it hurt," he said, and I pushed away from the lie of it instinctively.

I had seen the mess he left in the room that night. He had torn my parents apart—literally cut them to pieces—and I couldn't bear to see it happen. I couldn't bear to feel Athelas do it as if I was the one doing it. Couldn't bear—felt sick to feel—the almost tender wonder that permeated Athelas, or the dark, bloody joy that rippled over it and took over the whole of his mind as he moved to do his work.

I pushed away from the memory entirely, tears rolling down my face, but this time I didn't escape from the memory so much as I dipped out of it and back into it later on. No—not later in this exact memory, but into another small memory that was attached—or maybe it was woven in, I wasn't sure. Before I could free myself from the cascade of memory that began at my parents' murder, I found myself in that other, smaller memory. A mirrored memory of the one I'd just escaped was playing, right up at the front of Athelas' mind; bloody, hot, and ruthless, it showed everything that I'd tried to escape—the murders themselves. I pressed myself to the other side of Athelas' mind, and heard Lord Sero's voice say coldly, "I see that you're getting better at keeping the useless details to yourself. Very good. Our briefings may well get to a reasonable length of time at this rate. The heirling attached...?"

"Will never leave the house, my lord," said Athelas' voice, smoothly. "I made very sure, as you saw in the result of my night's work for yourself just now. I used the bone knife—even could all of the separate parts be gathered together, there isn't a necromancer in the worlds who could cause those bodies to set a foot outside the house."

"Enough," said Lord Sero, releasing the memory. "I have no

wish to be incriminated should the king begin to ask questions. Tell me no more than you must."

The memory sank, but not far, still hovering at the front of his mind and obscuring other memories as Lord Sero's version of the burrowing information worm turned in on itself in a coiling of Between and fae magic that ate itself and then disappeared.

Athelas' mind didn't exactly become less cautious, but it did seem to uncoil slightly, and I slipped out of the memory while I could, shaken and sick in equal measures. I wondered if Athelas knew how close he'd come to being killed by Lord Sero that night as a direct result of his own hubris. Probably. He might even have delighted in it, for all I knew. Playing games with my life and my parents' lives and then living to tell the tale even after defying orders in order to play his games.

The shattered and slowly uncoiling inner corridor of his mind hadn't suggested that conclusion, but I knew that there had been many moments where Athelas had genuinely enjoyed being with me. The most reasonable explanation I had for that was that Athelas had delighted in the trickery he had been engaged in. The cleverness of it—the twistiness of it.

Maybe even the danger of it, though that suddenly made me think again of both sides of the memory I had seen of the moment I had offered Athelas the dryad. He had been so tempted to take it, in that moment.

What I did know was that if Lord Sero had caught sight of the part of the memory that held the bargain Athelas had made with my parents—or any hint of the part that contained me and the command for me to never leave the house—Athelas wouldn't have left the manor that night or ever again.

I floated where I was for a moment to catch my breath and caught it on a sob instead. I don't know when I'd started to cry, but it felt as though I might have been crying for a while.

Athelas' voice said, "Did I not say so, Pet? Will you never learn?"

"Nope," I said, tears gliding down my cheeks and my voice rough with the ache in my throat. "Doesn't look like it. Can't hang around: I've still got more to find out, so if you'd stop trying to warn me about things I already know, that'd be nice."

I heard Jin Yeong's voice in the real world and knew that the tears must be falling out there, too. I felt a sudden rush of warmth and slightly unsteady happiness: it couldn't be fun for him to sit out there, not able to help, just watching me cry. But there he was. A little bit of pressure around my hand—a warmth around my shoulders.

I would have to give him a kiss when I got out of this torturously twisty world that was Athelas' mind.

"There is nothing more for you here," Athelas said sharply, and the environment around me grew spiky and poisonous.

I knew then that he was preparing to fight me for every memory I went after—and I knew then that for all the things he'd hidden that had come to light, Athelas had still more he wanted to hide.

And I knew, with cold, spiky certainty, that I couldn't let him stop me now. There were things I needed to know—questions that needed to be settled—and so much more to discover about the things that Athelas didn't want to be found.

"It is time, I think," he said, "for you to leave."

"I told you," I said, and my voice was harsh. "I'm not here to ask questions, I'm here to get answers. Don't reckon you can stop me."

He tried to stop me. He tried with an almost feral savagery, in fact, and perhaps I could have been gentler with him if my thoughts hadn't been so full of my dead parents.

It wasn't even necessarily that I thought it would do any good; I knew it would do no good. I suspected the kind of no good it would do, too; and yet I couldn't stop myself. I needed to know what other secrets lay in Athelas' mind. I needed to know them because although it wouldn't change how I felt about him, it would make a difference in what I did from now onward. It would make a difference to a lot of other things, too.

And perhaps I wanted to punish him—make him feel as powerless as my parents must have felt as they died. So I didn't try to be gentle. I didn't try to spare his pride or his pain—I seared through his mind like a hot knife through butter, forcing my way through, ripping memories from here and there. Finding anything that matched what I wanted to see, what I needed to know.

And when I had found them, I huddled them all together and sank into them, one by one.

CHAPTER FOUR

I was cold and aching from clenching my teeth by the time I came back out again. Jin Yeong was there as he always was, warm and present; I opened my eyes to see his face just a few centimetres away, his arms around me. Those black, bloody eyes looked right into the cold shock that must have been in mine.

"Shall I bite him?" he asked.

Athelas laughed behind him, soft and weary.

"No," I said. "We're probably going to need him later. And he's gunna pay what he's due to pay once everything's sorted out."

"What did you see this time?"

"I saw him killing people," I said. "Heirlings. Champions. A lot of people."

"You shouldn't have looked if you didn't want to see," Athelas said, as I touched Jin Yeong's cheek in a wordless thank-you and released myself from his arms.

Athelas didn't look at me—wouldn't look at me for quite some time, I suspected. I couldn't say for sure, but I was almost certain he had been taken aback at how swiftly and easily I had taken memories from him.

And I was almost certain that he was now very much afraid.

I met JinYeong's eyes for a brief instant before a tumble of movement in the doorway drew our attention. Les, a fork in either hand and a wild look to his eyes, stared at us and then at Athelas.

He gabbled, "Lady! There's a bad smell about the place! Who brought it into the house?"

"A bad—" I stopped and stared at Athelas, whose eyes were fixed on Les as if he couldn't quite believe what he was seeing.

I don't often get the chance to see him so completely shocked, and I'm not gunna lie: it was flamin' satisfying.

"Still alive," he murmured to himself. "Truly impressive: an almost cockroach echelon of survival skill, in fact."

"After all the times you tried to kill him, you mean?" I asked. "Don't worry, Les: I won't let him have another go at you. He can't get out."

"Can't is as can't does," Les said, with unexpected severity. "Lady, you can't keep bad smells in the house! They get in the curtains!"

"I can assure you that I've no intention of lingering in the curtains," said Athelas, showing his steel-lined cuffs. "And I would leave if I could, but alas…"

"You're not going anywhere until we've got a few more answers about a heck of a lot of things—and definitely not until Zero's back to take you wherever criminals get taken Behind."

"Indeed?" he said, and the raw fear I thought I had seen was gone as if it had never been. "Well, no doubt we will weather these things as we must. I've a suspicion that you're going to be rather too busy outside the house to allow your attention to dwell on me."

"I know you worked pretty hard not to die up until now," I told him. "But even a good run has to end some time, and I reckon you're about at the end of yours."

He shrugged one shoulder, entirely at his ease again. "All good things must end, after all, Pet."

"You know what's flamin' irritating about you?" I asked him. Of all the times he should be afraid, now was the time. Whether or not I got into his memories, he was going to die at the end of this—why was he more afraid of me taking his memories than he was of dying?

"I'm certain you're going to tell me," he said mildly. "I believe I'll save my strength."

"Every time we peel a layer off of you, there's another even twistier layer underneath. It's flamin' annoying."

"Lady," said Les, even more urgently, "you shouldn't stay in this room. Whoever smelt it dealt it, and—"

"I might point out that this is one of the more irritating conversations I've had," Athelas pointed out, his eyes dwelling coldly and emotionlessly on Les in a way that made me shudder. "The pain is not wholly your own, I assure you."

Les must have felt the same menace that I did, because he backed toward the doorway and sidled through it into the lounge room. I heard his voice say, "Lady, I hie me," and then his bare feet trotting across the carpet. Goodness knows where his shoes had gone this time. I'd have to get him another pair when I could.

"Don't threaten my friends," I told Athelas.

"That," said Athelas, "is not a friend. Nor should it be."

"For a bloke who pretended to be my friend and tried to kill me, that's flamin' rich."

"Good heavens, what an appalling habit I seem to have formed!" Athelas said, more to himself than me. "Comfort yourself, Pet: I'll refrain from useless warnings."

"Will you though?" I said, meeting his eyes just before they dropped. "Because that's one of the things I'm not sure about. I'll be back to pinch a few memories from you later, as well."

"I see," he said. "Am I to be shut in my own mind again while you're presumably about your business? I won't take it so easily this time."

Jin Yeong rose with a small sniff of a laugh, drawing the cold look of dislike from Athelas once again, and offered his hand to me.

I took that hand and let him pull me up. "You'll just have to wonder about that until you find out," I said to Athelas.

"I really do wonder why you bother to search my mind for things you already know."

"Yeah, but I *don't* already know 'em," I pointed out. "I know what you've told me, and nothing else. You can't expect me to trust what you've said after everything you've done."

"And thus we have another layer," he said, smiling faintly as he leaned back. He closed his eyes as well, but if he thought that was going to do any good, he was pretty quickly going to learn otherwise.

"Yeah. You're a flamin' onion at this point," I said, and slipped back into his mind one last time to bind him safely within his memories.

ONCE WE WERE DOWN in the kitchen again, I said to Les, "You gotta stop skulking off to other places without letting us know. I keep thinking something has grabbed you."

"I know all the doors, lady," he said.

I managed to stop myself from rolling my eyes as I went through the freezer for the last of the bread. "Okay, but tell me next time you're going somewhere, all right?"

"I know the *doors*," he said again, with unexpected emphasis. "I can go in and out where I need to go."

"Are you telling me not to worry about you?"

"That one would live through an explosion," JinYeong said dismissively, leaning around me to grab a blood bag as I took the butter out of the fridge.

"Worry is not currency, lady," said Les. "I accept food and drink only."

He toddled off into the living room again as if he'd made

perfect sense and I went on with the breakfast, though I said to Jin Yeong, nodding at his blood bag, "You're eating a lot these days."

"I should be ready to fight," he said. "If I do not eat, I will not fight as well."

"Weird," I said, staring at him. "Thought that was just hunger. You fight better after blood?"

"I fight verry well, all the time."

"Yes, but you fight better after blood?"

Jin Yeong gave a faint, assenting tilt of his nose. "*Keurae*. Blood is always necessary."

"Better make sure you stock up for when we know the king's name, then," I said, and ducked into the cupboards to see how many cans of baked beans we still had.

Daniel came in with Chantelle and Kevin while I was cooking toast and beans and leaned on the kitchen island as if he was too restless to sit down. He probably was.

"What are we doing today?" he asked. "We can have a bit more of a look at the underground section of the Hobart Rivulet, but there's probably not too much more to find that's worth the time looking. There's a map you can look up online, too."

"We'll have to take our chances with the rivulet later," I said. "I already know enough about it to be comfortable there. I need you to go see Five: Jin Yeong and I need to get rid of the brownies and find a portal for him today."

"Why are we—"

"Most of the stuff that the humans left with Tuatu is filed in a behindkind sorta way, apparently," I told him. "Wonder if they— ah, that's not important. I reckon they had a bit of behindkind help in the old days as well. The important thing is, Marazul reckons we'll be able to go through it all a lot easier and find names a lot more easily if someone with behindkind access and a behindkind portal goes through the lot of it."

"Can't the leprechaun go Behind and find one himself?"

"Nope," I said. "You remember how I said someone was sent to kill me a little while ago?"

He stared at me. "That was the dropbears thing out Huon way?"

"Yeah. And they've blackballed him from Behind because he wouldn't kill me. So we're gunna find him a portal—he deserves a bit of fun after all of this, and we could use the help."

Practically, Chantelle asked, "Where are we going to get a portal for the leprechaun?"

"Thought you lot might know," I said. "What about Upper Management? They had a lot of machinery there last time we snuck in."

"We did not sneak in," JinYeong said. "We walked."

"Stalked, more like," I said.

I could still remember the stark terror of striding down the halls of Upper Management to meet with a harpy named Richard, expecting to be lynched the entire way down the hall. Pretending not to be afraid. Pretending that we were the ones who ought to frighten everyone. It felt like a lifetime ago, but it hadn't even been half a year.

"What about that place your lot cleaned out when you collected the leprechaun? You told me it was a whole setup out there in the Valley. They'd have one, wouldn't they?"

I threw a look of admiration at Daniel. "Look at you, using your brain and everything! I reckon they might have; there was a lot of stuff that we just left there. Zero seemed to think that someone would come to clean it up, but it wasn't that long ago, so they might not have got to it yet."

"We will find out," said JinYeong. He seemed brighter and more energised than he had earlier, as if the blood bag he'd sucked dry had been half sunshine.

I knew better—JinYeong was happy because today meant mischief. Whether that mischief was losing a group of brownies somewhere along Campbell Street or fighting them off somewhere Between, it meant that there would be blood. Like any self-respecting vampire, Jin Yeong delighted in blood.

Almost as much as he delighted in making trouble.

"Today, we are dating again," he said, and that explained a bit more of the smug mischief in his eyes. "You should wear the clothes."

"We're going to have to go Between as soon as we lose the brownies," I pointed out. "We've got to make it to the Huon Valley, and I'm not gunna fight whatever we meet on the way in a silk shirt."

Jin Yeong pouted slightly and said, "There is a suede jacket. It is warm for Between and it will slow a blade."

"Fair enough," I said. Until we wanted to lose the brownies, we wanted to lull them into a false sense of security, and there wasn't a better way to do that than to start out exactly as we had yesterday. "But we're going to have to lose the brownies. We don't want them knowing that we're looking for a portal, and we definitely don't want them following us Between *or* to the Valley. You're wearing your best tie."

Jin Yeong gave a small sniff of amusement and grinned expansively enough to show his teeth. The tie was definitely not his best, and he had caught the joke. "We will have a verrry enjoyable date," he said.

Daniel rolled his eyes.

I said to him, "I'll text you Five's address: let him know that we're working on getting a portal for him and ask him to meet us at the house—no, take him around to Vesper's place. If the brownies go back to the house to find someone else to follow or to wait for us, we don't want them to know what all of our connections are."

"Got it," said Daniel. "Good luck. Call me if you need us to come and clean up a few brownies so you can get away."

"Will do," I told him, and went upstairs to get my jacket.

· · ·

IT WAS a warmer morning than I'd expected when I got outside with JinYeong. The sunshine made the suede jacket and leather trousers uncomfortably hot, but I ignored the discomfort. We'd be going Between before long, and it was always at least a few degrees colder there—not to mention far more likely to see bare arms or legs scratched up with something that could paralyse you, kill you, or both.

At least I had the satisfaction of knowing that JinYeong was equally uncomfortable, though for a different reason. I'd made him carry the backpack we would need to carry a portal away with us, despite his protests that he would just *carry* the portal and his piteous complaints that a backpack was **not** a thing he would wear. I knew too well how easy it was to drop stuff when you were fighting for your life.

We'd compromised: he carried the backpack, even if he didn't wear it on his back. I could afford to sweat a bit in recompense, as it were.

"Where d'you wanna get rid of this lot?" I asked him in a low voice as we headed down toward the centre of the city. The brownies had begun following us as soon as we left the house, just like yesterday.

We could catch a bus down there and take forty minutes to drive out to the Huon Valley like normal people, or we could find a way to lose the brownies and duck into the soft, cool shadows of Between and be there in twenty minutes or so.

The bus gave us less chance of being attacked by behindkind, but took significantly longer, and like Daniel, I was anxious to get things done as quickly as possible.

"We can fight," JinYeong said, but he looked doubtful. "They do not fight fair, so it will be messy."

"So we try to lose them instead of killing them? Sounds good." I preferred to be non-lethal as often as possible, despite knowing that when it came to Between and Behind, it more often *wasn't* possible. "You wanna try to lose 'em on the way down to the city centre, or once we're down there?"

"There are more ways at the centre," Jin Yeong said.

He wasn't wrong; and as soon as we passed the first pub, I knew exactly how we could do it.

"Oi," I said to Jin Yeong softly. "How long do you reckon it'll take 'em to change their appearance?"

Jin Yeong's dark eyes flicked over to the pub for a brief moment before he grinned. "Ah. But do you think they will let you in? I think not."

"I'm eighteen!" I protested.

"Then you have your identification?"

"Nope, but I have a vampire with me," I remarked. I didn't have any form of ID that required a photograph—didn't have any at all, if I was going to be completely honest about it. "A vampire who can be very persuasive if we get into trouble."

"You think it will stop them?"

"There isn't a pub owner in Hobart who'll let kids into their pub," I said. "And I reckon the brownies know that. I don't know how long it'll take 'em to change their appearance, but with any luck it'll be just long enough for us to skip sideways and Between. If we're careful, they won't know where we've gone."

I grabbed him and ducked in through the doorway before he could say anything else, and we found ourselves in a cool, beer-scented entryway that led down into a darker lobby and through to the bar beyond.

"This way," I said gleefully, dragging Jin Yeong along with me. I already knew where we should try to get out: I'd spotted a huge old floor vase on the way in, all painted up with dark green leaves and branches that seemed to move a bit when we got closer.

"I do not want to go into that," complained Jin Yeong, but he followed me when I ducked around a patron and slipped right through those feathery leaves.

I heard the sounds of a hubbub in the doorway that was just

out of sight behind us, but by the time we broke into a trot and passed around a ferny corner, all sounds from the human side of reality were gone.

We were already Between, so it seemed easier to keep going than to pop out again and try for a bus.

"Hope you know the way there," I said to Jin Yeong, my eyes constantly scanning the smooth road ahead of us.

I was mostly kidding, but not entirely. I knew the way to Huonville via the main road, but Between, anything could happen. I was pretty sure we were on Macquarie or Davy Street by now, travelling along what could have been a dystopian version of the real street except for the fact that the long road that stretched ahead of us seemed to be on the point of turning into a river. If we went any deeper Between, it probably would.

"*Eung*," murmured Jin Yeong, worrying me.

"You do know the way, don't you?" I asked, more insistently.

"I came with *Hyeong* to rescue you that time."

"That was *Judbury*," I said, worry deepening. "We had to come back to Huonville to get the human hive. We don't need to go all the way out to Judbury—we just need to go as far as Huonville."

Still, we seemed to be going in the right direction whenever we passed through a thin enough part of Between to show where we were in the human world, and it wasn't until we came to a familiar sort of bridge after about twenty minutes' walk that my suspicions were confirmed.

White rails peeked out of the stony bridge beneath our feet, creeping with moss and not quite as horizontal as they ought to be.

"Hang on," I said, catching a glimpse of white horses a long way below that weren't quite horses, all water and savage teeth and wild, hungry blue eyes. "Reckon that's the Huon?"

"They are a river," Jin Yeong said, his eyes wary. "Do not try to feed them."

"Heck no!" I said hastily. "They look like they'd take an arm off if I did."

"They do not like flesh, just skin," he added, more disturbingly.

"Oh what, they'll *only* take my skin? Nice of 'em."

Jin Yeong sniffed a small laugh, then said, "Ah. We went too far. *Yogi isseo.*"

He stepped out of the world Between, and though we had been just crossing the river a moment ago, now we were well on the other side and somewhere near the Huonville roundabout.

I managed to not tell Jin Yeong that I had already told him about not going too far and eyed the building in front of us doubtfully.

"Glad you remember what it looks like," I said. I'd been a bit tired from having to run away from dropbears and bringing things through from Between last time I was here; I'd followed Zero like the good Pet I was, and that was it.

I remembered the inside, though, even if it wasn't exactly how I remembered it being. If the outside was old and disreputable, the inside was solidly concrete—it had an aged look to it now that it hadn't had last time I'd been there. It could have been the shade of Between that had begun to overgrow it as soon as we stepped through the doors, lacking any human presence to keep it carefully at bay in the corners of the eyes, but it could also have been the very real greenery that had sprung up all around the lobby and trailed over pretty much everything in the room.

"Heck, talk about nature taking back!" I said, blowing out my cheeks. "It hasn't even been half a year! How quick does Behind take things over?"

Jin Yeong shrugged one shoulder. "It was already close, *ani*? Of course it will fall more quickly. I think no one comes in here."

"Yeah, probably not," I agreed. "Right. We gotta get upstairs if we want the portals."

He tilted his chin toward the elevator. "There is that."

"Reckon the elevator still works?" I asked. Mind you, it was more a question of if the elevator worked in a way that we were going to be happy with. "There are stairs. We'll use those."

But when we took the stairs up to the next level and opened the door, we walked straight out onto a roof that was surrounded by a low wall all around and a brick façade toward the front that was just a bit higher.

"Elevator it is, then," I said gloomily. I had a bad feeling about it, and not just because it presumably hadn't been used in the last several months. "Reckon there's anything nasty in it?"

"*Caneungsongi noppa*," Jin Yeong said discouragingly.

"Right, you're going first, then," I told him, and headed back down the stairs.

I'd only been joking, but when we got back to ground floor, Jin Yeong sauntered ahead of me while I took another look around the lobby for signs of danger, then pressed the elevator button and stepped in front of me when the doors opened almost at once.

It was suspiciously empty.

"Great," I said gloomily. "That means something's gunna come for us once the doors are closed."

Jin Yeong sauntered into the elevator as well. "I think you don't like elevators," he said.

"Too flamin' right, I don't. You're stuck in a box that can kill you if it breaks down, and this box is Between, where anything else can kill you."

He pressed the *close doors* button and the doors slid more-or-less smoothly shut. Nothing popped out at us, and we started upwards without too much of a shudder as well.

"See?"

"Maybe it's waiting for us upstairs," I told him. "Don't get too bright and bubbly yet."

Jin Yeong grinned, eyes dark and bloody, and said in English, "Yess. That is the fun."

"You've got a flamin' weird idea about what's fun," I said sourly.

Still, there wasn't anything waiting for us at the top floor when the elevator doors hissed open again, and even if it didn't look exactly like I remembered it looking, we actually made it *into* the top floor instead of to the top of the building.

"Getting pretty green up here, too," I said, staring around the cubicles as I walked down one channel between the waist-high boxes. Most of the cubicle boxes were still there, even if one or two had been tumbled down at the corners, but they were overrun with vines and deep green shadows that suggested the walls of the building were only as thick as you thought they were. What walls there were inside the office itself had been replaced by a treeline long enough ago that grass was growing down the carpeted section I walked along between the cubicles.

There was a pretty fresh breeze coming from the treeline that should have backed on to the street out front, too, which meant other stuff could probably come through there.

I added, "Dunno how I feel about nature reclaiming stuff in the middle of Huonville, though. It's not like there's more than grass and trees out there beside the road—it'll look a bit weird if everything goes to bush around here."

"This is not nature," Jin Yeong said, stalking along parallel to me through the cubicles on the other side of the room with one hand in his pocket. "Not human nature. Between eats everything, in the end."

"So long as it doesn't eat me," I said, with a faint shudder. "Oi, have you seen a portal yet? They used to be here on the desks— looked like computers but weren't."

"There is one here," he said, leaning over a cubicle wall and immediately retreating with what was very close to a hiss and a distinctly bleached look to his suit coat at the waist. "Ah, they do not wish people to take them."

"Yeah," I said, stepping up and onto someone's desk to cross into the next cubicle on Jin Yeong's side of the office. All of the cubicles I'd looked into had obvious spaces where portals had once been, and a froth of vines—or sometimes still wires—where they should have connected. "Figured that. Oh, hey! There's one in here, too! Looks like they've had to make a couple trips to get everything. Or maybe they just got tired and gave up. Which one should we take?"

"That one," said Jin Yeong decidedly, grimacing at his bleached front. "This one is...too clean."

"Something the people who took the other portals did, or something Betweeny?"

"It is not Between," he said. "I think it is cleaning for removal."

"Looks like it," I said, grinning, as he put the despised backpack up on the desk beside the portal I'd found. "Whatever it is, this one seems to be okay. I don't know which cords we should be taking with us, though. Reckon this one's important?"

"Take them all," Jin Yeong said. "The leprechaun will kick me if there is one missing."

"That's 'cos you kidnapped him."

His nose lifted slightly. "It was necessary. One should not hold a grudge for that reason. *Hyeong* has kidnapped me, and—"

I pretended not to notice that the sentence had trailed away and stuffed cords that were half vine, half electric into the front pocket of the backpack. "Dreamed about Zero last night," I said, as I did so. "They're doing all right in there, you know. Zero's playing dad, Morgana's playing...I dunno, scary vodka aunt? And none of 'em are dead."

"I am not worried about *Hyeong*," Jin Yeong said coldly. "What are you doing? I said I am not worried."

"Forgot I can do this now," I explained, hugging him a bit tighter. "Now that we're dating, I mean."

"I will accept the hug, but I am not worried; I am *concerned. Hyeong* should not have had to go this far."

"I'm concerned, too," I said, more soberly. I let Jin Yeong go and held the backpack open so that he could slide the column of the portal into it. If I looked at it like a regular human, the portal looked like a computer tower; looking at it with the ability to see Between made it appear...very different. "You reckon Five will be able to use this thing without a Between monitor? There isn't one in the room."

"If not, we have lost nothing but time," Jin Yeong said, shouldering the backpack. "Let us go see the little old lady. She will give us cake."

Since I was feeling much the same way about the possibility of cake, I cheerfully followed him. My phone rang on the way out, as we were passing cubicles toward the elevator that were more hedge than cubicle. Luckily, that didn't stop the elevator from working, even if it did groan a bit.

I saw North's number on the screen and said cheerfully, "How's it going? Got anything for us?"

"Maybe," said Tuatu's voice. "You remember I said I'd found out that a bloke with the name you're after had married in Hobart and had a wife and kid who died?"

"Yeah, I remember," I said grimly, grabbing Jin Yeong's arm as the elevator bounced to a stop.

"Well, it turns out that it was maybe only the wife who died," he said. "The kid might or might not still be around—but under a different name."

The elevator doors didn't open all the way, but that might have been because they were more tree than elevator by then. I glared at them as we stepped out, because I was pretty sure they were just doing it to be difficult. Even if it hadn't taken long for the place to be taken over by Behind, there was no way it should start disintegrating so much more quickly now that Jin Yeong and I were there. There were far too many trees in the lobby now, crowding around the walls and extending in small projections of twos and threes into the centre of the room. They curled all the way around between us and the exit now, too, and that was more concerning.

"What, a witness protection sort of thing?" I asked Tuatu, warily eyeing them.

"Reckon it was more of a fly-by-night thing," the detective said. "That's what North thinks, anyway. The records from your human friends suggest pretty strongly that the group at the time was doing rescue work like that—and that they were active over the time when the boy disappeared. We've got an address for you, anyway. North won't let me send it to you by phone, so we'll come by later on."

"Come 'round to Vesper's place instead of ours," I said, turning around one last time to gaze at the length of the lobby we'd come from. We were nearly at the front doors, but it was starting to feel crowded with all the trees, and I wanted to make sure we weren't missing anything that might be sneaking up on us. "We're trying to avoid the brownies today."

"From what North said, that's a good idea," he said grimly. "All right. Are we setting up base there instead?"

"Nah, just stashing our leprechaun," I said cheerfully. "See you later!"

Jin Yeong, who had been waiting for me to hang up, said, "It is good news, yes?"

"I reckon," I said. I was feeling pretty good about life in general right now. I might not be able to get to Zero and Morgana, or any of the other heirlings, and we might still have a lot of work to do, but we had come out to the Huon Valley without incident, had almost finished our job without incident, *and* we had a very good lead when it came to finding the name we needed to find.

"*Johah*," he said. "Then we can have some fun with those."

"Ah heck," I said sharply, turning on the ball of my foot to see what he was inclining his head toward.

I saw more trees: the usual gum trees that you'd expect to see around this area, even if you didn't expect them to be inside. All bumpy in spots and smooth in spots—and now moving far more than you'd expect a tree to move, even in a high wind. Definitely more than they should have been moving while we were inside.

There were also a few more of them than I remembered there being when I was looking toward the way out a minute or two ago. The mixed bumpiness and smoothness of those extra tree trunks segued from the original trunks all around us until there was double the number of trees, and the trees that had separated from the others were somehow more human and less tree, though I was pretty sure they still had bark.

"What the flamin' heck are these?" I asked Jin Yeong.

"I have not seen them before," he said. "Not in my country, not in any other."

"Fantastic," I said gloomily. "More Australian-specific behindkind."

"All travellers must stop here," said one of the beings closest to us.

If I'd been going on creep-factor alone, I would have drawn swords already; not only were the creatures as ugly and unchancy as all heck, their voices sent the kind of shivers down my spine that you get from nails down a chalkboard. Nails down a chalkboard that could and would kill you at a minute's notice.

Since I was trying to be reasonable and they hadn't actually made more of a move toward us than telling us we had to stop, I didn't draw anything.

I said, "Right. Well, we've stopped. What's the go?"

"You must pay a toll for passing through."

Jin Yeong and I exchanged glances. "I do not pay tolls," he said, with finality. "My face is my passport."

"We have no use for your face. Payment is in magic or blood."

"First of all, *rude*," I said. "He doesn't like it when people don't appreciate his face. Second of all, nobody told us we had to pay in magic or blood to get anywhere around here. No signs, no nothing."

"You have passed through our territory," said one of the beings. "You must pay the price."

"Yeah, we passed through it before, too," I told him. "On our way upstairs—there wasn't a peep out of any of you then. You can't tell me that you didn't notice us going through."

"You may come, but you may not go."

"That would have been useful to know on our way in, mate. Why didn't you tell us then?"

It stared at me with cold eyes as it said, "Lack of knowledge is no excuse for wrongdoing."

JinYeong made a small *pft* through his nose. "It is not wrong-doing to us. We do not live by your laws."

"If you pass through, you must pay."

I said in disbelief, "This is really a shakedown?"

"A payment is required, in magic or blood."

"It's a shakedown. Look mate, you're not getting my magic, and you're sure as heck not getting my blood."

"Then you have chosen death."

"No, you've chosen to be a pain in the flamin' neck, and we're about to become a pain in *your* neck."

"Verry painful," agreed JinYeong silkily, his feet shifting almost imperceptibly until his weight was on his back foot.

Ready to push off and leap for the closest throat at the first sign of attack.

"You got the portal nice and secure?" I asked him softly. "Don't wanna go breaking that. I'm pretty sure there was only that one more we could take, and I don't reckon we'll be able to get back up via the elevator."

"I shall be very careful," he said.

"Blood," said one of the tree beings, and shuffled forward. The others shuffled forward after it, deceptively quick, until the lobby around us was filled with the susurration of tree limbs that said *Blood, blood, blood.*

Jin Yeong sprang for the throat of the nearest while I hung back to source a couple of weapons. There was nothing nearby, but a quick lunge backward scored me a couple of half-size umbrellas that had been mouldering away in an umbrella stand for the last few months. I pressed the trigger button on each, striding forward again, and ducked just in time to avoid a flying Jin Yeong, who tumbled over my head and skidded to a barely-graceful stop on his knees.

I backed up, swapping the umbrella-turned-sword in my left hand to my right, and hauled him to his feet.

"Good thing we got you that backpack," I said. I added, grinning, "Good thing you can fly."

Champing his teeth against something far too gluey and aromatic to be blood, Jin Yeong said in utter outrage, "It is *sap.*"

"That's a bit tough," I said. "You can't kill 'em?"

"Not in this way," he said, cold rage in every syllable that hissed through his sap-coated teeth. "I will *tear them apart.*"

"Go for it," I said, tossing the second sword back into my left hand.

It should have occurred to us that tree beings might not be as susceptible to vampire bite—or any bite, really—as most other beings. It should have occurred to me that nothing short of an axe would do any kind of damage, too, but it wasn't until I swung and connected with those woody bodies that I realised how much trouble we were in.

The trees weren't just impervious to Jin Yeong's particular brand of slaughter, they were proof against any of the cuts and thrusts I could direct at them with my swords. I slashed and cut, but I hit wood and my blades either bounced off or cut too deep and were nearly torn from my hands.

The trees seeped sap, but I couldn't say that they were bleeding—or that they were even injured. And they moved more quickly now that they were annoyed, sweeping, shuffling, never too quick to quite stop me dodging in and out between them, but not slow enough to let me rest, either.

It was a game of slash and duck, where my slashes didn't hurt the enemy and the ducking only served to save me for a few moments and tire me out.

"You keep up with the game of tag," I panted at JinYeong, who seemed to be finding out the same thing. "I'll get an axe or something."

JinYeong darted forward as I darted back, and I skimmed around part of the tree-line that was far too alive and quick for comfort, looking for anything I could use. There had to be something that I could turn into an axe; it was too late to try and persuade my swords that they wanted to be axes instead.

Under cover of JinYeong, I foraged a bit too far and had to retreat again when a section of trees started to look like moving in for the kill. As I ducked back again, I saw something straight and wooden between a few of the tree creatures that pressed in on JinYeong. Somehow or other, he had taken off one of their branches.

I grinned savagely and made a lunge for it, low and fast through the moving roots of the tree creatures. I had my hand on it when one of them smacked me sideways and into the one next to it, leaves and twigs snatching at and just barely missing me. I ducked and rolled again, hastily getting myself out of reach, and collided with one of the couches that were in the lobby. One of the creatures, seeing its moment, lashed out at me, and this time I wasn't quick enough.

A limb that was very nearly a tree-branch tore open my jacket from the breast to the end of my left arm, dragging me forward and very nearly right back into the tree beings.

I shook myself free and leapt backwards, the arm of the jacket flapping against my bark-roughed skin, and stopped to take stock of which limbs were still attached. They were all still there, but the entire left side of my formerly pristine suede jacket was in tatters from shoulder to cuff, hanging on by a few threads at the collar and the seam at the cuff.

I didn't expect the spike of pure rage that stabbed through me. "You glorified and overgrown bunch of garden stakes!" I said wrathfully. "This was my best jacket!"

"*Nae mariya*," Jin Yeong said, panting.

Blood, blood, blood, droned the trees, shuffling closer.

"Fine," I said, taking the heat in the room and tweaking it with Between to send a molten, whispering line of fire down each of my blades that licked back upward toward my cuffs too. The jacket was toast already—might as well see what I could do with fire. "Let's see how you lot go with forest fire."

I swung down from high, crossed blades, wide and fast and fiery, and this time when the edges of my swords hit the closest creature, I felt them bite in like they ought to. I expected a reaction, but I didn't expect the huge shuddering of wailing that began and swept the trees backwards, each of them catching alight with fire as voracious as it was bright.

"*Heck!*" I said, catching my breath as I fell back to allow them to retreat. The lobby around us grew quiet and treeless in no time, but I still heard that voiceless wailing somewhere in the distance.

Throwing a narrow, molten look around, Jin Yeong said, "I think they will not come back," and swiped the back of his cuff angrily against his mouth, smearing sap.

"I'm not waiting around to find out," I said hastily.

I stripped off the ruined jacket, leaving it to moulder away into the ground with everything else that Between would eventually take over, and headed toward the door.

Jin Yeong, still gnashing his teeth and grimacing at the taste of sap, followed behind me, grumbling beneath his breath. "I want to drink *blood*."

"You're not biting me with that stuff on your teeth," I told him. "You can have a blood bag when we get home."

I was pretty cranky, too. If it had been one of my hoodies, I wouldn't have been cranky at it being ruined. Most of them *had* been ruined already, if it came to that. But it was the suede jacket Jin Yeong had bought me, and it had been beautiful and strong and made me look *very cool*, and now it was in tatters on the floor of a behindkind portal to the world Behind.

"I will buy you another one," said Jin Yeong. "You do not have to be upset."

"I'm not upset," I said crossly. "I'm frustrated."

"Yes; you are not upset, and I will buy you a new jacket," he said. "For now, we will go and eat cake with the little old lady. Later, there will be blood and more clothes."

CHAPTER FIVE

THE PORTAL WAS STILL IN ONE PIECE WHEN WE GOT TO Vesper's street, which was pretty flamin' impressive. We also weren't being followed by brownies, which was about as good news as we were likely to have all day. Hopefully, they'd gone back to our house, from where we could conveniently lead them astray again if we needed to.

In the meantime, it was just a matter of checking that there weren't any unusual signs of activity in the ground floor level of the units on our way up—or any behindkind loitering in the stairwells. I dunno, maybe it would have relieved some of my irritation to have been able to fight something. I wasn't given the chance for it; we got safely up to Vesper's unit, and she opened the door to us, beaming, which pretty much did for the irritation anyway.

"You'd better come in and have some cake," she said to me, and pinched Jin Yeong's cheek. "Your friend is already here."

Sure enough, there was a short, stumpy figure sitting in one of the couches when we got inside. It was Five—541, if you want his full name, but I always just call him Five. Leprechaun, peglegged, and ridiculously fond of biscuits, he could follow a money trail through any system of records, human or behind-kind. And it looked like he wasn't holding a grudge for being kidnapped and hoisted in front of a window about a week ago, either.

"Didn't I tell you?" he said to Jin Yeong, who was still behind me. "Can't keep *her* anywhere she doesn't want to be. Wasn't any need to be dragging me out of house and home, legs flapping, to get her out of anywhere!"

"G'day, Five!" I said, heading for the other couch. "Got you a portal—well, Jin Yeong has; it's in his backpack."

Five opened and closed his mouth a few times before he huffed, "In a backpack? For all that's gold, in a *backpack*!"

"Figured it was safer if we had to fight," I told him. Then, making Five sit up and splutter into his tea in outrage, I asked Vesper, "He been causing much trouble?"

"He's a charming young man," said Vesper serenely.

Five went about five shades redder and seemed to expand at the chest. When he caught sight of my grin, he snapped, "If you've damaged my portal by letting that vampire carry it, green and gold—!"

"It's because he was carrying it that it isn't in pieces," I said, still grinning. "You should have seen him playing tag with the trees! How's the leg?"

The leprechaun tucked his peg leg behind the other leg. "It's happy where it is, so I'll thank you not to eye it off!"

"No worries, I have better weapons these days," I told him. "Ones that aren't curmudgeonly about changing into useful things."

"It's already useful where it is!" he snapped.

I saw the moment his eyes grew beady with excitement and knew that Jin Yeong must have taken the portal out.

"At last," he muttered, almost feverishly, wriggling down from his chair. "Madam, if I may...?"

"Oh yes, the coffee table is free," agreed Vesper. "I don't use it at *all*, but it does slow down the shadows that come through the windows from time to time. Very useful."

Jin Yeong and I exchanged glances for the second time that day.

"You have a problem with shadows?" he asked her. "I will fix it."

"It's not what I'd call a problem, as such," Vesper said. "But it is rather uncomfortable on rainy days. Sometimes it's quite the charge from my chair to the kitchen, and they do like to coil in among the wool."

"We'll take a look outside," I said. "Has it gotten worse lately?"

Vesper's eyes dwelt on me warmly. "It got much better after you visited, my dear. In fact, it wasn't until a few days ago that the shadows started. After the house died, I should think."

So Ralph's house was completely dead, was it? I felt a bit bad about that: I was pretty certain that there were more than a few people still trapped in there. With any luck, they'd been kicked out in a not-too-dangerous part of Behind or Between—or, even better, into the human world again.

Five, setting up the portal with short, practised movements that made a mockery of the amount of time it had taken Jin Yeong and me to uninstall it all, huffed, "Green and gold! Is it just a few shadows? I'll take care of it for you tonight, so I will. It's the least I can do for a good bed and a good meal."

"And the cake," I pointed out. There was a pretty big piece of it next to his cup of coffee, and I was pretty sure it wasn't anything like his first. "Has Daniel already gone?"

"Brought me and left an hour ago," Five said, his eyes never leaving the portal. "I'll need a monitor, you know."

"Figured," I said. "We'll have to bring you one tomorrow."

"You can use the tv, dear," Vesper said to him. "I only use it for the noise anyway."

I didn't ask her what she wanted the noise for: given that it was Vesper I was talking to, the answer could have ranged anywhere from it being a tool to avoid paying too much attention to the odder things in her life that came as a consequence of living too close to what basically amounted to a haunted house, to it being a simple remedy for loneliness.

Five got to work on the back of the portal, leaving a series of cords-that-were-nearly-vines trailing from the backpack while I watched, and JinYeong ate his own cake as well as Five's. Vesper brought more cake, then went back to the knitting she'd probably been working on before we arrived, serenely untouchable.

"This looks a bit like the setup Abigail and her lot were getting done in their place," I said, after a while. "Computer cords turning to vines."

"That's what happens when you work with portals," said Five briefly. "The behindkind network isn't like your human network."

"So this is basically computer systems and natural internet," I said. What had the humans been doing with a behindkind setup? Abigail was—had been—very anti-fae. "Marazul said there wasn't much like this around."

"There's not," Five said, disappearing behind the tv. "Not like his—not like this, either. Leprechauns are the only ones who got into any sort of localised data entry and retrieval, but the way it connects and runs is different to how your human computers and internet run. What we've got is more of a private network, and it has its limits—your human internet has far wider reach and the search functions are different."

"Yeah, Marazul said you'd do a better job with the files we need you to look through because you know how to search the behindkind way."

Five, obviously trying not to look too pleased, vanished behind the tv again. "Very kind of him to say so," said his voice. "When I think of the things he does with magic and human systems—green and gold! A very good compliment."

"Figured you two would get along," I said, grinning. "Next

thing you know, you'll be sending people to and fro via intercompany memo."

"If I send anything via intercompany memo, we'll be visited by a few enforcers from the revenue investigations unit," Five said, climbing back up onto the couch.

"That you asking for a bit of protection?" I asked him. "You reckon you could run into trouble using this setup?"

"The dogs will come back," Jin Yeong said, before Five could reply. "We will not leave this place unprotected."

"Well," said Five, hesitating. "I won't say no, but only because I'd as lief not bring trouble on my hostess."

"You didn't mind bringing trouble on me," I said, grinning. "All right, all right, no need to pinch my cake! I take it back. Here, pinch Jin Yeong's cake instead; it's his second slice anyway."

I spent that night with Jin Yeong, both of us sprawled on the upstairs living room floor and neither of us sleeping. The house was a lot quieter without Daniel and the others, and I didn't really like leaving Athelas alone upstairs, even if it was no different to leaving him alone in the house with only one of the lycanthropes for a guard.

Jin Yeong didn't seem to mind the quiet, nor was he inclined to talk. I don't know what he was thinking about, but I was pretty sure he was murmuring maths to himself for a little while, and as for me—I didn't quite dare share my thoughts just yet. They were still too unformed and dangerous, and I needed to think them for longer before it would feel safe to say them.

So while Jin Yeong muttered maths and occasionally, absently kissed the hairline above my left ear, I thought my thoughts and tried to bring them into a more reasonable, useful shape. The problem was, while I could find a way to bring them into a useful shape, I wasn't sure it would ever be a reasonable shape. I wasn't sure if it was a shape I could live with, either.

Far too long before those reasonable shapes ever eventuated, I started to see something else instead. I don't think it was exactly a dream; I wasn't awake, but I don't think I was asleep, either. I could have been having a visitation from my Nightmare, except that there was no Athelas and no house—nothing at all, in fact.

But I heard someone breathing, and maybe someone crying quietly, before the darkness grew less bewildering and shapes began to coalesce into some sort of meaning. I saw a glimmer of moisture on a face, and recognised Sarah just as she wiped the back of her arm over her face. A darker trail spread in the wake of that swipe—blood, I was pretty sure.

Ralph's voice said in a subdued sort of way, "I can look after *myself*," and I strained my eyes to see the sharp, disagreeable face, because it sounded like he might be on the point of tears, too.

"I told you," said Sarah. "You're my brother now, and I'm not going to let overgrown water bugs eat you. It's only a scratch, you idiot."

"Bind it up," Zero's voice said briefly, and I finally understood the meaning of the huge mass of shadow that now began to glow white with my understanding.

It was good to see his face, even if I wasn't exactly seeing the real thing. He had a bit of blood and dirt up around his collar, but he looked like he was in pretty good nick despite that, and I felt the squeeze of my heart relax a little bit. I hadn't expected to see him dead when I next saw him, but I'd expected it to be a fight in the arena, and it was nice to see him relatively whole.

He said, "Do it quickly: we leave in five minutes whether or not you're cleaned up, and if there's a blood trail it won't matter how far we run."

"I've got it," said Morgana. Her back was to me; all shifting shadow and deep darkness that moved far too much to be just hair. "I saw how to do this on tv. Just tell me if it's too tight, because they said that can cause trouble, too. Don't want your arm to drop off—sorry, forget that. It's fine. It looks fine. Definitely won't drop off."

"How long will it take them to find us?" asked Sarah, her eyes on Zero and her arm resolutely held out to Morgana's ministrations.

"If they find a trace, a few minutes. If they don't, we've got a good chance to stay hidden for as long as it takes the king to think of a new way to drive us out of hiding. Zombie, do you want to move to the front? I'm expecting more trouble from the rear."

"Nope," said Morgana, looking at him over her shoulder. I caught a brief glimpse of deep shadows that covered the lower half of her face, and her eyes burned a deeper kind of darkness. "I'm hungry: the rear is mine."

"Think you mean the brain is yours," muttered Sarah. "Right, that's it. I'm ready to head out. Let's get moving."

I shouldn't have been smiling when I woke up. I shouldn't have been okay to hear that they were running for their lives. But all I could seem to remember was that I had heard every one of the voices and seen every one of the faces that had been in my house until a few days ago.

Every one of them was alive, even if they were missing a few pieces. And Zero was still there to keep them alive.

I just had to make sure I got them out while they were still that way.

I DON'T THINK it was morbid curiosity that made me slip into Athelas' room the next morning. I could have just gone downstairs to make coffee and breakfast for myself and Jin Yeong—an easier task now that the lycanthropes were all with Vesper and, presumably, eating her out of house and home instead of me—but there was still too much I didn't understand. Still too much I needed to know.

None of what I wanted to know would help me in my quest to

find the king's name, but I couldn't help wanting to know more about the why of Athelas' betrayal. It was part of those thoughts that were useful but not reasonable, and I wanted to know exactly how useful they could be.

JinYeong caught me at the door, but only said, "You are going to talk to the old man again."

"Yeah."

"I will not make coffee."

"Good grief, no!" I said hastily. JinYeong might make better coffee than the lycanthropes did, but it still couldn't be called good. "I won't be long. I've got an idea about what we can do while we're waiting to hear back from Marazul and Five."

"Then we will buy coffee," he said. "And I will go and drink blood."

While JinYeong went to get a blood bag, I boiled the little jug that someone had brought upstairs to sit next to the lamp by the wall and made tea from one of the teabags that were in a tupperware container in front of it.

No fancy tea for Athelas these days, but it was tea. There were biscuits, too; just like the tea, they weren't the delightful things that Athelas had been used to eating, but they would hold him over until lunch time.

I took the tea and biscuits in with me when I went into the room. It was stupid, but I preferred to have a physical reason for being in his room. I don't know why: it wasn't like Athelas would be fooled by it. Maybe it was because it gave me the illusion of being able to leave as soon as the job I was supposedly doing was done. I only had to wait around until Athelas finished eating his breakfast, and then I could leave.

It gave me a reason to go away again if I needed to. It gave me a length of time I could count down if things were too horrible to stay in there for a long time.

This time, Athelas woke nearly as soon as I entered the room, without any need for me to enter his memories as well.

"Ah," he said, opening his eyes. "I see that it's morning once again. How pleasant."

"Got some breakfast for you," I said brusquely.

"So I see. The collective household taste seems to have suffered a decline while I've been gone—is this what you subject your guests to?"

"Tuatu doesn't care what tea he drinks," I said. "And we don't keep a fae-who-betrayed-us tea selection on hand, so this'll have to do."

"I see that you're combative this morning."

"Nope. Just not making myself be polite. Are you gunna eat and drink this lot, or not? I can take it away if you don't want to eat it."

"There's no need to be hasty," Athelas said mildly. "Since I'm awake, I might as well eat. Perhaps you would be kind enough to put the biscuits on the arm of the chair."

"All right, but if you throw them at me, there's gunna be trouble."

"I shouldn't dream of it. I'm surprised you're not accompanied by your pet vampire, by the way."

"I am here," said a cold voice from the doorway.

"How very maladroit of me," said Athelas complacently. "Evidently I must make a habit of checking the doorway before I speak amiss."

"You can see the doorway from where you're sitting," I said. There was a clear line of sight to the door from the bureau mirror, which Athelas must have been looking straight at, since I was in front of—and not wider than—the mirror.

"One assumes you did not come to see me for the purpose of being offended," Athelas said. "Might one enquire exactly why you did come to see me? Ah—are you here to wring more memories out of me?"

"Just asking questions this time," I said.

"How novel," said Athelas, sipping his tea with the faintest of grimaces.

"Don't complain about the tea," I told him. "Traitors and friend-murderers only get bog standard tea."

"A logical standard to insist upon. What do you wish to know, Pet? Perhaps I shall answer you."

"Why didn't you just kill me when you got rid of my champions?" I asked. "You could have done it then, nice and easy—you wouldn't even have had to play games with my parents. I was there in their power, and then I was there in your power."

"There's no fun in doing things that way," Athelas said. He was back to his old, grey self again, the way he'd been just before he tried to kill me and left. "When one becomes content merely to kill, life has lost its spice."

I had the feeling he was just trying to bait me—or maybe that he was trying to wring any kind of emotion from me—so I only said, "Doesn't look like you're enjoying life much these days, either."

"Oh yes, but one's satisfaction is contingent upon the quality and durability of one's work, after all! One need not be working presently to appreciate the work of one's past."

"Is that how you look at your life before now?" I asked, and I was surprised to find that the first emotion that surfaced above the absolute, barren hopelessness of my soul was pity. "Sitting here, you're pleased with how things have turned out?"

"One doesn't like to sound so vain," he said, but his eyes didn't quite meet mine. "However, I'm moderately satisfied with the general trajectory of my work."

"Good to know," I said, pushing away from the bureau drawers. "C'mon, Jin Yeong; we've got somewhere we need to be."

"That was relatively painless," called Athelas after me. "Are you perhaps softening?"

"Nope," I said, stopping in the doorway and turning a little to look at him over my shoulder. "Just making sure I'm doing things in my own way instead of yours or the king's."

LUCKILY FOR MY peace of mind, Kyle—or maybe it was Kevin—arrived just before Jin Yeong and I were about to leave. It wasn't as though I hadn't done my best to shut Athelas up in his own mind again, but I still didn't like leaving him alone.

"I'm here to babysit the creepy old tea-drinker," Kyle said. "I'm not feeding him, though."

"That's all right; we'll be back before lunch," I said, hoping it was true.

There wasn't too much we could do until we knew the king's name—if we ever did find out what it was—and all I had to take Jin Yeong out for was a chase after certain loose ends that had evaded us until now. We'd been a bit busy trying not to die to follow through on some of our earlier leads.

"No schoolkids today," I observed to Jin Yeong, as we left the front yard.

No schoolkids, but there was a group of what looked like yobbos hanging around the house down one and across the street —leaning up against the fence or sitting on the metal top post, all flannel and trakkie daks and narrow eyes.

He chuckled darkly. "I think they were not happy about yesterday."

"Reckon they know we lost 'em on purpose?"

"*Arra.*"

"Yeah, that's what I figured."

Unless I was very much mistaken, the brownies were making absolutely no attempt to blend with their surroundings. It wasn't so much that they had given up their guise of being schoolkids, or even the fact that a group of twenty-something blokes moving down the street together were downright threatening: the most obvious clue that they wanted us to know that we were being watched was the way they...well, *watched* us.

They watched us like they were planning on mugging us behind the first convenient car or down the first convenient street. Maybe they were.

"Reckon they want a fight," I said. "Either that or they just want us to sweat. We're definitely not gunna lose 'em by diving into a pub again."

"Clumsy," muttered Jin Yeong dismissively. "We will go and drink coffee and make them wait."

"Suits me," I said. "You want pancakes?"

"Yes. I will pay."

"You mean pay, or talk yourself out of paying?"

"*Nega arraseo halkae*," he said, sauntering on with his nose in the air and the hand that wasn't around mine in his pocket.

"You know we don't have to pretend we're dating anymore," I pointed out, since I knew it was no good trying to talk seriously about vamping people when he was in a mischievous mood. "You don't have to hold my hand anymore."

"I wish to hold your hand."

"Okay, I was just saying."

"I will always wish to hold your hand."

I shot a look up at him and found that he was pouting.

"What? What did I do?"

"You are *supposed* to say that you wish to hold my hand as well."

"Oh. Well, it's not like I *don't* want to!" I protested. "I'm just not used to holding people's hands."

Jin Yeong gave an unconvinced sniff but said, "It is enough. For now."

We took our time wandering down to the centre of Hobart, the brownies following behind in a loud group that made people cross the street to avoid them, and found ourselves in a small shop that promised coffee and pancakes. The brownies settled across the road again, this time at the outside tables of the pub there, where they fit in very well. The pub owner eyed them uneasily, and I didn't blame him: they looked like exactly the kind of yobbos who would start throwing stuff into the street if they had a few more drinks.

"There is no news from the leprechaun or the merman?" asked Jin Yeong, when our coffee and pancakes were brought out to us.

"Nope," I said. "We'll catch up with both of 'em after lunch if we haven't heard anything until then."

"Then what will we do today? Are we to annoy the brownies?"

"I reckon we've got a few things we can catch up on," I said, grinning at the sudden light in his eyes. "Stuff we didn't get to do because his royal-pain-in-the-backsideness decided to bung us all into the Heirling Trials."

"That letter box?"

"Got it in one," I said approvingly. "That kid we shook down said he checks the P.O. box once a week, so even if we don't catch whoever's emptying out the letter box he delivers to, we should be able to get a good idea of when they'll be back next. We can also have a bit of a look at whatever is in there."

Jin Yeong's eyes dwelt on me thoughtfully. "You still think it is someone from Upper Management?"

"Not exactly," I said slowly.

I wasn't sure exactly what I did think, but I seemed to sense Athelas' meticulous and secretive hand in everything lately. I fished in my pocket for a moment before my fingers found the irregular shape of a key hiding in there; I put it on the table between us.

"It might be Upper Management. Might be not. But there are still a couple of things that don't fit yet: Athelas left behind a key, his network badge, and a ring."

"A ring?" Jin Yeong's brows rose. "Here is only a key."

"Heck," I said softly. I'd forgotten about the ring, even though I'd automatically mentioned it. It had rolled under the bed in

Mum and Dad's room while I was grabbing the network badge a little while ago. I hadn't stopped to scrabble for it because a curious lycanthrope had been watching me, and it had seemed somehow secret.

And now that I thought of it, it tickled away at a memory that wouldn't quite come out.

I would have to try and winkle both ring and memory out later.

"I'll show you later," I said. "Forgot to bring it with me."

JinYeong turned the key over between his fingers. "This belongs to the old man? I think it is a human thing."

"Yeah," I said. "It's even money between him wanting me to find it or just not wanting Zero's dad to get hold of it. Either way, it might connect to what we're doing today, or might not. Figured it might come in handy, so I brought it along anyway."

"There will be something," he said. "If not today, there will be a moment, a time, when it fits. Until then, we can do nothing."

"Figured that," I said gloomily. "Okay, we might as well go find the letter box, I suppose."

JinYeong leaned back casually and tilted his head very slightly in the direction of the group of brownies. "What of those ones?"

"Let 'em follow us," I said slowly. "We'll just have to be careful about finding interesting stuff when there aren't any people around."

"Will it be dangerous for them to know what we find?"

"Reckon Athelas is at the end of the line anyway, which would mean that nothing we find out here will make the king any happier if he finds out, too—or help him out at all if he does. And if we deal with the king in the arena—"

JinYeong slid his forearms across the table and leaned on them, crowding the pancakes. "You are still concerned about the old man."

"I didn't say that," I said uncomfortably. "I just meant that—"

"—even if we do find something, it will not hurt him," said Jin Yeong, nodding. "*Arraseo.*"

I narrowed my eyes at him, but it wasn't exactly as if he was wrong. "It's rude to tell people the truth like that," I said.

"Yes," he said. "You do it *all the time*."

I couldn't help laughing. "Yeah, you put up with a lot. Don't know why you want to date me."

"Ah," he said. "That. I wish to date you so that I can persuade you to marry me."

I gazed at him for a while before I said, "You've got kangaroos in the top paddock."

He grinned. "Even when you are rude, I love you."

"Yeah, and that's the bit I don't understand," I said. "It's all well and good to dance around answering my questions, but—"

"I love you because you don't bite your friends when you are hurt; you get up and fight, and then fight again," he said. And then, while I was still staring at him, he leaned just slightly further in and kissed the end of my nose. "And I love you because you are warm."

"All humans are warm," I said.

Jin Yeong leaned his chin on his arms but didn't take his eyes off me. "They are not warm like you."

"Pretty sure humans are all equally warm, give or take a few degrees," I said.

"That is not what I meant."

There was probably a time and a place for being flustered by your vampire boyfriend, but under the gaze of a score of brownies wasn't exactly it.

I cleared my throat and said, "Eat your pancakes."

CHAPTER SIX

WE HAD A PRETTY LEISURELY BREAKFAST, THEN TOOK THE
brownies for a walk with us up around the outskirts of North
Hobart, this time heading more toward the old brewery and
Mount Wellington than home. Luckily for me, I'd written down
the address we needed to visit—it was a place we'd learned about
from an erstwhile pattern-making student called Jonny just a little
while before everything went to pieces. The house had apparently
burned down, but someone sending letters to the letterbox there
had been not only paying the power bills of Morgana's and my
houses but had been taking care of a few others—all of us with
either dead or seriously changed parents—not to mention
keeping the water connected.

They'd been doing it in such a circuitous way as to make it
very hard to know that it was the same person doing it, too—let
alone making it possible for anyone to find them. But with the
help of Five and Tuatu, Jin Yeong and I had found that person, on
paper at least.

Now it was time to find the person hiding behind the paper, if
we could. At the very least, we could find the letter box. Whatever we found there, I was pretty sure it would only lead back to

Athelas, though I wasn't sure exactly how quickly. He was the one who had had Tuatu collecting all the information that had given me the heads-up about someone having paid off the power at not just my place, but Morgana's and Ralph's houses, too. I was less sure than ever that it was the smoking gun I'd hoped for—more sure that it was something Athelas had meant me to find all along —but I knew I wanted to know for sure, given what I'd seen in Athelas' memories.

And as we approached the block that had the right number on its dilapidated letterbox, another thing caught my attention.

"There are neighbours," I said in surprise.

"That is surprising?"

"Since when do people who want to hide what they're doing make sure they have witnesses?" I pointed out, walking across the nature strip to the letter box as if I belonged there.

"There is respectability in everyday life," Jin Yeong said, and followed me in the front yard.

"You telling me that it's less suspicious to keep coming and going from a burned out house where there are other people coming and going, or what?"

"*Maja*. It is sensible."

"Yeah, but there's a thin line between being less suspicious and opening yourself up to dangerous scrutiny," I complained. I looked the place over in one glance and sent another down the street to see how far away our followers were. The whole space was just a burned-out wreck of block and rubble, though it looked like there was more if I took a moment to check out the shape of it Between. "It's weird, that's all."

"This is a dirty place," Jin Yeong said with disfavour. "We will look and then go."

"Don't reckon it's as burned down and dirty as it looks," I said. Looking at it Between, there was almost an entire house there; probably a copy of what it had been when it was still standing.

Or maybe the whole place was still there and it just *looked* burned from the street?

"Wonder what it looks like from next door?" I muttered, putting my hand out to touch the latch on top of the gate. "Heck, here come the brownies. What now?"

"We check the mail," JinYeong said, as if pointing out the obvious.

"Can't," I said, pointing at the lock that kept the top of the letterbox flush with the bottom half. "Reckon whoever it is who comes here doesn't want people getting their mail."

"Maybe," said JinYeong, narrowing his eyes at the lock, "you can use Between."

"Can't do that, either," I said after a brief, abortive attempt to fiddle with the threads that ran through the lock itself and, failing that, an attempt to push my hand right through the substance of the letterbox while pretending it was a kind of Between. "Whoever did it has used magic, not Between. We could try to find some bolt cutters, but—"

JinYeong raised a brow at me. "What? You are angry. Why are you suddenly angry?"

"Flamin' heck," I growled, digging the key I'd taken from Athelas' room out of my pocket. "If this works, I'm gunna—actually, I don't know what I'm gunna do, but I'll probably kick someone in the shins."

He instinctively stepped back, which made me grin.

"Not you," I told him. "Can't ruin your trousers. I'll kick Athelas when we get home."

I put the key in the lock, and in it slid, quiet and soft and just right. It turned without a hitch when I twisted it, too. JinYeong gave a gleeful chuckle and snatched the lid up as I took the lock away, revealing three or four envelopes.

"Flamin' heck," I said sourly once again, looking from the key to the letters and back again.

It wasn't like Athelas couldn't have gotten the key somehow, through his own little machinations, but I had a bad feeling that it went deeper than that.

"Right," I said, grabbing the envelopes. "Off we go."

One of his brows went up, and a gleam of amusement lit his dark eyes. "We are going? Already?"

"Nope," I said, those letters firmly in hand. "It looks like my idea was right, and I don't flamin' like it! It doesn't make sense. We're going to see the neighbours."

JinYeong's hand on my upper arm dragged me back softly but inexorably.

"Oh yeah," I said. "Brownies. Reckon we can do a sneaky and skip over the back fence?"

He nodded sedately. "*Kurae*. That will be better."

"You up for vamping someone?"

He blinked a little. "We need to vamp them?"

"If you reckon that someone isn't gunna be pretty flamin' uptight about strangers skipping over their fence and coming into their kitchen, you've got a big surprise coming. We wanna talk to them, not have 'em call the cops on us."

"There is no house," JinYeong pointed out, but he followed me when I grabbed the latch of the gate once again and let us both in. Then he said, "Ah. This tricky old man."

The house was there, as if it had never been gone. Now it wasn't a ghost structure just barely sketched amidst the ruins, it was a solid presence of brick and façade.

"Thought so," I said in satisfaction. "Let's go."

"Perhaps the brownies will follow us anyway," he warned. "The door is old and not very strong."

"Since when do behindkind use doors, anyway?" I asked. "We'll have to risk it. It's better than siccing them on the neighbours instead."

The front door was locked when I tried it, which wasn't surprising; I could have just looked around a bit and then tried to walk through it as usual if no one was looking, but it occurred to me just in time to try the key on that lock, too.

The key turned without a hitch once again, so I let it go and said to Jin Yeong, "After you."

He grinned and turned the key himself, then stepped through the door. Apparently the invitation thing isn't entirely a myth, and things are easier if there's an invitation; turning the key in the lock seemed like it would be a good compromise.

I followed him through the door, half expecting to have brownies on my back at any second, but I managed to shut the door behind me before anything happened. I did hear the creak of the wooden stairs as several sets of feet climbed onto the patio, but the weight attached to those feet settled in a few different places around the patio without trying to get through the door.

That was nice. Couldn't have Jin Yeong ruining his tie today.

I grabbed the back of his suit jacket as he passed through the dining area on his way to the back door, and when he looked enquiringly at me, said softly, "Hang on. I wanna have a look at these letters before we go jumping any fences. I know what they're gunna be, but I want to double check."

I opened two of the letters in quick succession while Jin Yeong opened the third, and we laid each of the thin sheafs on the dining table to stare down at them. Three bills looked back up at us: two power bills and a rates notice—each of them with a familiar address attached.

"What is it?" Jin Yeong asked. "These are the same as the ones the policeman found."

"Yep," I said, short and quiet. "I'm pretty sure Athelas has been paying the bills on my house—Morgana's and Ralph's, too. That's why we're going over to see the neighbour; I reckon they'll confirm it for us if we ask."

Jin Yeong's eyes danced unexpectedly. "It is just like the old man. What do you think he meant by it?"

"That's the question," I said, gathering up the papers along with a truly impressive amount of dust. "And no matter how hard I think about it, I can't find a good answer. Not one I like, anyway."

"There is a good answer," he said. "But I think there is no happy answer."

"Yeah." I leafed through the notices once more, double-checking to make sure that I hadn't missed anything. There was nothing else. Nothing surprising, either.

"You already knew what we would find here," Jin Yeong said accusingly.

"Not *knew*," I said. "I definitely suspected. You can't go deep-diving through Athelas' memories and not start to realise that he's so twisty he's turned back on himself. He wasn't on our side, but I don't know that he was on the king's side, either—I don't even know if he was fully on Lord Sero's side."

"He was on *Hyeong*'s side," Jin Yeong said unexpectedly. "But not in a way that makes *Hyeong* happy now, *kuchi*?"

"Yeah," I said again. "I reckon that's about as close as Athelas gets to picking sides—doing everything for Zero and...I don't know what else, yet. But I reckon he expected to make Zero king, whether or not Zero wanted it. That's why it's hard to tell if he was on Lord Sero's side or not—they both wanted the same thing."

"The old man understands power," said Jin Yeong, with one shoulder shrugging up. "And when he loves, he tries to give power. Why do you think he wanted the detective to gather all of those things?"

"It was either really dumb or really smart of him," I said. I'd been thinking about that, too. "And Athelas—"

"The old man is twisty, but not stupid," agreed Jin Yeong. "He wanted you to find out?"

"I reckon," I said. "If not me, Zero."

"You think he wanted you to know he was the murderer?"

"No," I said slowly. I had the feeling that all of this had been part of a carefully orchestrated series of falling dominoes—a piece in Athelas' plan that was perhaps marked merely as *closure*. "I think he was maybe trying to be kind to Zero. I think he wanted Zero to understand everything after he was dead, and Zero was king."

Jin Yeong sniffed a small laugh. "The old man did not expect to live after he returned to Lord Sero. I think he was too twisty."

"That's what I reckon," I said. "He's been dancing around Lord Sero's orders for years, I reckon; probably figured it'd catch up with him when he went back. He must have known that Tuatu would do everything he could to make sure he let us know what was happening if Athelas forced him to do something—and he must have expected me to tell Zero."

"Probably he thought *Hyeong* would find out for himself," Jin Yeong said.

It was my turn to sniff, but it was a bit more on the sharp side than Jin Yeong's had been. "Well, he wasn't wrong about Zero doing what he wanted, anyway," I said sourly. I was still a bit sore about Zero pinching back the information I had pinched from North.

"I just wish I could figure out exactly what he meant by all of it," I said. I had a suspicion or two, but I didn't particularly want to acknowledge them. There would be too much else I had to acknowledge first. "He had a lot of opportunities to kill me before he signed the pet contract—and if all he was doing was trying to put Zero on the throne, it would have been a lot safer to kill me. He killed most of the other heirlings."

"Ask him," said Jin Yeong. "See if he will tell you."

"Reckon that's about as dangerous as digging through his memories," I said gloomily. I'd already asked, anyway. "All right, we might as well get a wriggle on. You think the brownies will stay on the patio?"

He nodded. "If we do not go Between, they will stay where they are."

"Right, out the back door like normal people it is, then," I said, suiting the action to the words. "Here, givus a boost. I don't have your flying abilities."

Jin Yeong primly gave me a boost that put me right on top of the shoulder-height red brick wall, and elegantly threw himself over it while I was dropping down to the grass on the other side. The owner of the backyard met us at the sliding glass door to his backyard, a scowl on his face and his mouth opened—probably to demand to know what the heck we thought we were doing in his backyard—but before he could say anything Jin Yeong looked brightly at him.

"*Annyeong*, friend. You would like to invite us in, I think."

"Come on in!" the bloke said, the scowl vanishing straight away. He gave us a good grin, too, as if he really was glad to see us.

Nice bloke, I thought, feeling a bit guilty. Probably had a nice little barbeque out the back somewhere, too, and a lot of steak in the freezer.

"Lot of people out there on the street today," I said, as we slipped through the sliding back door.

"Yeah, it's a bit weird," he said. "I should probably check it out; we don't usually get many people coming along the street. Last time we had a bunch of yobbos along out here, they burnt a house down."

"I don't reckon you wanna check this bunch out," I told him, catching Jin Yeong's eye. I shook my head when the man wiggled his kettle questioningly at me and added, "Nah, no need for a cuppa; we'll be heading off pretty quickly."

"I would not go outside this afternoon, if I were you," Jin Yeong said to the man, his eyes warning.

"Fair enough," he said, putting the kettle back down. "They gave me a bad feeling, anyway. Either of you want a beer? I don't have much to eat at the moment, but I can do you some salt and vinegar chips."

"We're all good," I said, grinning at Jin Yeong's baffled expression. Apparently he hadn't tried salt and vinegar chips yet. "Oi, someone comes past to collect the mail every month, don't they?"

"Oh, that. Yeah. I don't know why they don't just redirect it like normal people. There isn't even a house there anymore. Maybe they like giving the old bloke a job."

"Old bloke in tweedy sorta suits with elbow patches and grey eyes?" I asked, my heart beating just a bit too fast.

"That's the fella. He seems to like taking a walk up the street to get the mail, and he's always friendly enough if I'm out in the front garden."

I exchanged a look with Jin Yeong. It wasn't like Athelas to be seen or remembered unless he wanted to be remembered. "Waves to you, does he?"

"Stops for a chat every now and then," the man explained. "Last time he told me about some computer trouble he was having, and the time before that it was a pet that was making life hard for him."

"The flamin' *cheek* of it!" I muttered, caught between an aching, bitter kind of amusement and pure outrage. Not only was Athelas stopping to talk with random neighbours while he was doing secret business, he had the absolute gall to complain about me while he was doing it!

"Yes, that pet was very troublesome," said Jin Yeong solemnly, but there was a wicked glint to his eye that the bloke didn't see. "Did anyone else come to the house?"

"No one ever came except the kid that delivers the mail, and him with the tweed suit—not until the two of you. And now there's a group of bogans camped out on the patio."

"Don't worry, we'll get rid of 'em when we go," I promised him. "You just keep inside for a couple hours after we go, all right?"

"I won't go out this afternoon," he said, echoing Jin Yeong earlier. "Oh, are you not staying?"

"We better keep moving," I said. "Just wanted to ask you about our other mate."

It felt odd and uncomfortable to call Athelas that; after everything that had happened in the last week or two, it probably wouldn't ever feel normal again. I caught myself up and thought fiercely, *It doesn't* have *to feel normal. It's not normal. He's not one of us and he never will be again*, but that only left me feeling hollow and sick again.

"We will go now," said Jin Yeong, tugging lightly at my sleeve. "We have some trouble to take away with us before it becomes bored."

"Right," I agreed hastily, and followed him out the sliding door and into the back yard once more.

There was a scattering of brownies that I fairly *felt* as we passed back through the abandoned house before Jin Yeong flung open the door and sauntered out onto the patio and down the stairs. He didn't pause, despite the fact that he must have seen the last brownie playing at high-jump with the fence at the front, and when I caught up with him at the front gate he was grinning in a dark, bloody sort of way.

"Are you spoiling for a fight, or are you just enjoying the fact that Athelas' devious hands are behind pretty much everything we dig up?" I asked him.

"He is such a sneaky old thing," Jin Yeong said, his voice deep with satisfaction. "My Ruth, do you wonder—do you wonder why those dead heirlings are still so troublesome? They are dead, yes, but they are *still here*."

"Yeah," I said, slipping my hand into his almost by instinct and trying not to notice how bright it made his eyes. "I wonder about that a lot."

Daniel and the other lycanthropes were back by the time we got home—for lunch, apparently. Someone had brought home four roast chooks and a huge tub of mashed potato that was revolving in the microwave to reheat, while North perched on the arm of the couch Tuatu was sitting on and sniffed curiously from time to time.

"I thought you didn't eat," I heard him say, as we came into the living room.

"I don't have to," she said. "But that smells *good*."

"I don't know about you," he said. "But I'm not going to get between that lot and their food."

"There's enough for everyone," Daniel said shortly. "No one will get bitten."

He slung plates out on the table with a couple of deep lines between his brows. I stepped up into the dining room to join him while Jin Yeong skirted around the lycanthropes to get a blood bag out of the fridge.

"Had a dream last night," I told him, since I knew exactly why he was distracted.

"Yeah?" He looked at me briefly. "Wait, what sort of a dream?"

"One where I saw everyone in the arena. Morgana, Zero, Sarah—the whole lot of them."

His hand paused, still holding the last plate. "What were they doing?"

"Running, mostly," I admitted. "Just thought you'd like to know: they're dreams, but they're really not. And everyone's definitely still alive."

Daniel, the tension leaving his shoulders, blew out his cheeks and put down the last plate. "I kept hoping for that, but it's still a relief to hear it. Do you think Zero can actually kill the king?"

"Save us pulling out the king ourselves and going through all the trouble, you mean?"

It wasn't like I hadn't thought it—wasn't like I hadn't wished I could just let things run their course like that.

Daniel nodded. "If they're still alive and doing well..."

"No," I said plainly. "If it was just Zero by himself—yeah,

maybe. But he's trying to keep them all alive, too, and if there's anything I know about the king of Behind, it's that he goes for the soft parts and the young ones first."

"So we're still going ahead with the plan," he said. "All right."

"How were the shadows over at Vesper's unit last night, anyway?"

"The shadows are lively and too real for my comfort," Tuatu said grimly, turning around to lean on the couch back. "And as soon as the portal was up and running this morning, they started coming out from every corner. One of 'em touched me, and it was so cold it burned."

"Did you have to run for the kitchen?"

"No," he said, showing a darker colour around his brown cheeks. "Vesper threw me her circular knitting needles and I garrotted a few of the beggars with them—apparently hers have a steel core instead of the usual brass, and they didn't like it much. Five got a few of them with the vacuum cleaner, too, once we figured out he had to throw salt as well."

"Sounds like fun," I said, grinning.

"It wasn't," Daniel said coldly. "I don't think they'll be back for a while, though."

"So long as you got some info for us on the king's real name, it's worth it," I said. I hadn't been the one doing the fighting, of course, but Daniel still nodded in agreement. "You did get some info, didn't you?"

"It took a while, but we were able to find a few records there," said Tuatu. "It would have been quicker if he could have down-loaded everything straight from my phone, but there are a few firewalls that the portal couldn't get through—he says they need another kind of computer. When we were able to get to the right files, we cross-referenced the couple of names Marazul sent us, and came up with a few possible records."

"Spit them out, then," Daniel said impatiently.

"A Doctor Lucas Lin who was married to Emily Simmons—"

"That's the one we had earlier, right? The woman who died, but whose son might not have died?"

"That's the one. We found the son by cross referencing the wife's maiden name with school records and the family birth records. We found a Tammy Simmons listed at one of the most prestigious boarding schools in Melbourne, but no birth record for him."

"Let me guess," Daniel said. "There was a birth record for Tammy Lin."

Tuatu nodded. "It turns out that the son was sent to boarding school under the mother's maiden name, but on the money of a Lynden Thompson. There aren't records of a Lynden Thompson anywhere but at the bank."

With something bright and meaningful tickling at the back of my mind, I said absently, "So he turned up one day, opened an account, and then just disappeared again?"

"Looks like it. His money was used to finance a few different ventures around Hobart, but there's no record of him actually owning anything—or of being born, living, or dying."

"Sounds like our bloke," I said.

"Whoever he was, he even owned a speakeasy back in the day," Tuatu added. "*Reason and Rhyme*, he called it—the outside was a poetry club; inside, it was a bar. His money spotted it, anyway."

"Weird," I said. "We didn't have the prohibition here."

"I don't think it was that kind of speakeasy," Tuatu said significantly.

"Oh! Right," I said, processing the new information. "It was a behindkind bar."

"The only place you could meet with a lycanthrope at one table, a vampire at another, and a group of fae at the bar," North said, nodding. "Even a human or two, every now and then. I remember places like that. You don't see them much anymore."

"Hang on!" I said, caught by a sudden thought that was joining itself to a few others in quick succession, a webbed, wildfire of ideas that suddenly all made sense. I sputtered a laugh, and muttered to myself, "Flamin' fae: always thinking they're *so* flamin' clever and everyone else is so flamin' stupid!"

Jin Yeong's eyes grew bright. "Ah," he said. "You know something. You have found someone to kick?"

"Yeah," I said. "You know what? I'm always saying how fae think they're so clever, but I forgot something, too. He's gotta have some human in him—the king, I mean. He's gotta have some human in him way back in the line. And he's *really* old—old enough to either know some really old stories, or to have been the one who started them."

"You know his name?" said Jin Yeong, his voice deep with satisfaction.

"I know his name," I said, a bubble of laughter in my throat. "He's old-school—even the way he named his son was old-school. All of his human names around Hobart reference the same name: Lukas Lin—Lynden Thompson, for pete's sake!—and they all have references to the old poems and stories. Even the speakeasy —*Rhymer*!"

North made a small, contemptuous puff of air. "That old story? It was about him?"

"No, but I reckon his parents might have had a bit of inspiration from real life," I said. "And I reckon the story is probably a lot different when you tell it from Behind. He had to get his necessary bit of human from somewhere, and I'm pretty sure he carried the name with him to remind himself to keep the human bit of him secret and safe."

Daniel exchanged looks with his lycanthropes and then with North, who shrugged at him. "It's not like he would have had to worry about anyone Behind knowing the story and guessing his name," he said. "Only half-and-halfers like us would have a chance of knowing both sides of the story, and most of us don't really go to human schools. It's too dangerous for the humans—and for us, if we get caught."

"School was not necessary for me," North said, shrugging again.

I saw the way her eyes grew a bit distant, though, and I knew Tuatu did, too. There was a time when North had gone to school like a normal child and had loved it—and had given it up so that the human child she'd replaced could have her life back.

"I still don't know what you're talking about," said Dylan, or Darren. "And I went to school before I turned."

"You were probably pulling on little girls' pigtails," I said, grinning. I poked Jin Yeong in the ribs and said, "I s'pose you're gunna tell me that they don't have the Thomas the Rhymer and Tam Lin stories in Korea?"

"Our behindkind stories are different," he said.

I added, "Flamin' heck, even his kid's name is a derivative! *Tammy*, you said, didn't you Tuatu? The flamin' cheek of it, thinking that no one would get what he was saying!"

"I did say that," Tuatu said. "For pity's sake, Ruth, just tell us what it is!"

"It's Thomas," I said, in quiet satisfaction. "His name is Thomas."

CHAPTER SEVEN

I suppose we could have started for the arena straight away, but not even Daniel protested when I stipulated on starting out tomorrow. I still had a few things that needed to be done tonight to give us the best chance at making it out of the arena alive, and I had a lingering hope that I would have one more vision of a lively, protective Zero with all his charges alive and well.

Not to mention that we were all going to function a heck of a lot better on a full night's sleep. Sleep doesn't matter too much to fae or zombies, but it makes a heck of a big difference to humans —not to mention the fact that you don't want to be around sleepy lycanthropes, in battle or in the living room.

Mind you, that was providing we could manage to fall asleep at all.

We all meant to go to bed early—planning on getting up early as well, of course—but all of us seemed to have the same problem with actually falling asleep. Jin Yeong didn't need sleep, so it wasn't surprising that he'd stare at the ceiling for hours, but I listened to the others turning and huffing and at last snoring for several hours without being able to do more than close my eyes ineffectively.

North, who never settled for sleep or anything else, left the house to give everyone else a chance to sleep—or that's what she said, anyway. I saw her eyes linger with a curious mix of longing and affection on Tuatu as she passed him on her way out. He sprawled out on the couch with two of the lycanthropes curled up against him, and although he wasn't snoring at that point, he wasn't far off.

"And they're worried about *us*," I mumbled to JinYeong, who turned on his side to wrap his other arm around my shoulders and tuck his face into my neck. "Don't bite me while I'm trying to sleep."

"*Ani*," he said. "I will bite you tomorrow instead."

I didn't sleep much, but I still got up early the next day and decided to take a long shower before the sun was up. It wasn't so much that I needed the shower as that I needed the time to think —or maybe to *not* think—and stand still and try not to panic. I would have liked to have gone and looked for the ring I'd told JinYeong about, but I very much didn't want to do that with Athelas still in the room.

The household wasn't awake when I headed for the shower, and North hadn't come back, so I sent Tuatu upstairs with a cup of tea for Athelas and crouched with my shoulders under the running water to help wash away the anxiety.

I came out with slightly damp hair and a few bits of potpourri on the shoulders of my shirt that the banshees had thrown at me on my way out, to find a pale-faced Chelsea hurrying to meet me.

"He's gone!" she said, her voice sharp with fear. "The boss just went up to see why Tuatu didn't come back down and found him sitting up against the wall."

"Flamin' heck," I said softly. I hadn't realised how exposed and frightened I would feel at hearing the news. Even though I knew it would be the wisest and most sensible course for Athelas to disappear, never to be seen again, it still frightened me that he was loose and out in the world. I asked, "Is Tuatu okay?"

"Just sleepy, by the looks of it," she said. "He seems to be coming out of it, but you probably better come up and have a look at him."

I followed her upstairs, and my conscience pricked me when I saw how grey Tuatu had gone, propped up against the wall and dazed around the eyes, breathing a bit too slowly.

"Sorry," I said to him, rubbing one of his hands between mine. "I shouldn't have sent you up alone."

"I'm sorry," he said jerkily. "Couldn't...stop him using me. But I told him...it was the last time."

"Your debt," I said, nodding. "Good work."

"It wasn't good work!" he snapped, and to my relief, that made his colour deepen a bit. "I let him go!"

"Yeah, but you're not dead, and you're not indebted to him anymore either," I said. "How'd he do it?"

"He was already awake, and he said you probably had the room and restraints attuned to all of us to stop any of us hurting ourselves. The cuffs unlocked with the key from my own cuffs."

"Yeah," I said, breathing in deeply through my nose. "I figured that someone would touch him—or that he'd try to use his restraints as a weapon. It's my fault; he shouldn't have even been able to wake up properly. Here, try to get up. I think we should get your blood circulating a bit—I reckon he used a bit of magic once the cuffs were off to make sure that you stayed put long enough for him to get away."

"Get North in here," suggested Chelsea. "She'll get his blood going."

Tuatu, looking very fed up, said as he got up, "I'll be fine. Just give me some tea, and we'll see what we can do to fix this."

"No time to try and fix it," I said. "You lot head downstairs, I want to have a closer look at the room."

Jin Yeong obviously didn't consider himself part of the *lot*, and I suppose I mustn't have thought about him as part of it either, because he didn't go and I didn't tell him to go. He just stood with his shoulders against the wall while I grubbed around under the bed in all the dust and at last laid my hand on a smooth, rounded citrine ring.

"Got you," I said, and wriggled back out from under the bed to look at it more closely.

As soon as I saw it in the morning light, I knew exactly where I'd actually seen it last. I hadn't been able to tickle the memory free because the memory I'd seen it in hadn't been my own memory—it had been Athelas' memory, from the night he killed my parents.

"Heck," I said, a bit thickly. Jin Yeong raised an eyebrow at me and I explained, "It's Mum's. Saw it on her finger in one of Athelas' memories."

"Ah," he said. He didn't seem surprised, and I suppose I wasn't surprised, either. "Why did the old man have it?"

"Dunno," I said, and put it in the coin pocket of my jeans. Maybe it would be good luck. Maybe I'd one day have a chance to ask Athelas why he'd taken it from my mother's finger. "Reckon he took it for a reason, though. Let's go down and have breakfast."

"I do not need breakfast," he said chidingly, but he followed me downstairs and into the kitchen, where seven lycanthropes and a cold, worried detective were already waiting for us.

"What are we going to do now?" Tuatu asked, as soon as he saw us.

"We're gunna have breakfast, and then we're gunna get the king out of his arena and into ours," I said, trying to sound soothing.

"If we go quickly enough, it shouldn't even matter that the old man escaped, should it?" asked Chantelle. "We're going to be shut into the arena no matter what happens—no one in and no one out, that's the deal, isn't it?"

"Yeah," I said, crossing into the kitchen to boil the jug. "Even if he knew what we were planning and tried to report to someone, it wouldn't do him much good. I don't know who he'd report to, either; Zero's dad is dead."

Daniel shot me a brief, unimpressed look and sat down at the bench. "You don't reckon he knew everything that was going on?"

"Could have," I said. Instinct said that it was more than possible; knowing Athelas, he would somehow have figured out how to hear what was going on in the house despite being confined to one room. "It doesn't matter too much at this point."

"You don't reckon he's trying to help the king?"

"He could be," I said. "But even if he is, how will he tell the king anything about us?"

"They will not report," agreed Jin Yeong. "Not yet. It is their nature; they will not report until the time when they should report, and to the person they ought to report to."

"Gotta love bureaucracy in the fae world," I said. "When it works in our favour, anyway. Right, is everyone here? We need to make a few decisions."

Jin Yeong said, "The North Wind is gone and the crazy one is not here."

"Yeah, I noticed," I said. I'd also noticed that there were no forks left in my cutlery drawer when I opened it to get something I could stir my coffee with, so Les was probably out there doing what he usually did—whatever that was. He'd turn up again when he was ready—he might even turn up in the arena if it took his fancy—so I wasn't too worried about him.

It would have been nice to have forks too, of course, but they were replaceable. Just like all the spoons Les had taken while we were in the Trials.

"What do we need to decide?" asked Tuatu, dropping down heavily at the table.

He looked far too weary, which was a worry. He could just be struggling with guilt—or Athelas could have done something to him that would only come out later.

I was struggling with my own guilt and didn't much want to talk about it, so I just said, "I didn't sleep much last night."

I hadn't slept at all, and the vampire spit that was now running around in my veins was the brightest, most sparkly part of me. If it wasn't for that, I'd probably be tossing back coffee after coffee and buzzing in a completely different way.

Daniel's eyes were on me straight away. "You mean you didn't dream."

"Got it in one," I said.

"Does that mean—"

"It means I didn't sleep," I told him firmly. "That's all."

His voice was grim. "So we're going to have to go into our arena without knowing whether they're still alive?"

"Nope," I said. "I know someone who can give us a pretty good idea of what's going on in there—so long as you're happy to take the time to do it."

"Green and gold, *another* one?" muttered Five. "How many behindkind do you have at your call, kid?"

"Only the nice ones," I said, to disarm him. I shoved the honey and jam at Daniel and started piling coffee and tea on the tea tray to take over to the table. "This one is less of a friend and more of an acquaintance. I helped him escape from an Upper Management office one time—he's the sort of bloke who has really big ears."

Daniel shot me a narrowed look but took the breakfast things and passed them to another lycanthrope to put on the table. He did the same with the plates I passed to him.

"He's in intelligence?" he said. "What good will that do us? We don't need people who can find stuff out, we need someone who can—"

"—hear really well," I finished for him. "Yeah. Told you he has really big ears."

"Someone better explain so I know what's going on," said Tuatu, while Daniel and Five both stared at me, open-mouthed.

"You've got an *auris*?" Five said at last, taking a cup of coffee mechanically. "An actual, live auris?"

"Little bat-bloke?" I asked, grabbing my own coffee. "Big ears, four arms; hears really well and doesn't like being shut in a little cage just to listen to other people?"

Daniel leaned back impatiently to avoid Kyle and Kevin, who were slinging plates across the tabletop without regard to elbows. "Yes, but you've got one, that's what you're saying?"

"I haven't *got* one," I said, surprised. "That's the point. I let him out of a cage once when I went a bit further Behind than I meant to. He said if I ever needed him, I should just call out, 'Big Ears, Big Ears, hear my call' or something like that. Oh wait, it was *answer my call*."

"Had an auris, let it go!" uttered Five at the ceiling. "Of course! She throws someone else's pegleg at a dropbear!"

"He said he'd help," I pointed out. "It's not like he didn't say thanks."

"Careful, I reckon he's gunna pop," said Kevin, or Kyle, watching Five with a fascinated eye. "You think it'll come when you call?"

"Only one way to find out," I said, shrugging. "We don't have anything to lose, and it might help."

"Do it," said Daniel. "We'll do it. It's going to take us a little while to eat breakfast, anyway. We might as well use the time."

Five, crossing his arms over his chest, said crankily, "I am *not* dancing for it!"

I shot him a sideways look, but Daniel explained, "Auri usually ask for a price—and they don't have to help anyone and don't really care about anyone, so they usually get you to do stuff that makes you look stupid."

"That's why fae trap the little blighters if they can," Five muttered. "Keep 'em captive and they have to do as they're told if they want to eat."

"Yeah, I've noticed that fae don't like being made to look

stupid," I said, not even trying to contain my grin. "All right. I'll do any dancing he wants—the rest of you can sit there looking cool."

"Me too," said Darren, looking nice and toothy with anticipation. "I was in the school dance team for three years—I'd like to see it make me look stupid."

"We'll be lucky if it doesn't make the lot of you wear bonnets and bleat out 'The Shepherdess and the Goblin'," mumbled Five, the voice of gloom.

"I look flamin' good in a bonnet," said Kyle, leaning on his elbows. "It's my perky ears."

I called out, "Big Ears, Big Ears, answer my call," nice and loud before anyone could start fighting, and that made them all sit up straight and pay attention.

Something that was more movement—or energy—than sound made a pretty big *pop* near the centre of the table, and a small, furry creature with big ears picked its leg up and out of the honey pot, its four arms extended cautiously, fur standing on end. It didn't seem to know what honey was, but it sniffed the leg, cautiously licked it, then settled down happily to lick the rest of the honey off.

"I know what I'm not having on my pancakes," muttered one of the lycanthropes, then shut his mouth as the auris darted him a look.

"I don't know you," it said. "It will be expensive, and I don't think you want to pay what I'll ask. Who told you that you could use those words?"

"He didn't use them," I said. I would have snabbled the honey pot and replaced it if the auris hadn't grabbed it again. "That was me."

"Oh, it's you," the creature said, stopping mid-chug with its eyes bright and shrewd. "You didn't have to shout; I would have heard you anyway."

"Yeah, I see that," I said, and couldn't help my eyes sliding across to its ears. I'd forgotten how big they were—each of them was at least the same size as its body and maybe a bit bigger.

"I'd make you eat mouse parfait for that, but we're friends," it said cheerfully.

It didn't look like it was cranky, though; if anything, I would have said it was gleeful. It was a lot better for the wear than when I'd last seen it in a lot of ways, and that was nice.

It looked as though my friends found the auris' gleefulness more worrisome than hopeful—which was fair enough, since I wasn't the one likely to be eating mouse parfait in exchange for requests for help.

On the other hand...

I grinned suddenly, understanding. "You don't like owing favours to people," I said.

"No debts," it said, grinning back. It took another slurp of honey, then said, "You've got one request, and only one. You want surveillance? A name? A password? Recording of surveillance will be extra—*they* can pay."

"We don't need recording of anything," I said hastily, before Five could throw something. "We just need to listen to someone for a bit."

"Our friends—" began Dylan, but I cut him off before he could say another word.

"We want to listen to the king for a bit," I said instead.

"Pet—" Daniel cut himself off and firmly pressed his lips together.

"Yeah," I said. "It's better to listen to the king than to the others. We'll still get a good idea of how they're doing, and we might find out something that'll make life easier for us."

I turned back to the auris and found that it was looking at me with eyes that were fierce and bright.

"Ah!" it said. "Then you *are* the pet!"

"That's me," I said. This was another thing I wasn't sure was a good or bad thing.

"Blackpoint says hello and sorry he couldn't get back to you sooner. He also said that your interference is a bit much and can you stop it before you cause more problems."

I stared at the auris for a very long time, caught between rage and the awareness that I couldn't blame it for Blackpoint's messages or attitude.

Someone laughed bitterly, and maybe it was me, because it stopped when I said, "Figured he cared a bit more than that. If he didn't want me to poke my nose in, he should have looked after the humans better. He was the one who brought most of them into the Behind world."

"That's the fae for you," said the auris. "Don't care about much, very bossy."

"Yeah? Why are you carrying messages for them, then?" I asked.

"I met this one when he was pretending to be human," it explained. "You know where the king is?"

"Sort of. Does it make a difference?"

"It makes a difference to how long it takes me to find someone," it said, and ran its tongue around the inside of the honey pot for good measure. "The closer you get me to the right location, the quicker I'll be able to pick up on their vibrations."

"It might not be as easy as you think," I said. "The king's inside a Challenge arena."

"Very good, very good," it muttered, trotting back and forth on the tabletop, around cups and over plates. "Metaphysical space and Between is much easier to work with, and with his preference toward magic he'll never notice it."

I watched it rearrange the space and wondered if it knew exactly what I was asking it to do.

"Good thing Palomena's not here," I said, as it pushed the sugar bowl and the cylinder of serving utensils closer together, then sat down. "She'd have you for being a traitor. She's gotta report stuff like this to the king once he's out."

The auris propped its left ear against the sugar bowl and carefully curled the very top edge of it. It looked as though it was tuning a tv antenna, and I suppose it was.

"I suppose you're planning to kill him?"

"Yeah," I said, and Five gave a wordless howl of irritation across the table. It was only fair that the auris knew what it was getting into.

"Then I'll only be a traitor for as long as it takes you to kill him," said the auris. "I'll thank you to make sure you do it before he can send the Investigators after me."

I raised my brows at it. "They'd be able to catch you?"

"Of course not," it said irritably, settling back against the utensil cylinder and closing its eyes as if it was about to take a nap. "But it makes life difficult for me and I prefer life to be easy for me. I need to find a warm lap and stop working for hire."

"Don't we all," muttered Daniel. "Look, when are you going to start?"

The auris opened its mouth, but instead of its voice, what I heard was the king saying, "I can't give you reinforcements right now; you'll have to do your best with what you have."

"Your majesty, we're already thin on the ground—if you could assist us with at least some scraps of magic—"

"And what do you suggest I protect myself with while you're out playing tag-and-dodge with the people you should be killing?" enquired the king, and his voice was terrifyingly light and pleasant. "I'll recharge tonight when I'm sure I won't be followed—you'll have to make do until then. I will get you some reinforcements when I have the strength with which to call or make them."

I grinned, hard and sharp, and when I met Daniel's eyes I saw the same gritty satisfaction in them. If we acted today, within the next few hours, we would catch the king at his lowest ebb for magic.

"Between is coming in through the place where we lost the

younger Lord Sero," said the second voice again. It sounded as if it expected to be hit, and I wasn't surprised to hear the tone of the king's voice.

"What else does one expect of Between?" he asked acidly. "It does as it pleases, without regard to the whims of anyone else."

It probably just didn't like kings who tried to turn the worlds upside down to keep power, I thought, but didn't say so aloud. I didn't want to risk interrupting the auris and stopping our stream of information.

"Is there anyone who could—"

"Are you incapable of working through Between? If so, I'll be happy to relieve you of your position. You haven't yet proved to me that you can do more than waste my power in a fruitless search for a group of mostly-dead heirlings and their runaway leader."

"We'll work with it, your majesty," said the other voice hurriedly. "We do have an idea of where Lord Sero is, but their zombie is making it very hard to approach without being noticed, and there's a human who can do human magic—"

The auris' eyes snapped open, making me jump. "That's it," it said. "Your free trial is at an end. You can call me again but it'll cost you more than you want to pay and I might not help you anyway."

"Yeah, I heard that's how you blokes work," I said, pretending not to see the proud grin on Daniel's face, or the tears in his eyes. "You know the way out, don't you?"

"Down and out," it said.

I said, "If you're still looking for a warm lap, come back and find me. I know someone with a warm lap and too many shadows around the place—she makes a nice tea cake, too."

The big fruit-bat eyes glowed, but it said carefully, "Perhaps I'll do that. I'll look into it."

"Take care of yourself, all right?" I said. "Don't go getting stuffed into cages again."

"Speak for yourself," it said. Then it grabbed the honey pot and vanished into the woodwork.

Into the brief, pregnant silence, Five said, "Green and gold, I wanted honey with my pancakes!"

NORTH RETURNED SHORTLY after breakfast was on the table, looking windswept and wild-eyed and somehow more *other* than usual, her skirts in constant motion and her hair wafting around her.

"What happened here?" she demanded, her eyes immediately on Tuatu as she entered.

"He's had a run-in with Athelas," I said. "Athelas made him let him go."

North strode across the room but stopped short behind Tuatu's chair, her skirts and hair continuing the forward motion that she couldn't. Her hand reached out to his tense shoulder as he sat there with his eyes closed, his tea untouched in front of him.

"Wouldn't if I were you," I said, watching that hovering hand. I knew exactly why she'd gone out last night: the effect of being fond of a human while being the incarnation of the North Wind was dangerously humanising to North. Any kind of physical touch took away a little bit more of her power and brought her a little bit closer to being human—at least for a while. Touching Tuatu now would likely defeat the purpose of her deliberate distance— or at least hamper her efforts for a while.

North stiffened, but she pulled her hand back to herself and gave the smallest of nods in acknowledgement.

"What do we do now? Pick another location? The old man certainly knows too much."

"We've been discussing it, and we don't have the time," Daniel said shortly. "Morgana's been in there with the king for four full days—we know they're alive, but they'll be about the only ones who still are, and we've got until tonight to take the king away before he recharges."

"But he'll know *everything*," Tuatu said stubbornly. "We can't go walking into what could be a trap, for all we know! Shouldn't we at least change the place just in case he tells someone?"

"Nope," I said. "We're going to go ahead with our plan exactly as it is. We never discussed anything in front of him, and if Athelas knows what's good for him, he'll have run for the hills—it's not like the king is gunna be giving him any prizes for not killing me."

"He might think he can get the king's favour by turning up and killing you in the arena," Tuatu said miserably. "If he's the sort to make last ditch efforts."

"He's definitely the sort to make last ditch efforts," I said. "But we're going ahead with our plan anyway. There's not much else we can do; we need to get everyone out of the arena as quickly as possible. And if we get the king out in the next couple of hours, he's going to be as weak as he'll ever be. It's the perfect time and the perfect place."

"We go now," Five said gruffly. "That's decided. What else did we have to decide?"

"Well," I said. "I've got a plan, but it's more of an idea than a plan, and—"

"Business as usual," snapped Five. "Green and gold, the day *you* have a plan that isn't just running around and waving a sword at something—"

"Yeah, but doesn't it work out well?" I said, grinning. "You even got your pegleg back, and I reckon that's a win."

"What's your plan?" asked North. "Even if we do get the king in the arena, he won't surrender easily. His magic—"

"That's the plan," I said. "His magic is the strongest part of him, right? Even the auris said so."

"Strong enough that he's kept the throne for as long as he

has," Daniel pointed out. "But I don't have any personal run-ins with him, so—"

"He walks Between," I said, trying to remember every moment I'd spent in the king's company before I knew he was the king as well as after. "He even lives Between, in a way. But he doesn't *use* it—not to do stuff. He uses his magic and his brain."

North nodded. "You want to bind him? How?"

"Figured we might try a circle of salt and iron filings."

"That's a bit old-fashioned," Daniel said, exchanging a look with Five, who shrugged.

"Old-fashioned, but still effective," he said.

"Very effective," North agreed. "The Palmers kept their daughter safe that way for many years—I don't think they used salt, though. That's an interesting variation."

"I saw somebody use it once," I said, and that was another memory I allowed to run through my mind. I already knew what I needed to know from it, but it felt safer to check again, and again.

"What do we do once we have him?"

"We've got to try and bind magic," I said. "We won't be able to get him out of the circle until we do."

"What if we can't bind his magic?" asked Daniel.

"We kill him, of course," said North, prompting a startled and mildly horrified look from Tuatu.

"That's one of the bits I'm not sure about," I admitted. "I don't know if he has to die or if I can just keep him captive and end the arena trial. I don't know if anyone would even try and hold him responsible for anything he's done if we do take him captive and end the trial."

"He's got to die," Daniel said flatly. "And I'm all for incapacitating him first. The less of us he kills, the better."

"I agree," said North. "Whatever happens, he has to die. If he doesn't, he's still king and we're still traitors. I'm too busy to be killed."

"I'm too busy to be killed, too," said one of the lycanthropes.

"Also, I just don't want to die. If we're going to fight the king, we might as well kill him."

"Okay," I said, even though I felt sick to my stomach. I knew the king had to die—I knew that if it came right down to it, I could be the one to have to do it—I was even very sure that it was the right thing to do. It just made me sick to think about doing it outside of a fight, as if I was an executioner. "Then we agree that the king doesn't leave the arena alive."

Everyone nodded, but none of us looked exactly cheerful about it and I could understand why. At least I wasn't one of the king's subjects.

Chelsea asked, "When are we heading out?"

"After breakfast," I said, helping myself to another piece of French toast.

If you have to have a last meal, breakfast is a nice one to have: there are pancakes, French toast, bacon, croissants—anything slightly brunchy and delicious is up for grabs.

If some of us were gunna die today, we were gunna die well-fed.

We gathered beneath Hobart's central business district in the darkness of the Hobart Rivulet tunnel around mid-morning. It wasn't completely dark; there had been some attempt at lighting the place for the walking tours that used to happen, but most of the lights were darkened by mildew or had blown their bulbs a while ago. The lights that were still working gave a kind of heavily-shadowed half-light, but more luminous by far was the sheer amount of Between to the place.

The shadows weren't green in any way that could be seen by the eye, but they *felt* green. They felt as though they were sieving reality to me through the filter of Between, and in the glow they created around them, I saw things moving that shouldn't have been real.

"This is gunna be good," I said, more to myself than anyone else. Memories came back to me, thick and fast, and I knew then for certain that we couldn't have settled on a better place.

Jin Yeong, looking around with narrowed eyes, sniffed slightly. "I think the king will also like it."

"Yeah," I said. "But that can't be helped, and we already know he's more magical than Between-focused. I don't reckon you can bend the rules for as long as he has and expect the system to love you, even if it is a twisty system."

He shrugged one shoulder. "I do not know about Between."

"You go through it all the time," I said, looking up at him in surprise. "What do you mean, you don't know about it?"

"You breathe air all the time," he said, slightly sulky. "So you should make a hurricane."

A breeze whipped up my hair around my face and pushed Jin Yeong's carefully coiffed hair askew.

"I can do it," said North.

"Yes, but you are abnormal," Jin Yeong told her. "That is my *point*."

"Right," said Daniel, pointedly speaking a bit louder. "If you want to know where everything is, listen up. Once we're shut in, it'll be a bit late to try and get your footing."

"Yes, boss," I said, and two of the lycanthropes snickered before Daniel scowled at them

"There are two main ways in and out—where we came in here near the hospital, and up toward the top of Davey Street heading toward the brewery. There are access tunnels here and there, plus a few viewing holes near the Mall and Wellington Court."

"Anywhere for us to hole up and defend ourselves if things go wrong?" asked Tuatu.

Daniel cocked his head sideways, indicating a faintly lit series of blocks. "That's the Wellington Bridge. Sandstone, I think. Most of it is still the same as it was when it first got built, so it'll probably keep off a bit of magic—what do you reckon, Pet?"

"I reckon someone did a good job laying the sandstone with magic and steel," I said, looking it over. "Fae don't like stuff that's been built with the help of metals, do they?"

"Nope," he said, grinning. "And there's magic there, right?"

"Yeah," I said curiously. "More than I would have expected. This can be our rallying point, I reckon. There isn't much behind it: just a bit of tunnel until it exits out onto the street. We can't get out that way, though—it's barred."

Where we were, the tunnel arched over our heads, made of brickwork done some time in the 19th century; below our feet was the uncertain edge of cement and, right in the middle, the rivulet itself. If we took the bridge as our rallying point, we wouldn't be able to get out, but anything fae—such as the king—would have trouble getting to us. I had a feeling that they might not even know we were there, with the amount of metal and human magic threading through it.

On the other hand, if we really needed to run...

The tunnel wasn't very wide here, and if we had to run after trying to fight the king, there was nowhere to go but back up the tunnel, and precious few turns to it, if the tunnel I remembered was correct.

"It's going to be hard to fight properly," I said.

"Yep," Daniel said. "There are a few places where there's space to fight, but mostly it's stuff like this."

I touched the curving brick wall beside me and felt the muffled mix of human work and Between tendrils, and perhaps even a few threads of what felt like human magic. If I needed to get through the walls, I would easily be able to do it.

"Let's go a bit further," I said to Daniel. "I want to make sure I'm remembering everything properly. If it comes to a fight, reckon I can do a bit of expanding around the walls."

"I wish you wouldn't grin at me like that. It makes me feel like something's about to go for my throat."

"Don't worry, it's not your throat it'll be going for," I said.

I was beginning to feel reasonably hopeful about everything. The entire underground area of the rivulet felt familiar and usable in a way that was all the best bits of human and Behind combined—a Between of familiarity that was no doubt a result of my human magic and Between abilities meeting in a space that seemed exactly designed to give me the best of both of those worlds.

I was certain that I could use this place as an arena with all the ability that the king was now displaying in the arena he'd chosen. More than that, I was certain that someone like me had once worked here—had once helped to form the walls and overhead arches that ran with such a welcoming sort of magic.

"Right," I said. "First we'll have a bit of a walk through; then we'll find the perfect spot to call the king in and do a bit of trapping. We've set up our emergency meeting point: back at the bridge."

"We should divide into two companies," North said.

I grinned, but she wasn't wrong. "Don't trust me, huh? All right, don't panic, Tuatu; I'm just kidding. You and North wanna take the cascade side of the tunnel along with Five? You can check to make sure there's nothing nasty ready to jump out at us later and then come back here. I should have found a good spot to lay everything out by then."

"The rest of us will go with you," Daniel said.

North nodded in agreement and disappeared into the darkness with Tuatu and Five. I left the lycanthropes and Jin Yeong behind as I strode eagerly through the tunnel in the other direction, looking for somewhere to call in the king without having us too closely packed together in case something went wrong, and that was uneven enough to hide a sprinkled circle of salt and iron shavings.

The king's magic was the most dangerous part of him, and that danger would need to be dealt with first. I couldn't exactly bind his magic without him being there—I didn't even know if I could do it with him there—but for the time being, I could bind the whole of him, body and magic, within the same sort of working that my parents had once bound Athelas. I knew better than to leave enough physical trace so that he could use it as Athelas had done. Once that was done, it would be a matter of trying to remove his magic from him—or of deciding exactly how we were going to dispose of him.

It was probably going to be a long process, I thought, stepping up from the uneven bricks and onto cement as the tunnel widened out. But if we got the king out of the arena and away from Zero and the others, at least they would be safe. I wished I could have thought of a way to bring Zero in here as well; he was bound to be worried once he figured out what had happened. It would also have been nice to have at least one more very large, very good fighter.

I let myself think briefly and regretfully of the times when I had walked into a fight with all three of my psychos, and then pushed those thoughts away. There was no time to be thinking of Athelas right now—it did no good, and it looked as though I'd found the spot I was looking for, anyway.

Opening wide, with the ground across the rivulet paved with cement rather than the previous brickwork, the area I had walked into seemed to be a utility space for powersheds, generators, and abandoned scaffolding.

Workmen only, said a placard on the wall. I passed it and climbed up an incline to look at the area properly.

It had a high, uneven ceiling that was stippled with what were probably bats, along with a few metal protrusions and even the odd chain or two—probably left over from whatever construction team had cemented the place and put in the "workman only" areas. It looked as though they'd clipped the chains to weighted boards to swing building materials across the rivulet.

I jumped across to the slightly higher ground across the rivulet and found a couple of utility doors there in the wall that also said

Danger. No admittance. If I looked down from here, I could see the edge of the concrete but not what was directly below it. It was darker toward the edges of the concrete, too; all moss and secret green that would be very useful for hiding what I was supposed to be hiding.

I gave the place a pretty thorough once-over as Jin Yeong arrived silently in the shadows to watch me, and by the time I was back on the concrete platform I could hear the boisterous sounds of the lycanthropes catching up, too.

"Who's got the salt?" I called out to them. "And who's got the shavings? We might as well get going on our little containment job so that we can start pulling the king out of our hat. Reckon this is a good spot; he won't be able to see the circle from up here if I don't manage to get him directly into the circle first go."

Chelsea and Kyle crossed the rivulet, each with a ten-kilo sack of salt, and loped up to me.

"Round the edges," I said, bringing them with me to show them exactly where I wanted it laid. "And make sure you lay it so that he can't grab a handful or anything."

"What fae maniac would grab a handful of iron shavings and salt?" Daniel asked, horrified. "It'd go straight through them!"

"Yeah," I said, with the lingering remembrance of Athelas' memory at the back of my mind. "It did."

We laid the salt and shavings, clearing away anything that was big enough to provide a stepping stone or a break in the belt of salt, and at the same time had too much surface to hide the fact that there was salt spread across it. By the time we'd cleared the areas we needed to clear and had resprinkled dust and dirt after the salt and shavings to make the area look untouched, North and Tuatu had come back with Five.

Looking over the area worriedly, Tuatu asked, "Ruth, are you sure this is really going to stop him?"

I couldn't blame him: if you looked at it from an outside point of view, there wasn't much to be seen.

"'Course," I said soothingly. "It doesn't look like much, but that's a design feature, not a design flaw."

Our work mixed with the dirt and dust already on the concrete and blended so well that even when North lit the place with a ball of magic, it didn't glint off the shavings.

"It's just so…" Tuatu trailed off, and North supplied, "Fragile?"

I couldn't help grinning. "Catch any fae in one of these and you'll see if it's fragile. They can't use their magic while they're inside; saw a memory about it once."

"You saw a—never mind. Is it all right for you to be standing inside it while you're making it?"

"Don't reckon it'll do any harm," I said. "It's not a trap for me, so as long as I make sure I don't scatter anything on my way out, it'll be fine."

"I don't think you should stay in there with him, anyway," Tuatu said.

"Not to worry," I said, carefully stepping over the salt to the other side of the circle before I closed it with a final shake of the bag of iron shavings. "I'm human; it won't bother me. I can go in and out as I want."

"Yes, but can he hurt you if you're in there with him?"

"Nope," I said happily. "Not with magic, anyway. That's the point of it all."

"He will try to hurt you another way," Jin Yeong said.

"True," I said. "I'm not planning on staying in there with him, but he'll be a bit sus if I'm all the way over here and he's right in the centre."

"Does it matter if he's suspicious?" asked North. "Once he's here, he's trapped. Let him work it out as quickly as he likes; he can't change it."

I gave the salt-and-iron circle one last check and said, "Yeah, that's fair."

North stepped lightly across the rivulet as if floating and paced carefully around the whole of the circle, double-checking the work. The lycanthropes scowled a bit, but I was happy to have another set of eyes on it. The less we got wrong now, the easier things would go for us later—and it wasn't like I was an expert on capturing fae, either. I just knew what hadn't worked, catastrophically.

I waited for her to finish her inspection, moving over on the concrete platform until I was just outside the circle, with Jin Yeong beside me and a utility door behind me.

Then I asked, "You lot ready to go?"

There was no putting things off any longer. It was time to start, whether or not I felt ready.

Mind you, there were enough of us there: North and Tuatu stood side by side on the other side of the rivulet, blending into the darkness of the wall there by virtue of North's hair, which flowed around them both like seaweed on the tide; Daniel and the lycanthropes were just behind them, grinning wolfishly in the luminous areas of Between that seemed to draw them like cool shade to a panting dog; Five was muttering somewhere nearby, too. I was pretty sure that the old mad bloke was around some-where: not so much because I could see him, but because I couldn't—and because there hadn't been any forks left in the kitchen drawer when we left.

Jin Yeong still stood by my side, insufferably beautiful and very well aware of it. His eyes were dark and bloody, and there was the faintest of curves to his lips—he was obviously ready and eager for the fight.

I shouldn't have been so glad to have them all here. In all like-lihood, at least a few of us were going to end up dead. More of us would probably be injured if we didn't manage to get the king under control with this little trick. But it was comforting to have the assurance of them all at my back, and despite the danger of it, I couldn't help wishing that Zero was here too.

"You can back out now if you like," I added, flicking a look around at them all. "I don't know how well this will work, and I don't know how many of us will be killed even if it does work properly. I don't know what's gunna happen at all."

"We know that it'll get the king away from Morgana and the others if it works," Daniel said abruptly. "That's enough for me."

North shrugged and said, "I agree with the boy. If Sarah is freed, that's all that matters. I don't care about the others."

"That's why we're all here," Tuatu said, shooting her a look. "So that *everyone* has a chance to get out alive. We all know the risks, Ruth. We're willing to take them if it means getting the others out—and getting rid of the person who's been making Hobart a nightmare to police over the last few months."

"All right," I said. "But if you die, you flamin' better not haunt me, because I warned you."

"I am already dead," said Jin Yeong in my ear. "So I shall haunt you anyway."

"Yeah, you still haven't bought me another jacket," I said. "Looks like I'll be the one haunting you if I die."

"You may not die," he said. Graciously, he added, "You may haunt me. I will permit it."

Daniel threw him an irritated look. To me he said, "You know you can do better, Pet."

I picked up a rock and flicked it at his shins, sending him scuttling backward in a hurry, swearing. "You want me to go telling Morgana how much better she can do when we get her out?" I asked him threateningly.

"All right, all right! I was just saying."

"Don't say," I told him irritably, and elbowed a far-too-smug Jin Yeong in the stomach. "Stop smirking."

"For pity's sake do the thing!" snapped Five. He had his hands shoved in his pockets, and he looked about as uncomfortable as I felt. "The sooner we have the slippery old twister in our hands, the better."

"Agreed," I said, wiping my hands on my jeans. I cleared my throat, stared right at the centre of the salt-and-iron circle as if I could already see the king there, and said, "Oi. Thomas Lynne, King of Behind. I'm calling you, so get your backside over here."

There was a moment of absolute silence and stillness, then at least two of the lycanthropes snickered and the centre of my salt-and-iron circle quietly replaced the air that had been there with a person who had not.

It was the king, and he was directly in the centre of my circle, his eyes drilling into mine.

"G'day," I said. "Thought it was time we had a few words."

CHAPTER EIGHT

IT TOOK THE KING A MOMENT TO GRASP WHAT I'D SAID, AND another to formulate a response that wasn't already there and waiting. "How in the *worlds* did you get me here?"

I shrugged at him, feeling the knob of the utility door brush briefly against my back. "You're the one who was playing silly beggars with humans in the human world, chucking around names and smiling up your sleeve. You can't do that sort of thing and not expect people to find out your name."

The king gave a short laugh. "Is that so? What do you want with me, Pet of Lord Sero?"

"I didn't call you here as someone's pet," I said. "Otherwise, I would have bitten you by now."

"Don't think I don't know exactly how Lord Sero senior died," he said flatly. "I won't give you the chance to do the same to me, trust me on that."

"Yeah, I didn't figure you would," I said. "I don't have to bite you to get rid of you."

"If you wanted so badly to meet with me, I'm not entirely sure why you weren't in my arena," the king said, looking around. He didn't do the looking around very obviously, but I knew he was looking around despite that—carefully, meticulously, figuring out where he was and how to make it work for him.

I would have been doing the same thing.

He added, "We could have settled this in the arena like participants instead of you dragging me away from my business mid-blow."

"Yeah? Well, you didn't invite me along to the party," I pointed out. "Flamin' rude, that was. You can't tell me you would have politely met with me in the arena when you didn't even call me there."

"I called you," he said, and now his eyes were diamond-hard. "You didn't appear. I am *very* curious to know how you managed that, human."

I couldn't help the chuckle that escaped me, sudden and explosive. "Heck! You actually *did* call me? Mustn't have done a very good job of it."

Because I knew, suddenly, exactly what he had done wrong.

I was pretty sure he spoke through his teeth. "I assure you that I did as good a job as I knew how. They do say that all is well that ends well; I hope to prove the truth of that today."

"I don't think you'll be proving anything that you want to be proving," I said. "But if it's just an arena you want—reckon you're in the right place. This one's mine, but since I've called you here, you're obviously welcome."

He laughed. "So you have called me here to kill me?"

"Yes and no," I said. "I called you here to give you a chance to give up your throne without the bloodbath. You don't deserve a chance, but I figured I should give you one anyway."

That was a complete bluff, of course. There was no way he'd give up anything, and I didn't expect him to.

"You're very brave with your allies at your back," he said, but the amusement was gone from his eyes. "I wonder if you know you left the strongest of them outside the arena?"

"Someone else was monopolising him," I said, shrugging. "There's enough of us here to take care of you, though."

"You think that the North Wind will be strong enough to bind me, I take it," said the king, contempt in the line of his lips. "Do you know how compromised she is? Barely more than a gifted human, at this point. I know she's been spending more time than is wise with the human beside her. Incarnations really do have to be careful about how...fleshy they become."

North smiled at him coldly. "There is more to the wind than brute strength."

"Who else do we have?" He did a full circle, deliberately turning his back to me. "A handful of lycanthropes, a vampire, and two humans! And this—a *leprechaun*! What an interesting team to assemble!"

"Don't you read books?" I asked him. "It's always the little blokes that come out on top."

"A very comforting fiction reserved for novels," said the king. "I'm as fond of reading as the next person, but it's never a good idea to put too much trust in the idea of underdog justice."

"Yeah, that's what the all-powerful bad guys usually say," I pointed out.

"I'm no more the villain of the piece than you are the heroine: everything is a matter of perspective in this life."

"Pretty sure the law isn't going to care about perspective," I said. "That's why we're here."

"I have a right to reign; it was won and bought in blood, as the law demands. I haven't strayed from the letter of the law—in fact, if there's an antagonist here, it's you."

I shrugged. "I mean, it wouldn't be the first time someone has said I'm antagonistic."

"Not to mention that every one of you is subject to me," he said, a current of disbelief rising in his voice. "Repent and renew your service to me; I can be merciful when I please, but I won't wait for you to think better of your choices if you betray me now."

"I'm not your subject," Tuatu said. "I'm human."

"Yeah, me too," I said. "Sorry."

"I am not subject to any king," North said flatly. "I am subject to nothing but my own whim."

Daniel said incredulously, "Since when does the behindkind throne recognise lycanthropes? We've been outlaws all our lives because the throne doesn't recognise our rights or our citizenship!"

"I'm blackcarded," Five said, crossing his arms. "Green and gold, *you* threw *me* away! I have no allegiance to the throne Behind."

"I see," said the king, his gaze dwelling on each of us in turn. He might as well have gotten out a notebook and started taking names, for all the threat that was in his eyes. "You'll pay dearly for your treason, I promise you. Don't think I won't kill you without a second thought if you really raise a hand against me."

"Hands, teeth." JinYeong shrugged. "It is all the same. You are an old dog that many people would like to see hanged. Your time is at an end."

That was the first thing that really made an impact, I think. I didn't see the king's expression change—except maybe it grew a little less good-humoured—but he stepped forward swiftly, his hands sweeping away from his sides, before the edge of the salt-and-iron circle pulled him up short.

I saw the involuntary grimace that pulled at his upper lip as he realised the reality of his entrapment, and felt a profound sense of satisfaction.

"Having a bit of trouble moving, are we?" I enquired.

He stared at me. "You have the unmitigated gall to entrap me in an iron circle?"

"That's me," I said. "One hundred percent unmitigated gall. What are you going to do about it? From where I'm standing, you don't have too many options, and no matter how much you try to threaten us, it's not going to do a lot of good."

"Think again, Pet," said the king. "Think one last time before you commit yourself to this attack. I knew a child, not so long ago, who walked through Between and approached me without fear. That child had a great deal of human magic, but like all humans didn't seem to know it."

"Garbage," I said. "I knew it flamin' well. I just wasn't allowed to remember I knew it."

He shrugged. "Perhaps you knew a little, but I knew more. Don't think that you can possibly know any kind of magic as well as I do—or that you know mine anything like as well as I know yours."

"That's a lot of words for someone who actually believes what they're saying," I said. If I had been bluffing earlier, the king was bluffing now. He was trying to put me off my game.

"Very well," he said. "If you will not be warned, we'll begin. Let's see how well you've learned how to use your magic."

I'VE ALWAYS HATED PROVERBS. They're smug, self-righteous, and too flamin' pithy.

You know: *Be careful what you wish for; you might get it. Don't put all your eggs in one basket. Even a monkey sometimes falls from the tree.*

What's sauce for the goose is sauce for the gander.

In other words, I forgot that even if the king hadn't been able to bring his little henchmen in with him, he was just as free as I was to draw from the world around us with whatever ability he had. And I definitely forgot that he knew the world Behind a heck of a lot better than me—well enough to know what was in the water here below the city, at any rate.

And it's not like he didn't warn me, either. That was nice. I felt the pull of Between below our feet, a call running from within the trap that held the king—a clumsy call that ran straight into the rivulet and demanded something big and squishy.

I had been right that he wasn't easily able to make something out of Between or reach Between and pull something out. I hadn't considered that he could still call things through Between—and that he was still the king. Whatever he called would do his bidding.

"Something's coming from the water!" I yelled, my heart rate speeding up.

Daniel swore, and said savagely below his breath, "He's not supposed to be able to use magic when he's imprisoned in iron!"

"He's not using magic," I said. "He's calling something through Between. We knew he'd be able to use Between; that can't be helped."

"You know he'd be able to call up giant leeches?" asked Daniel, going furry around the ears.

He swore once more and went full wolf, shedding clothes and voice alike. Around me, the rest of the lycanthropes did the same, and I heard Five say, "*Green and gold*, what's this monstrosity!" as dark, nightmarish creatures rose from the rivulet.

They were glistening, leech-like creatures, too big to have been hiding in the human side of the rivulet and seeping with a kind of viscosity that made them seem as though they were melting away as they poured themselves onto the concrete. At least five of them divided our group, each of them with a circular maw filled with teeth that dripped the same kind of viscosity their skin leaked.

"Ah heck," I said, and then there was a sword in each of my hands, though I hadn't picked up anything to turn it into a sword. They were my own swords, and I had pulled them through Between from somewhere in my bedroom.

I didn't have time to wonder at that, because then there were teeth and slippery, tough hides slithering past too close for comfort. The leeches went for the lycanthropes first, and I heard yelping as I charged after them; I didn't know why until I leaped the rivulet and the first droplet of leech goop flung itself onto my forearm, burning off the hair there.

I hissed between my teeth, wiping it away frantically on my shirt as I ran, and heard Tuatu yell, "Mind the mucus, it's acidic!"

"Flamin' heck it is!" I snarled, and plunged a sword into the closest leech.

The flesh gave, plump and yielding, but sprang back almost as soon as I wrenched my sword out, and the mucus that spread over the dimpled wound seemed to seal it up.

"Great!" I snapped. "They're self-healing!"

I was talking to JinYeong, but he wasn't there. I had only a brief moment for the shock of loss that discovery caused, and then another of stark, terrified worry, before a scented cannonball whipped past me at the end of a needle-pointed chain suspended from the arched ceiling above and embedded itself into the side of the leech I'd just stabbed.

JinYeong, springing up from the metal rod he'd thrust through the leech and up onto its back with another length of chain flying from his right hand, disappeared over its back—presumably to attach it to the metal rod on the other side.

I heard his voice yell, "*Chigeum, chigeum!*" and the chain snapped tight, dragging the leech backward. It rose in the air as it struggled against the pull, then, with disastrous suddenness, the metal rod tore upward through flesh like a backwards cheese slicer. JinYeong tumbled from it and hit the ground at a roll, avoiding the falling leech half that flopped down in front of me.

That left me looking at a bifurcated leech corpse that was weeping mucus—a nice way to start the fight and probably some sort of demented omen about how it was going to go. As I stared, something huge and shadowy barrelled through the air, and I ducked just in time to avoid a wind-borne leech but not the displaced air that curled up from the floor in its wake and tossed me sideways.

Someone grabbed my arm as I nearly took a nose-dive into the rivulet, tugging me back up and away from the water. I caught a brief glimpse of Detective Tuatu's taut, terrified face and gasped, "Thanks! Don't stab 'em—slash 'em!"

He seemed to choke a bit, then pointed over my shoulder. "What's he doing?"

I turned in a hurry, because Tuatu was pointing toward the imprisoned king, and that was definitely not a good sign. I was just in time to see the entire length of a leech flop heavily over the thick barrier of salt and iron filings, following a barely noticeable thread of Between that called it away from the fight.

Unlike Athelas, who had nearly torn his body apart to free himself from the trap laid by my parents, the king was happy to coolly tear apart one of the monsters he had called to his aid to get free.

I leaped for the writhing creature and saw at least two of the lycanthropes and North do the same, but we were too late. Stronger in its death throes than it had been in the peak of health straight from the water, it sent us flying again and again until it was a shrunken, shrivelled mass of blubber curling in on itself in the salt and iron.

I drew closer to the ruined circle again, but I could already see that it was too late.

The king was gone. Gone without a fight, without a word, vanishing into the darkness of the tunnel so thoroughly that not even his footsteps could be heard.

"Flamin' heck," I said softly. "This is *not* good."

One of the lycanthropes yelped again, short and sharp, and I heard Five bawling, "Pet! Move your skinny backside, girl!"

"Salt!" I yelled. "Get to the salt and throw it at 'em!"

I threw my swords aside and went for the bags instead, grabbing handfuls of the salt to hurl as I ran. The smell of salt and burning filled the air as everyone else followed suit, salt burning through mucus and mucus melting through everything else, and for a few minutes it was all I could taste and smell.

The king was well and truly gone by the time we met in the centre of those blobs of black slime that curled in on themselves and checked to make sure that everyone was alive and still fully-limbed.

"Right," said Daniel, his hair burnt out in patches from leech slime and his eyes more feral than usual. There were burnt patches across his bare chest and legs, too; in fact, most of the lycanthropes were looking the same. "That didn't go as well as we thought it would. What now?"

"Now, we gotta find the king before he manages to get himself a little army of leeches," I said. "He'll be looking for somewhere safe, and he can't use the bridge, so I reckon he'll head further up toward where the rivulet is more powerful."

"He'll need to recharge," agreed North. "But if he can only call leeches from the water, it won't be a great challenge to any of us. We've got enough salt left to kill any amount he throws at us, and you've still got a few filings to make another trap, don't you?"

"Don't reckon we'll be able to catch him like that again," I said. "And I've got the feeling it won't just be leeches, either—he'll have access to any of his subjects who were in the arena when we started."

"That's all we need!" groaned Five. "Giant leeches, goblins, brawlers—"

I grimaced. "What the heck are brawlers?"

"Those four-armed bozos," said Darren, shoving a foot into one leg of the many pairs of spare trousers the lycanthropes had brought along and trying not to fall over. "All they're good for is fighting, but they're pretty good at it."

"I've met a few of them," I said, my heart sinking. Brawlers weren't too bad to face when you had Zero, Jin Yeong, and Athelas all together, but I wasn't looking forward to having to fight them with only one of my psychos and an assortment of lycanthropes, humans, leprechauns, and the incarnate version of the north wind. Especially not if there were a lot of them.

"He'll have called up something else to help," Daniel said. "He smelt bad—sweat, mostly—so he'll get someone to guard him and go to ground anywhere he can recharge."

"Yess," said Jin Yeong thoughtfully. "He was verrry afraid."

"That's what I figured," I said.

North said, "If so, we should try to get him while he's recharging."

Tuatu stared at her. "You want to go after him straight away?"

"Not a bad idea," I said thoughtfully. "Let him know what it feels like to be hunted for a while. He's going to have trouble doing much while he's in need of recharging anyway—let's make him use up as much energy as possible and call out as many behindkind as he can."

"We'll have to fight all the ones he does call out," Tuatu said.

"Yes," said North. "But what else should we do? Wait until he's bright and refreshed enough to fight for himself as well as keep up an army?"

"We'll go ahead and see what we can sniff out," Daniel said, jerking his head at the other lycanthropes. "If there's no other trace, we'll be able to smell him."

Darren stopped trying to pull up his trousers and joined the others as they changed once more, sinking back toward the slimy cement in an explosion of fur that covered their nakedness. They spread out between the leech carcasses with their noses to the ground.

I reached out to the shifting miasma of Between that curled through the dead leeches, wondering how the leeches could have fouled up the feeling of Between as badly as they seemed to have fouled up the rivulet on the way out.

"Flamin' heck," I said, realising the full cleverness of the king. "He pulled them up because they make a mess Between as well as in the water. I can't even see where he was, let alone where he is."

"He can't have gone far," Five said bluntly. "There are only two ways to go: backwards and forwards."

"Not exactly," I said, and North nodded.

"There's something not quite right," she said. "He's pulled something sideways and I can't tell where it is because of all the mess."

"What mess?" asked Tuatu, but North only added, "You can't see it. Don't worry about it."

"I'm very worried about it," he retorted. "I don't know whether I'm going to have a knife stuck into my back from one of the walls or not."

"I won't let anyone stab you," she said.

"I'd like to see you try to stop a goblin from stabbing anyone," muttered Five, and received a cold look from North for his troubles.

Ahead and just out of sight, Daniel snarled; if he could have spoken, it would have been, "Got him!"

The lycanthropes took off together at a lope, leaving the rest of us to scramble ourselves together and chase after them. When I caught up with them, they were prowling outside one of the utility doors—this one had a sign that said *Danger! High Voltage!* which was pretty fitting under the circumstances. They didn't change back to human, but they paced impatiently enough that the message was clear: through the door.

"All right, we'll go through," I said, still trying to peer through the murky mess left behind after the leeches. "But I can't see real well at the moment, and there could be something waiting for us, so you'd better all be ready."

"How are we going to break through the door?" asked Tuatu, and then seemed to have an annoying memory. "Oh, right; you're going to do that thing where you walk through walls, aren't you?"

"Yep," I said grimly. "And we're gunna take you with us."

"Fantastic," he said.

He reached for North, but I grabbed his arm instead.

"Nope," I said. "You should try not to touch North right now. She needs all her strength while we're in here, and if you're too close she won't have it. Just grab my shoulder."

Daniel, as if he'd only been waiting to make sure that we knew what was going on, plunged on through the door before I could first—which was probably safer for Tuatu but left me feeling as though I needed to rush after them and make sure no one was hurt.

I was meant to be leading; I was meant to be taking the risks of the first in line. With Tuatu in tow, I couldn't stop Jin Yeong from going on ahead, lean and alert, or even keep up with him. He wasn't as soft and easily damaged as Tuatu, but the raw irritation of anxiety that jibbed inside me didn't acknowledge that.

North must have been feeling something similar, because instead of sweeping past as I was pretty sure she wanted to do, she hung behind Five, bringing up the rear and gusting a series of scurrying, impatient breezes up through our ankles and toward the rapidly vanishing tails of the lycanthropes.

I would have liked to have slowed down to check ahead, but there still wasn't much to be seen with Between; I hurried on through the darkness of a utility cupboard that was far longer and colder than it should have been, following the slick, leech-slimed shoulders of my vampire to make sure that nothing had a go at him where I couldn't see or stop it.

The same mess still clung to my own clothes and even my skin, slowly burning, slowly eating away at both. In fact, the whole greasy film seemed to have followed us, clinging to shoulders and hair, much like the—

"Flamin' heck," I said, irritated. "Hang on! We have to stop and clean the mucus off us; that's why Between is so murky right now."

"We don't need to be able to see Between; it works for us regardless of—oh." North stopped. "You'll be able to look ahead and see stuff more clearly if we're clean?"

"Yeah."

"We don't have time to stop," Five said gruffly. "If we stop, we run more of a chance of losing him."

"If we don't stop, we've got a flamin' good chance of walking into a trap," I retorted.

"Yes, but—"

"Stop now," said Jin Yeong, with a cold look at him. "We will clean ourselves."

Up ahead, Daniel seemed to be of the same opinion as Five, because he snarled and dashed back toward us as if to indicate his impatience. He must have indicated to the other lycanthropes to stop and wait despite that, though, because they dropped to their haunches while the rest of us pushed through the thickness of Between to the nearby rivulet and gingerly waded into it. Here it wasn't so much the rivulet as a trickle of it escaping to seep through bricks of the walls, but it was big enough to do what we needed it to do.

The water didn't feel like it was doing much, even though we were a little way Between, but the mucus sloughed off on the water that fell back as we splashed our clothes and burnt skin, tainting it with the same kind of film I'd seen just before the leeches rose in the water.

And as the taint of it skimmed along the surface of the water, the miasma in the air finally began to clear.

"It's working," I said, splashing more vigorously as Daniel changed back to human with an expression that wasn't any less irritated than it had been as a wolf. "I can see again. Well, I can see more again."

"What can you see, though?" asked Daniel impatiently.

"Far off? Not much. I can tell the king is out there somewhere, though—and that we're going in the right direction."

"What is nearby?" asked Jin Yeong, wringing out his suitcoat and putting it down on the concrete that was still somehow the floor of the utility cupboard.

"About twenty brawlers who are *flamin'* well armed considering they've got a weapon for each hand."

Daniel swore. "I was hoping he'd be too weak to command anyone else. How much magic does he *have?*"

"More than we thought," I said grimly. "Definitely more than he ought to have at this stage. He's been king for too flamin' long, I reckon."

Daniel asked, "So you didn't manage to do anything about his magic at all while he was in the circle?"

"Nope," I said, and heard Five groan.

"Green and gold, that's all we need! The king of Behind, free to pick us off one by one with his magic intact and freshly recharged! Brawlers in the hall and leeches in the water."

"That's a cheerful way to look at it," Tuatu muttered.

"Don't worry," I said. "I've got another plan."

JinYeong shot a look down at me and said, "We will not use you as bait."

"Rude," I said. "You haven't even heard the plan!"

"I already know it," he said, sniffing. "I know you."

"I don't mind using you as bait," said North. "That's your choice. But I won't agree if I don't think the plan will work; we'll only have a moment to make it work, and he'll be suspicious. Old dogs are the wiliest."

"Oi," said Kyle, changing back. I had the feeling he had changed back just to say it. "Watch it."

North just lifted an eyebrow at him and turned back to me. "We should try to end it now—if we can break through the brawlers to the king, we can get to him before he recharges."

"I think so, too," JinYeong said. "Then there is no need for using bait, or people. Just blood and tooth."

"I vote for ending it now, if we're putting it to the vote," Daniel said. "I don't see why anyone should be used as bait, either; not when we can just break through and take them down physically. If he's only called on twenty-odd of the brawlers, that means his magic is still really low, even if it doesn't feel like it. Any king should be able to call out every one of his subjects that are in the vicinity—and I'm certain there are more of his subjects here than twenty brawlers."

"What if it's a trap?" I asked.

JinYeong glanced down at me. "You feel it is a trap? *Wae?*"

"Not with Between," I said reluctantly. "But it just feels wrong instinctively."

"What do you see Between?" asked Daniel.

"I see the twenty-odd brawlers and I can sense the king a little bit further on, as if he's come to the end of how far he can move Between. We're pretty deep in the walls here, and his forte isn't Between so..."

"Then we should fight," JinYeong said decidedly. "I agree with the wind and the wolf."

Tuatu said slowly, "I feel like it's too easy, too. But I'll go with the majority."

"Me too," I said, but I said it reluctantly.

"This lot want to fight now," Daniel added, and before anyone could say anything, added faintly defensively, "They just told me— I'm not pretending."

"Yeah, we wanna go," agree Kyle.

"We fight now, then," North said, nodding. "See if we can end this without giving the king a chance to power up while we're working out our trickery."

Tuatu's eyes met mine, and I shrugged a bit and pulled out a cricket bat from Between. Somewhere out there some kid's bedroom lost a cricket bat, but it wasn't like I could do anything about it—Tuatu needed a weapon, and I had no way of knowing where to return it when we were finished.

"You gunna put this back when we're done?" he asked, trying to grin.

I grinned back. "What, with the extra blood? Nah. Oi, you're more of a blunt instrument bloke than a stabby one, aren't you?"

"I suppose that's one way of putting it," he said, taking the bat. "This is fine. If I can't have a gun, I prefer this to a sword."

"I've only ever pulled a gun out of Between once," I said doubtfully. "And that one wasn't just someone's gun that I got from somewhere, it was something that decided to be a gun to help me. I don't know if I could do it from straight Between."

"I don't know that I want to try it, anyway," he said, as there was a general movement forward among the lycanthropes. "If we're within the walls right now, I wouldn't like to see the kind of ricochet a discharge would make."

"Me either," I said, and started forward with Jin Yeong at my side.

The brawlers didn't see us until we broke cover from the shadows that seemed to confine the space we were in to a single long tunnel just like the utility cupboard it was still pretending to be, and out into the area of free Between.

When we did enter the open space it took them a moment longer to realise that we actually intended to fight them. That gave me precious time to look around to see all that I could see with both Between and human sight and, having looked, to glimpse the king himself with my regular sight. He was far away and up on rising ground with what I was pretty sure was a power generator next to him, and from the amount of magic coiling up and around him, he was recharging as fast as he could.

"Flamin' heck," I said. "He's using the power generator—it's a hydro one."

The brawlers stared at us and we stared at them before North said, "Get out of our way and we won't hurt you. We only want the king."

There was a brief moment of stillness before one of the brawlers laughed, and that must have annoyed the lycanthropes, because a wolf knocked down the one who had laughed, going right for the throat, and life became a hot, blood-soaked melee.

Somewhere in the mess and the fight, I copped a good stab to the left leg from the nasty little dagger in a brawler's hand before JinYeong went for his throat. I knew the lycanthropes were taking a few hits, too, because I heard more yelps amidst the snarling as time went on. I couldn't help them as much as I wanted because Tuatu was nearby, smashing purposefully with his bat, and he was the softest of the lot of us. Neither of us had teeth to defend ourselves with, but at least I had training and the ability to pull stuff out of thin air.

North hovered, sweeping brawlers off their feet for the lycanthropes to savage, but never getting too close to Tuatu. JinYeong, a bloody shadow, darted between arms and weapons, blood spurting in his wake, and as more of the brawlers fell and we pushed on to higher ground, I saw the moment the king's eyes opened across the cavern.

They opened only briefly, then he closed them again and the coils of magic around him seemed to become busier—or maybe just more frantic. Recharging as I knew it was supposed to be a serene, peaceful experience; I wondered if it had ever been that for him, always grasping at his power to keep it safe, or if this was a new, uncomfortable experience for him.

I had a moment of fierce delight in the knowledge that all we had to do was cross the rest of the ground and climb up toward the cement platform he'd sat himself on, before I felt a stirring in the king's magic.

My eyes snapped back to him at once, and I barely avoided an assault from a dying brawler that Tuatu batted a bit too close to me, but the magic around the king hadn't changed.

So what part of the king's magic was still working, disconnected from the rest? There was nothing between us and him, because as the lycanthropes snarled in satisfaction, the final brawler fell and we pressed toward the figure on the ledge above.

But I still felt that magic stirring, strong and forthright and authoritative, digging into the walls and air around us—and then, below and behind, curving around the empty space, were more and more brawlers. They scuttled out of seemingly nowhere without a touch or stirring of Between to announce them.

I only had time to gasp out, "Get climbing, you lot!" before the others saw them.

Jin Yeong swore in Korean and, grabbing me around the waist, threw me up onto the next level of concrete and rubble, the lycanthropes springing up around us and North sweeping all before her.

If I'd known that the arena I picked was home to so many behindkind, I would have chosen somewhere a lot more barren. If they weren't going to be on my side anyway, it would have been convenient if there were significantly fewer of them.

"Doesn't matter," Five shouted. "Once we're through to the king, they'll be easier to take care of."

"Wouldn't bet on it," I said, but I said it between my teeth. There was a sharp, stabbing pain in my ribcage that I had an idea was my rib threatening to break again, and I could still feel the blood oozing down my leg every time I lunged forward to climb upward.

And that was when the brawlers began to come at us from the sides as well, trying to pincer us into the bunch behind. We pressed forward anyway, because it wasn't much use trying to go back; there were too many brawlers there. All we could do was go forward, fighting furiously to get through the brawlers in front, and leave North and Jin Yeong at the rear to sweep back the line of fighters with a combination of gale-force winds and blood-stained teeth.

But I couldn't help looking for ways out as we fought our way up to the king, regardless. If something went wrong and the brawlers still went for us after the king was dead—if we even managed to kill the king—we would need a quick exit. North was slowly tiring and so was Jin Yeong, and the rest of us couldn't hold a candle to them in terms of strength.

One of the lycanthropes yelped, high and sharp, as I saw our hope of escape. Up there, behind the king and his generator, was what I was pretty sure was the back-side of another utility door. We were on the inside, but if we could get to the outside and make a run for the bridge along the actual rivulet itself...

I looked around wildly and saw that Kevin or Kyle had gone down in a pile of fur and blood, and stopped where I was, with a clear line of sight to the king.

Daniel changed back as I hesitated, all blood and bare skin. "Go *get* him!" he snarled. "I'll look after my kids!"

Anther lycanthrope changed and crouched beside Kevin, bare and shivering—probably Kyle. "We've got him," he said.

So I left them and ran with Jin Yeong beside me, blood flinging wide in arcs as we ran. Behind us a storm of wind whipped around the fallen lycanthrope and sent the brawlers below tumbling back into their brethren, the momentary lull urging us on.

I expected a blast of magic or more brawlers at the top, but all I found was a pile of clothing and the swiftly disintegrating coils of magic that I had seen from below—the coils of magic that had proved that it was the king I was seeing.

There was a brief lull in the wake of North's tempest, and the lycanthropes joined us on the platform with Tuatu helping Kyle support wolf-form Kevin.

"You got him?" Daniel said sharply.

"He's not here," I said disgustedly. "He never was; he's probably somewhere down by a fast-flowing part of the rivulet and recharging as fast as he can, surrounded by leeches—it was all magic and a few scraps of clothing."

"How did he get enough magic to do all this when he's nearly at the point of recharge?" Daniel said in disbelief. "He shouldn't be able to do more than call a last few subjects to his aid and maybe throw a glamour on one of them!"

Jin Yeong, all moody eyes and pouting, bloody mouth, said to me, "You were right. He has more power than he should have. He has more power than the old man, too."

"Reckon that's what happens when you've been king as long as he has," I said. "How's Kevin holding up?"

"Not good," Daniel said briefly.

He wasn't looking too good himself, but I knew that the blood all over his chest was no longer seeping out of any wounds: he had changed back to human, spurring his body to start healing itself. He might be naked and feeling a bit more vulnerable, but at least he was healing.

I asked, "Can Kevin change? Or are we going to carry him back like this?"

"We can't leave the king out there," North snapped, leaping up beside us. "We need to get him now, while there's hope! If he's as strong as this now, what will he be when he's had his chance to recharge?"

"We're not likely to do much good in this state," Five said bluntly. "Green and gold, we've got two naked boys, one wounded wolf, and two humans with extra holes in them!"

"Kevin can't fight, and I'm not leaving him here," Daniel said. "And it doesn't look to me like the king is any weaker than usual, either. We should retreat to the bridge for now; we'll talk it through and decide what to do somewhere we're sure the king can't sneak up on us."

"Good point," I said. "Let's go back, tuck ourselves in, and try not to get killed while we patch everyone up."

"That'll be a bit hard with that lot down there," Tuatu said grimly. "Are we going to fight back through them all? I don't know that we'll make it."

North, her small, mulish chin setting, said, "I will make a path. If we're not going after the king, we should get back safely at least."

"No need," I said, and opened the door beside me. "We've got another way out. Let's get out of here."

CHAPTER NINE

Daniel did what he could for Kevin with bandages and I did what I could with my human magic. If we could keep him healthy enough to gather the strength to change, he would be able to heal himself from there—or at least, that's what Daniel said. He had his deeply worried dad look on, which meant that he, at least, wasn't sure whether or not Kevin would make it to the point of being able to make the change to human.

I wasn't sure, either; what there was of my human magic wasn't exactly strong, and I didn't exactly know how to use it to the best advantage. I'd once known, and now that I remembered I had known it was easier to remember small ways I'd once used it —but I was still missing some fundamental muscle memory-type instincts. I wasn't even sure that I was going about trying to heal in a way that did more than waste my own energy.

Zero and the others must be out by now, though. The thought was bright and delightful: a sort of secret joy I could hug to myself despite the maybe-dying lycanthrope curled up in the shadows beside me. Despite the battered look to our little crew. Despite the still-burning patch on my arm, the dull ache from the hole in my leg that was only slowly healing despite a fresh bite from

Jin Yeong, and the thought that the king was still free and growing more powerful by the hour.

"Morgana's probably stomping around the house by now, trying to figure out where we are," I said softly to Daniel, and his brow cleared just a little bit. "How long d'you reckon it'll take them to go see Vesper or Marazul to try and figure out where we are?"

"As long as it takes the big man to stop shaking down anyone else he thinks might have carried you off," Five said bluntly. He seemed to be trying to sand down a deep scrape on his pegleg with a bit of fallen brickwork, but I had the feeling it was more to take the edge off his mood than because he was worried about the smoothness of the wood.

"Are you sure the king can't see us in here?" Daniel asked in a low voice. "If we need to move in a hurry—"

"If anyone needs to get out, we'll make sure we look after Kevin," I said. "And no, the king can't see us here. I can feel him out there, sending bits of his magic out to try and find us—they're getting stronger and stronger, but he doesn't know how to see human workings properly, and this bridge was made with iron tools and human magic. The little bits of magic that do get this far are just sorta...I dunno, not really bouncing off. More like wafting away because they think this is the end of the tunnel."

"All right," he said. More loudly, he added, "Sorry I didn't listen to you before."

"It was a majority decision," I said, shrugging.

"Still," he said. "You're usually right when it comes to instincts, so—"

"You said you have a plan," North said abruptly.

I had the feeling that she was trying to stop herself from apologising, too, and was grateful. From the exasperatedly fond look that Tuatu sent her way, he seemed to think the same thing.

"Yeah," I said. "But I had to change it a bit—now that I know how strong the king's magic is."

JinYeong's dark eyes rested on me. "This plan. Is it more dangerous or less dangerous now?"

"Lots more dangerous," I said cheerfully. "But only really for me. Well, unless I die, and then it'll be more dangerous for the rest of you—but at least the arena will open again. I'm the only other heirling in here, after all. If I die, the arena opens."

"There are other plans," said JinYeong. "And I wish to—"

"Where's our harbinger, that's what I'd like to know," muttered Daniel, interrupting him. "He could have helped a bit!"

"It's better if he stays out of it," I said. "Not much use him being killed while he's out prancing around the arena, and it's not like he'd stay put if we asked. What happens when your harbinger dies?"

"Better not to find out," said North dryly. "I don't think it would end well for anybody."

"Especially the anybodies in here?" Tuatu asked.

"You," said North, her eyes resting on him, "are safe. Nobody will hurt you."

"That's very nice, but I want everyone else to be safe, too!"

North said as if explaining to a child, "Yes, but I can't keep everyone safe. The vampire looks after his human, the wolf looks after his cubs, and the leprechaun—"

"The leprechaun looks after himself!" snapped Five.

"Don't worry, I'll look after you, too," I said, grinning. "Now that I've got a vampire looking after me and so much flamin' free time!"

That should have made JinYeong grin, too; instead, to my surprise, he scowled away into the corner, eyes dark and angry.

North only said, "It wasn't meant as an insult."

"You're just trying to make us all feel better," I agreed. "Don't reckon it's working real well; you might wanna work on your pep talks."

"It is not time for pep talks, it is time for planning," JinYeong said, turning a sulky look on all of us.

"Fair," I said. "I told you I had a plan. You saw how much power the king has even when he's nearly depleted—he's just going to keep coming for us until he gets us."

"If you're saying we need to get rid of his magic, I agree," Daniel said. "But how are we supposed to do that?"

"Saw a nifty bit of Between working the other day," I said. "A nice little bit of can't-see-me that wasn't like anything I've seen before. I spent a bit of time figuring out how to do it, and if I'm close enough to the king while he's distracted enough not to notice, I reckon I can do the same thing to his magic."

North narrowed her eyes at me, and Daniel said slowly, "You're going to try and get rid of his magic by using a don't-see-me spell?"

Five gave a rude crack of laughter. "She's going to make him *think* it's gone with a don't-see-me spell. What sort of a distraction will you need?"

"Well," I said, and hesitated. "I reckon capturing me would be enough of a distraction, and it'd get me close enough to do the work, too. If I have to strain to do it, he'll see me straight away, though, so I'll have to be nice and gentle. It doesn't need magic—not mine, anyway—so it's a pretty good bet."

"That is half a plan," North said.

"Yeah," I said. "But it's the only one we've got, isn't it?"

"I," said Jin Yeong dangerously, "am a very good distraction."

"You're a pain in the neck," muttered one of the lycanthropes, poking him with the pommel of one of my freshly clean swords.

Jin Yeong snarled, "*Manjiji ma!*" and the lycanthrope snarled back, lunging forward.

"Oi, oi, oi!" I protested, darting in between them. "Jin Yeong, what the heck? What's bitten you?"

"Nothing has bitten me; I will bite *it*!"

"Yeah, all right, but settle down!"

Dark, bloody eyes glared at me. Jin Yeong said through his teeth, "I will not settle down, I will *bite* something."

"And I'll flamin' smack you one upside the head!" I retorted. "What the heck is going on?"

"You do not listen *anyway*," he said, and turned his shoulder.

"The heck?" I said blankly, looking toward Daniel and North for some kind of assistance. "What'd I do?"

"Nope," said Daniel. "Not getting in the middle of this. C'mon, you lot, let's go look at the outside through the bars."

He and the other lycanthropes vanished into the darkness, and when I turned around to see what had become of North and Tuatu, the softest flutter of breeze passed across my face along with a surprised sort of yelp that must have meant that Tuatu had been swept away unexpectedly. From the grumbling somewhere along the top edge of the bridge, Five was up there muttering to himself.

"You flamin' pikers!" I yelled after them all.

Jin Yeong, all stormy eyes and flashing teeth, said, "I am going for a walk, too!" and started out into the darkness of the dangerous side of the tunnel.

I grabbed his collar and hauled him back. Much to my surprise, he let me; but I wasn't the only one surprised. Jin Yeong's eyes, wide and startled, blinked at me as I pulled him back to face me.

"No," I said. "You don't get to have a temper tantrum and storm off. Sit down and figure it out."

"I do not wish to sit down!"

"Then stand there and fume—or start pacing around the tunnel! I don't care."

He stared at me, then removed my hand from his collar and said as though unsure if he was saying the right thing, "I am angry. Why are you yelling at me? You are not angry."

"That was just to get your attention," I said. I shoved him backward and he sat down involuntarily on the curb. "Sit there and work it out."

"I shall not work it out. I shall go out and bite something," he muttered.

"The heck you will!" I retorted. "If you get yourself captured or killed by the king, what am I supposed to do?"

"*Nae mari*!" he said, as if it was a protest.

"You're the one who said you have trouble with emotions," I pointed out. Despite his words, he hadn't moved, and the angry, liquid look to his eyes had faded into thoughtfulness, so I felt safe enough to duck back under the bridge and dig into the cooler for a blood bag. "You're never going to learn how to deal with them if you don't get any practise. Use your words."

"*Hyeong* would not make me sit down," he called after me. "*Hyeong* would make me fight."

"Yeah, and *that's* turned out great for your emotional stability, hasn't it?" I retorted, snagging a bag of blood and tossing it at him. He caught it and I sat beside him on the curb. "All right, what's the go? Why are you angry?"

"I am *trying* to be a good boyfriend," he said.

I stared at him. "What?"

"I am trying to be a good boyfriend," he continued stubbornly, "and you are making it very hard."

"I don't have the faintest idea what you're talking about," I said, bewildered. "I thought you were angry about the plans—what does you trying to be a good boyfriend have to do with going after the king or making plans to catch him?"

It was his turn to stare at me. He said slowly, as if to someone hard of hearing, "You said you will make yourself bait."

"I still don't understand how that has anything to do with you being a good boyfriend!" I objected. "Of course I have to be the bait! It's the only thing that makes sense—I'm the only one who would tempt him to make a risky move at the moment. I'm the only other heirling in here."

"Yes, but I do not want you to become bait, even if you choose to do it. But I can't ask you not to do it and so—"

"You're angry," I finished for him, with a sudden brightness of understanding. "Oh."

"Yes. Why should I watch you die?"

"Oh," I said. "All right, that's fair. Sorry. I didn't think about it like that."

Jin Yeong's eyebrow quirked up. "*Oh?*"

"Didn't think about it from your point of view," I explained. "Reckon I wouldn't like it much if you were trying to throw yourself into the king's arms as bait in a trap that might or might not work, either. We'll all go together like you and Daniel said earlier —if there's enough of a distraction while we're attacking, I might be able to get to his magic anyway."

"Ah," he said. "I thought I would have to argue more."

"Yeah, well, I would, but you're not wrong. I don't want you out there dead, so it's not fair to expect you to watch me die if something goes wrong. Who knows? It might even convince the king that it's not a trap—I don't think he expects me to use any of you as bait at this point."

That made his eyes dance. "Would anyone think so?"

"Dunno," I said thoughtfully. "But maybe the main thing will be making him think so for just a little while."

"FOR THE RECORD," said Daniel, as the filaments of Between I'd woven around us glittered and moved of their own accord, "I don't actually like this plan much."

"I don't like it either," Tuatu said. "But I like it a lot better than the first one. At least we'll all be together, and you won't be actually alone with the king."

"Just shouting insults at him across the divide," I agreed.

Turns out that Jin Yeong wasn't the only one who hadn't been so keen on using me as bait, no matter how sensible it was to do it that way. We had all come out together that morning after eating, checking on Kevin's recovery, and stopping to discuss exactly what we would do if things went wrong with our new plan—a plan which had more bait and less danger for everyone concerned, but still a pretty good chance of working.

Well, at least as good of a chance as my plans usually had of working at first glance.

We came out carefully, quietly, and shrouded in Between to keep us hidden from the king's attention as long as possible, keeping strictly to the real rivulet channel without trying to push into Between—yet.

"You know exactly where the king is right now?" North asked. She sounded vaguely suspicious, which was rude, but I could understand it.

"Yep," I said. The king might have been the most important and the most powerful in his own arena, but despite the fact that he still had subjects in here, this was a specially chosen arena of my own. I knew how it worked, I knew how to make the best of the human magic that ran through its walls like veins, and thanks to Between and the clearing of the miasma from the leeches, I knew exactly where the king was.

"Because yesterday—"

"That's the thing with us pets," I said. "We learn flamin' quick, and if you show us where the food is once, you don't have to show us again."

Five gave a short, satisfied laugh. "Figured out how he did it, eh? Good work, kid!"

"For instance," I said more quietly, sensing the approach of something large and many-faceted, "now that I know how he makes himself look like he's somewhere he's not, I can tell that he's pretending to be in about four different places right now. Each of them has little trigger points to tell him if anyone gets too close so that he can send out his little minions without having to come out himself."

"What trigger points?" asked Tuatu. "More importantly, what do they trigger, apart from a truckload of brawlers or leeches?"

"Trigger points like stepping anywhere on the concrete on that side of the rivulet," I said, pointing. "And stuff like insect-clouds that are roaming around in the little bubble he's made for 'em, just waiting to be let out."

"Green and gold!" huffed Five. "Murder midges!"

"Those aren't insects," said Daniel, staring across the rivulet with narrowed eyes.

"Yeah, I know," I said. Even if I hadn't been able to see the shiny silver finish of them, I would have been able to see them Between: clockwork scarabs with razor sharp wings and pinprick legs, swarming in the darkness. "I'm pretty sure they're self-swarming from all the bits of metal and leftover building materials that got left too long in Between dark—not sure they belong to the king exactly, but they don't look flamin' friendly and I reckon they've been stuck in that bubble since last night at least."

Jin Yeong, his eyes flitting around the tunnel in search of further threats, looked back briefly at me to ask, "How do you know which one of them is real?"

"None of them are real," I said, thinking involuntarily of a time when I had had to tell the difference between real and constructed versions of Jin Yeong. Then of another time when I'd had to tell who he was when he wasn't wearing his own appearance—and had outed him with a kiss.

He must have been thinking the same thing, because he grinned at me with sharp teeth and a soft, mischievous glow in his eyes.

I looked away hastily, glad that the duskiness of the tunnel hid the colour I could feel in my cheeks, and added, "None of the four kings he's put around the rivulet are the real king—the real king is pretty close to one of the fake kings, in a space that's very sure about not having a king there."

"We're sure it's not a trap?" Daniel said. He sounded suspicious, too, which was rude.

"Yeah," I said. "Because it's not magic that's telling me it's very sure there isn't a king there; it's Between. He doesn't really know how to use it properly, and it gets a bit passive aggressive when you get pushy without knowing how to do stuff."

"Probably tired of being sent into a new cycle every time he murders his way through another one," muttered Five.

"That's what I reckon," I said in satisfaction. "Anyway, we just need to avoid the triggers here as well as the ones that are nearby him, and we'll be right. We also need to be a bit quieter when we get closer to where he is, 'cos I reckon he'll be listening."

"Are there any other trigger points we need to avoid here?" asked North.

"Nope. I'll let you know when we get close to another one."

"Then we should keep going," she said, and swept ahead once again.

She obviously wasn't enjoying her time underground, and who could blame her? You're not supposed to shut the wind up underground.

We moved cautiously through the tunnel until we got closer to the second pretend king, then I took the lead and pushed through the walls and into the dusty, dusky area of Between. The wall stretched with us, opening the whole area out for us and doing away with the slight sensation of pressure that had come along with walking in the normal tunnel.

"We're getting closer," I said softly. I could feel the subtle shift of Between around us—from being just Between to being a place that was concentrated around a lump of magic it didn't really like. Like the miasma from the leeches, it infiltrated the air and left it noticeably different.

"How do you know?" Five asked, his voice grumpy. That was nothing new; it usually did sound grumpy. "I suppose you did a nice little reconnoitre while we were running for it yesterday."

"Nah, I'm just really observant," I said, grinning.

Actually, I'd sat there under the bridge like a bat for half the night, sending out bursts of the Between version of echolocation to try and see what the king had done with the arena. Now that I knew exactly what it looked like when he pretended to be somewhere, it was easy to spot what he'd done. After that, it had just been a matter of working out exactly where he *really* was, and threading tiny amounts of my human magic through the arena like glittering, insubstantial dominoes just waiting to fall.

"How close are we?"

That was Daniel. He sounded worried.

"Flamin' close," I elaborated. "Oi, you lot. Stop for a second."

"I'm not going to join hands or do the haka," Tuatu said suspiciously. "I'm not going to hug any of you, either."

"No one wants a hug from you, boyo," said Five, glaring at him.

"No one's giving or taking hugs," I said. "I'm *trying* to show you something! Everyone just belt up and pay attention."

One of the lycanthropes looked as though he wanted to open his mouth, but the look Jin Yeong shot him made him think better of it. Everyone shut their mouths, as a matter of fact—even North, who had been looking amused but was apparently ready to weigh in on Tuatu's behalf.

"This is our backup plan," I said, and jerked my thumb at the utility door we had just drawn even with.

It wasn't a real door, but that didn't really matter because it didn't lead to a real room, either. The door was the human-presenting part of a small tear in the wall that opened into a pretty big fissure in the tunnel wall—a fissure that was big enough to act as a sort of safe room for all of us. It was too close to the human-made tunnel and the remembered passage of humans to be quite present in the world Behind, and it was just a bit too sideways and not-quite-there to be completely present on the human side of the world, either. It was made of almost pure Between.

"Interesting," said North, reaching out to open the door.

It allowed her to open it, just as I'd hoped.

"If we can't make it to the bridge, or if too many of us are injured, this is where we've got to get to," I said. "Just open the door, everyone in, shut it again."

"Won't they just follow us in?"

"Nope," I said. "It doesn't open from the outside—not unless you're one of us. It only opens from the inside. And to anyone chasing, it'll look like we've just run Between; this place doesn't exist on either the human or the Behind side. Not until one of us touches the door handle, anyway."

North stepped inside, looking around for a brief moment while the soft glow of magic lit the room, then came back out.

"It's all Between," she said.

"Yep," I said. "Figured it was safer. The king is too good with magic—he might even be able to see what I'm doing if I do it with human magic, so I sorted this out last night with a bit of Between and a lot of fiddling."

"We'll be able to get back out again, I suppose?" asked Five, looking narrowly at me.

"Yeah, but we'll have to be careful about it, because if things get nasty, this is exactly where every brawler and his leech will be milling around for a good few hours," I said. "They won't be able to get in—they shouldn't even be able to see it—but there'll be a lot of them hanging around because of how close the fake king is."

"We'll be rats in a trap, in other words," Five retorted.

"Only for as long as it takes the king to redirect the brawlers," I pointed out. "He won't keep them there if he thinks the fake kings have all been busted. This is just a little hidey hole to stay in until it's safe to go back to the bridge—just in case anything goes wrong during the fight and we have to retreat."

"This is good," said Daniel, and I knew he was thinking of Kevin, alone under the bridge. "So that's why you had us bring half the supplies."

"Of course," said Jin Yeong. "If we are hurt, there will be a need for food and blood."

Daniel shot him a look. "Just make sure it's the right blood you're going after."

"I do not drink *wolf blood*," Jin Yeong said, his face the picture of disgust.

"Right," I said. "If you lot are finished bickering, we'd better get on to the last boss battle."

Morgana would have appreciated that joke. North only swept back out of the room without so much as a flicker of interest, Five and Jin Yeong looked confused, and Daniel rolled his eyes.

"Fine," I said, starting along the tunnel again. "Let's go get the king."

It didn't take much longer to get to the place I'd been looking for—and, having found it, for all of us to push through the softness of the tunnel wall and into the Between part of the world. I led them around by a more circuitous route than I would have had to if it wasn't for how close one of the fake kings was, and at last stopped at the mouth of a concrete valley that seemed to have been formed by the cleaving of a vast, ridiculously broad piece of cement.

"Here we go," I said, gesturing around the valley. It was the first time I'd seen it in real life rather than as an echo of Between, and I couldn't help gazing around along with the rest of them.

It should have been a crack in the concrete, but with the assistance of Between it was a whole valley, cut from the cement as it dried for the first time and then grew wet and dry by turns along with the seasons. There was ostensibly one way in and one way out, which looked pretty dangerous if you didn't know about the third way—which was only a way out, not in.

A breeze flitted its way around our knees, sweeping up toward the end of the valley; that was North checking the place out to make sure there were no hidden threats, I figured.

I pointed to the jagged edge of the left-hand side of the valley. "That's my spot, up there," I told them. "Reckon the king will come out at the other side to see what's going on and keep out of the fight. There's a nice little icing of magic all over the other side that should stop any sort of attack from getting through, so I know he's up there. Don't reckon he'll try to get down here, not when he could end up copping something that his wards would stop otherwise."

"What about your attack?" Daniel asked.

"It's not an attack," I said, grinning. "It's more of a show and tell. His magic won't even recognise it as a threat."

"You hope," said Five, not very quietly.

"We will be far away from each other," Jin Yeong said, measuring the distance with his eyes. "Still, you are closer to us than to him."

"And we're the ones in the line of fire," pointed out Five caustically. "Think on that, pointy teeth! He'll send them at us from behind and before, if he can."

That was something I wasn't exactly happy about, either.

"Why this area?" asked North.

She and Jin Yeong had been looking around ever since we arrived, their eyes flicking here and there, constantly on the lookout for attack. Five had been doing it to some degree, too, but in his case, I had the feeling he was looking for places we could retreat to and advantageous ground rather than potential threats.

In short, Jin Yeong and North were treating this like a trap, and Five was treating it like a battlefield. I hoped to prevent it being either, but things didn't always go according to plan, so it was better to have a back-up plan.

Good thing I had another back-up plan.

I grinned at them all and just waited for someone to see what was behind me.

"It is another door," Jin Yeong said, with narrow eyes. He sounded accusatory, and the finger he used to point at the door definitely was. "What is this?"

"This?" I said airily. "Oh, this is just a bit of a worm-hole—"

"If we have to face worms as well—"

"All right, keep your knickers on, Tuatu! I mean that it's a bit of a short-cut to our little escape door. If things get too hot to handle in here and the king manages to get you all surrounded, you just need to nip through the door here and get to the door *there*. They'll have to go the long way around."

Jin Yeong's eyes grew narrow. "How will that work for you?"

"It won't," I said frankly. "I'll just have to hustle down my side of the crevasse and make it to the door with you. If I'm fast enough, it'll be fine."

"What if it is *not* fine?"

"You've seen me legging it," I pointed out. "What do you think?"

"I think I will be happy when the king is dead."

"Fair. Are you lot ready?"

"That depends—do we have to work up surprised expressions, or can we just attack them?"

"Don't care," I said cheerfully. "You just need to keep them occupied for about twenty minutes while I mess with the king. Bonus points if someone can throw a bit of magic."

"I'll do what I can," said North, looking around one last time.

I took that as my cue and touched the first little glittery domino in the series that I'd so carefully set up last night. Lit with Between, it hit the next and set off a four-pronged chain reaction that would take us from frying pan to fire.

"Right, that's done it," I said, taking in a short, determined breath.

Tuatu looked alarmed. "What's done it? What happened?"

I grinned at him. "Just triggered every fake-king's hiding spot to make the king think we're there."

"You mean, apart from the one near us?"

"Nope. Not much use triggering all of them except this one: he'd know straight away that we're here. This way, he just knows that we're at one of them, but not which one. He's gunna have to send out a lot of personnel to deal with it, and I don't reckon he'll be able to recall them too easily when he realises where we really are. You lot just have to stay over this side of the rivulet and let the brawlers mess up the other side until I'm in position and you're ready to start being bait."

North threw a calculative look back toward the rivulet we had left behind in the human world—the nearest pretend-king location. "We'll have to account for those ones first, then," she said.

"Only when they realise what's happening. So just keep quiet for a bit until he's had a chance to send out *everyone*. Then you can come in and start making a mess."

"I can make a mess," said Jin Yeong, with a very satisfied snap of his teeth. "Are you going now?"

"Yeah, might as well," I said. "He'll come out to see what's happening as soon as he figures out that he's had to send brawlers to every location. I'll get him then."

"I'm glad you're so confident," muttered Five, unsheathing the short, tough little sword that he always seemed to fight with when he wasn't working with a bow.

It wasn't that I was confident—it was more that I had to be, because this was the only choice we had right now. The king's magic was so much stronger than I'd been prepared for—any amount would have been more than I'd prepared for, given that I'd hoped to have him still trapped in an iron-and-salt circle right about now.

So I said firmly, "We're gunna be fine. See you lot when this is over—or at the doorway if something goes wrong."

"Go," said North, drawing nearer to Tuatu but without quite touching him. "Work as quickly as you can: I feel something in the air."

"Got it," I said, and turned and ran.

When the North Wind says there's something in the air, there's something in the air.

I could feel what she meant as I ran, leaping up to the next rock and then the next, squeezing between two folds of concrete. I breathed in the air and felt as though it was loaded with dust motes or magic or possibilities. Heck, maybe it was.

Whatever it was, it felt like I outran it or maybe just climbed beyond it, because when I finally got to the top of the concrete escarpment it was easier to breathe despite the exercise. It felt like I'd climbed up and out into fresh air, and I fairly revelled in it.

No matter how good it felt to breathe clean air, I had to be careful; I stayed away from the edge of the escarpment—away from anywhere that could be seen from the opposite side—crouched against the rocky outcrop that was the inside of one of the walls of the tunnel, and waited.

It was hard to wait, but probably easier on me than it was on the others below. At least I could send out feelers Between to see if my little fall of dominos had called the king's attention in the way I hoped it had. North might be able to see more than the others, and Jin Yeong could certainly smell as much as or more than the lycanthropes, but they had only their immediate surroundings to inform them. I could almost imagine Five's pegleg drilling holes in the ground as he waited.

I found traces of movement heading toward each of the four locations that had a fake king installed—and waited. I felt the king himself stirring opposite me—and waited. Even when movement boiled over in the entrance of the crevasse, I waited.

Then, from below, I heard a shout and a death rattle. At least some of the brawlers had found my friends, which meant that before very long a lot more of them would arrive to help out.

Right. That should about do it.

I pushed away from the wall as I rose, and strode toward the concrete lip of the crack. Time to let the king know I was here. He might—probably would—think it was a trap, but I was pretty sure he would come out anyway.

I just had to make sure that when I began what I'd come to do, it wasn't seen as an attack.

It was gut-churning to wait—sickening to look down and see my friends fighting without me. It wasn't as if I was the best fighter in the group, but it was still hard looking down and feeling like I was doing nothing physically to help.

North swirled through the brawlers, as swift, strong, and untouchable as a cyclonic gale; Jin Yeong tore his way through them in a spray of blood, too swift and savage to be stopped. The lycanthropes and Tuatu made a strong, present rear-guard with Five sending small, deadly arrows into the thick of things and thrusting savagely with his short sword whenever anything got too close.

They were strong enough to push away from my side of the concrete crack and press forward, which was good, but it also meant they were a bit too far away from the concrete wall and the door to safety when more brawlers poured in from the left, circling in behind and forcing the lycanthropes to curl around tighter in a circular defence.

I threw a look down and to my left, my heartbeat quickening. Heck, there were more of them arriving. The king definitely knew we were here now.

He was also prepared to send in a good lot of brawlers without appearing himself.

That didn't seem fair, so I used a trailing edge of my human magic to weave Between around North and make her look a bit more kingly, and around the rest of them to make them look a bit more minion-y. To my inexpressible joy, it worked; the brawlers who had managed to circle in from behind turned against the other brawlers and fought furiously against them, opening up the way to our escape route again.

And then, just as I had known he would, the king came out to play.

CHAPTER TEN

HE SAUNTERED UP TO THE VERY EDGE OF THE CONCRETE LEDGE as if he didn't have a care in the world, but I saw the distorting magic all around him: protecting, nurturing, and confusing. There was also a strong outward projection of awe to it, and I had the suspicion that if I'd been a bit closer, it would have been very hard not to drop to my knees in abject fear. There was a nasty edge to the magic strongly suggesting I do it—nasty, and strong.

Which…I suppose might have been a nice boost to his ego, but was it really necessary? Was it even particularly useful?

"Pet of Lord Sero," he said, by way of *hello*. "Have you come to kill me again? I wouldn't suggest it—even a human with a small amount of magic should be able to tell how dangerous that would be."

"We'll see," I said. "I figured your little minions would be busy enough dealing with that lot down there that you wouldn't have anyone left at home to look after you."

Now let him figure out if it really was a trap, or if I was just bluffing!

His golden-brown brows went up; surprised retriever, I call that look. "Not unexpected, but one of my less likely scenarios," he said. "You think you can attack me from over there with your delicate human magic? Or are you hoping in whatever fae magic you might have been born with?"

"I don't tend to hope in fae magic too much," I said, shrugging.

Human magic was delicate, all right—but it wasn't anything like as delicate as Between, when you really knew how to use Between. Now *there* was a power subtle enough to slip through anything like a needle and coil itself in with all the king's fae magic, ready to weave and sew and sneakily lead magic into following it until it curved in and around itself and made a beautiful little spell!

I sent out a little tendril on its journey and added, "I'm not here to attack you. I'm here to talk."

Both of those things were true. Like my effort with the brawlers, I was more interested in making the king's resources turn on themselves than I was in outright attacking—and the longer I talked, the better chance I had of succeeding.

"What's happening down here?" mused the king, his eyes on the mass of bodies below.

I was pretty sure it was an insult to me, that deliberate focus of attention on something else, but I didn't care. It just gave me the leisure to keep going with the leading point of Between, weaving it through and around his magic, while his followed it: thread to my needle.

"A bit of a fight, by the looks," I said. "How long do you think it'll take them to get through to your side?"

"I wasted a lot of brawlers on the other locations, but I still have enough to be getting along with," he said. "Don't think that I don't have enough to protect myself with. How did you know I was here, by the way?"

"Why would I tell you that?" I objected. Just like the fight below, if he didn't know what was going on, or how it was going, that was his problem. I just needed time for the tricky bit of

Between work I was doing to complete its job. "You forgetting we're enemies or something?"

"Like you, I suspect, I'm just sparring for time," he said, shrugging. "Just until I find out what you're doing to make my brawlers think that they're on your side, mind you. Then I'm going to strip it away and kill all of your friends there to show you that I don't appreciate being called out like a child to play—ah! There it is. I think we'll undo that bit of magic."

I would have liked to have thought it was just a bluff on his part, but from the movement of the fight and the sour taste of magic undone, I knew it wasn't. The brawlers below now knew with crystal clarity that they were fighting against their own, and they weren't happy about it. I saw them turn and fight the line of lycanthropes and Five—saw Jin Yeong and North falter briefly in the throng as they too, realised what had happened.

They had a limited amount of time left for me to do what I had to do, and they were in danger of being cut off from the way out once more.

"Now," the king said, while I desperately tried to calculate how much time it would take for my touch of Between to keep weaving through his magic. "Let's see what we can do about this mess. The North Wind is an obvious first choice, but she has very few weak spots. It was kind of you to make sure the biggest is present with us today; I'll be sure to mark him as *very important* in this little fight—there, you see? They'll all go after him as a priority."

I couldn't stop the little charge of magic that went out from him—couldn't stop it sinking into the unknowing Tuatu with the behindkind equivalent of a hit notice. I saw the effect of it nearly straight away, though; the mob of brawlers moving backward and forward like waves on the beach, wary of Jin Yeong and North, pushed forward in a tidal wave toward Tuatu.

They engulfed and separated him from the line of lycanthropes, leaving two fallen wolves in their wake as Tuatu desperately fought to get back to them. North saw it and acted in a moment, decimating the shifting knot in one single charge that sent four-armed brawlers flying and screaming into the melee. I saw her a moment later, dragging Tuatu back toward the others, but there was blood staining the back of her dress and every footstep that touched the concrete below.

"Flaming heck," I said softly, because even if North had saved Tuatu's life, she was now very likely to die herself—along with everyone else in the group. With my eyes darting back and forth to make sure that Jin Yeong was still moving, still alive, I couldn't blame her. She was protecting her own.

I saw the boiling of more brawlers at the far end of the crevasse and caught the brief look upward that Jin Yeong sent me. I jerked my head vigorously at him. *Get out of there.* I couldn't see if the fallen lycanthropes were still alive, but I had a cold feeling that they weren't.

I knew that unless they retreated now, they would probably all die, and I still hadn't been able to complete my part in the enterprise.

Jin Yeong, snarling, held back the crawling mass of brawlers while North pulled Tuatu into the wall, the lycanthropes dragging their fallen with them while Five slashed with sword and bow alike, out of arrows some time ago.

I looked across at the king with sweat on my temples and saw that he was watching me thoughtfully.

"You'd better go and help your friends, don't you think?" he said. "It doesn't look like they're likely to last long without you. Or are you depending on the vampire to even things out? Things aren't looking very good for him—even vampires have a limit to how much punishment they can take."

"This one can take more than you can dish out," I said, but there was a cold feeling in my stomach because Jin Yeong *was* flagging. I saw him disappear beneath the masses of brawlers twice before he emerged again, fighting desperately to get back to the others.

"Perhaps," said the king, shrugging. "But I haven't got a stake in this battle: it's a matter of indifference to me whether or not he lives. I don't think you can say the same, and it makes me *very curious* about why you're still here."

He knew that something was wrong. He knew that something was happening, even if he didn't know what it was. He was edging back from the precipice even though on paper, it would have looked like he was winning.

He was moving back, and the tenuous link I had with him was verging on either failure or discovery.

In the last moment that I was near enough to do so, I frantically slipped that needle of Between back out of his mind and magic, out of sight and out of detection; then I turned and ran for it.

There was a sickness in my stomach that wasn't fear; it was a sickness of failure and dread that said I had gambled with my friends' lives —worse, that I had gambled with those lives and *lost*. I leaped down, fell down, tumbled into a brawler, and then I was fighting with no way out and no one beside me or behind me. I don't know where the swords came from, but they were in my hands and there was blood on my face, heat in my ribs, and a dreadful coldness in my legs while whiteness danced in front of my eyes, decorated with brown spots.

I stabbed and slashed and ducked, never quite quick enough to avoid injury but never slow enough to die, and then somehow I had broken free. I sprinted along the edge of the rivulet, my heart pumping dizzily in my ears, in my skull, and caught sight of the others ahead of me—too far ahead of me.

I saw the massive wave of brawlers spilling into the tunnel behind them too. They had to cross the rivulet to get into our hidey hole now, and it didn't look like I was going to make it in time to get in there too.

I ran anyway, because it's not much use saying things are impossible without trying. I ran because there were only three lycanthropes walking. I ran because all I could see of Jin Yeong was his head as North and Tuatu carried him with a trail of blood pattering out behind them as they ran.

And I stopped running when they began to cross over the rivulet, because another wave of brawlers was tumbling from the walls in front of me as though being birthed from the stone. Five saw me and yelled, but I couldn't hear what he said. Daniel caught sight of me too, and his jaw tightened—it looked as though he was trying to decide for a brief moment whether or not to acknowledge my frantic arm movements that meant *get in the wall right now, you wally!*

To my relief, he nodded at me a moment later. He would make sure that everyone who was still alive would live, even if it meant me being shut outside. He had already lost people today, and I didn't think he was willing to lose any more, especially with the amount of brawlers between me and them. Not when so few of the group were still in fighting shape.

Tuatu and North were still on their feet, but barely, and all I could see of Jin Yeong as he was carried in with them was torn clothing and blood fairly dripping from him. Even a vampire shouldn't lose that amount of blood.

I would have leaped the rivulet and made a good go of getting in with them if the water hadn't boiled up with something big and toothy as Five crossed over last with a bleeding half-wolf, half-human Kyle. Daniel grabbed Kyle as the leprechaun was pulled under, and when Five resurfaced, gasping, there were hands to drag him out before anything could pull him under again. Bereft of his pegleg and roaring, they carried him into the side of the tunnel with them, and I grinned a bloody, encouraging grin at Daniel when I caught his eyes in the last second before he shut the door in the faces of the approaching brawlers.

Those brawlers saw me from across the rivulet, and I ran. I

ran, but I didn't go far—or anywhere too hard to find—because there was no need. Even if there had been a need, I had no more strength and I was running pretty short on blood, too; it was far better that the king find me now, while I was still alive, and take me back to his side of the concrete escarpment so that I could finish the work I had started and failed to finish earlier.

This time I was going to do the thing my own way, without putting anyone else at risk. This time, I was going to—well, it was pretty likely that I would die. But at least I would manage to do what I came to do.

That was if I could stop myself from dying in the meantime.

I couldn't stop myself from falling. I hit the concrete hard but it didn't hurt, and from the sound of the rivulet, I was in just the right position: if I lived for long enough, either the leeches or the brawlers would find me—and when they found me, the king would also find me.

Hopefully he would find me quickly enough, I thought, and passed out.

THE WORLD WAS dark and cold around me when I was irresistibly drawn back into it by a familiar voice. "Dear me!" it said softly. "What do we have here?"

I managed to crack my eyes open and Athelas' face swam above me.

"Heck," I said, laughing around the ache in my throat. "You actually came. I didn't see you while I was looking around last night—I was worried you were long gone."

"Where else would I be?" he asked, laying a cool hand on my forehead that dripped with magic. "I didn't go through so much effort to keep you alive only to leave you to die before you achieve what I need you to achieve."

"Figured," I said, almost gasping in relief at the release from pain.

More than physical pain, I felt as though my heart was lighter. I hadn't been wrong. Athelas had never meant to kill me—he had very carefully done his best to kill me while I was still protected by a contract that wouldn't allow it and had taken the proof of his attempt back with him to Lord Sero.

I gave a snuffly sort of laugh and added, "Didn't see you sneaking around until now, so I thought I must have got it wrong. You better get moving if you want to live; there's a good few of the king's brawlers coming for me, not to mention the rivulet leeches. They're pretty nasty when they make skin-to-skin contact."

"I moved you from your somewhat perilous position," he said. "You don't need to worry about that for now."

"The heck you did," I said angrily. "Put me back! They're supposed to find me!"

"I shall certainly not allow you to die now that you're so close to achieving my revenge for me. You'll have to put up with being healed and hurled back into the battle at some later stage, I'm afraid."

"I *thought* you must have been after the king as well," I said grumpily, feeling tingly about the legs. I had the feeling they would start to hurt soon, which was probably as much of a good thing as a bad thing. It meant my body was healing, even if I'd prefer the kind of healing that came from vampire spit. That thought brought with it a sick kind of panicked feeling, so I pushed myself into speech again. "Once I figured out that you preferred me alive to dead, it was easy enough to see that. Reckoned you had Zero earmarked for being the next king, though."

"That is something I cannot control," he said. "This much— the absolute fall of the king, the order, and the ruling powers—is enough."

I sat up dizzily with Athelas' support. "So that's why you weren't too upset when Upper Management started killing all those fae VIPs. Figured you just liked to see people getting their hearts ripped out as a matter of business."

"One can always learn a few new tricks, even if one is an old dog," he said coolly. "It was interesting to me on a professional level. On your feet, Pet. Where are the others?"

"That's the problem," I said. "There's only one way to get to them, and it'll involve cutting through about fifty-odd four-armed blokes. They need to get out and then get back to the bridge—the king can't get to them if they're there, and they can get out safely from there once the arena opens. I don't think the king can even sense past it as part of the arena."

Athelas said, "They're badly injured, then?"

"Two of the lycanthropes are dead—the girls, I think—and I reckon Kyle and Dylan are close behind," I said flatly. "North tried a bit too hard to make sure Tuatu didn't die, so she's a lot weaker than usual, too. Five is still doing well, but I think he lost his pegleg when they crossed the rivulet before the power station—reckon they ran into something with a lot of teeth that didn't have a chance to grab 'em. Five went under for a minute, though."

"The mosquito?"

"They carried him in with them," I said, and an involuntary shiver spread through my body. "I don't know."

"And yet," said Athelas, observing me closely, "here you are."

"Yeah," I said. "I'm the bait."

"I see," he said. "And what is the trap, if you are the bait?"

"That's me, too," I told him, feeling the strength grow quietly and surely inside my legs and my lungs both. "The king's being a bit too free with his magic, and I need to get closer to him to be able to do anything about that."

Athelas glanced toward the rivulet as it bubbled with the scum of the passing of leeches. "I see; you intend to go back to him. Will you present yourself to him half-dead, then? These creatures won't drag you to him—they'll kill you and leave your carcass for the rats."

"Yeah," I said again. "Maybe. It was a calculated risk. That's where you come in now, though—with flamin' good timing as usual. You're about the only one the king would trust to drag me in by the scruff of my neck without thinking it's a trap."

Athelas' grey eyes once again rested on my face, their expression hard to read. "You expect me to bring you captive to the king?"

"Got it in one," I said. "You flamin' owe me—you know you do! The least you can do is take a couple of orders from me so that we can finish up this nightmare."

"You might recall, Pet," he said, "that we've had this conversation many times before."

"The one where you tell me not to trust you and I trust you anyway? Yeah, I know."

"Then might one inquire *why* you persist in doing the same things and making the same mistakes all over again?"

"Because I know you didn't kill all those people and spend so much time scheming just to keep the king on the throne. And because I know you wouldn't be here if you weren't here to help."

"I came to see my work through," he said coldly. "I'll see it to its end, and there's nothing you can do to prevent that. I've killed again and again to stay alive and undetected long enough to bring it about—you can't imagine that I'll balk at a few more deaths to see it through!"

"You can't stop me trusting you," I said. "And you know you owe me."

"There is no legal obligation—"

"I'm not talking legal."

"And no fae obligation—"

"I'm not talking fae obligations," I said, my voice tight and choked. "I'm talking about my dead parents and the fact that you can't ever make up for killing them!"

"A fine recompense," he said. "To take you to torture or your death. I'll go with you and set the others free; we'll regroup and find another way to get at the king."

"Nope," I said. "You're going to hand me over to the king, and then you're going to go and get the others out—they're going to need some help and some healing, and I'll be busy being bait."

"Why should I do any such thing? If you're not willing to take my revenge for me in the way that I choose, what would stop me from handing you over and taking it myself? Do you think I'm willing to throw away everything I worked so hard for just for your friends?"

"Can you just *stop* trying to make me think the absolute worst of you all the time? I've seen too many of your bloody memories! You never tell me an outright lie, but you lie all the time and I'm flamin' tired of it!"

A faint touch of amusement came to Athelas' eyes. "I suppose it's a little much to expect you not to think I'm trustworthy when I followed you in here. It's always been my best weapon against you, after all."

"Why do you think I let you out?" I said impatiently.

This time it was shock in his eyes, utter and complete. "I *beg* your pardon?"

"I let you out because I figured you'd either run for it or try and see everything through. You came to see it through so I'm expecting you to flamin' listen to what you're told and do what needs to be done!"

"Pet, am I to understand that you *arranged* for the detective to enter the room in which I was awake, fully understanding that he was still bound to me in bargain?"

"Why the heck else would I have sent him in there alone! I knew you'd use him, and I knew you'd be here when I needed you."

He gazed at me for a very long time, then opened his mouth to say not quite steadily, "Pet, I wish—I would give a great deal—"

There was no time for him to finish that sentence because I

already heard the slick, wet sound of leeches coming up from the water.

"Save it for later," I said. "We've gotta get going to hand me over to the king so that I can distract him while you get the others out. Reckon I'm in bad enough shape, or do you need to stab me?"

I saw the frozen, blank moment where no emotion at all showed in his face, then Athelas smiled humourlessly. "I believe I'll decline that particular job. You're in sufficiently bad shape outwardly to allay most suspicions, though I rather think my touch has done its work on your inner injuries. Perhaps we can agree at least to get you to the king in as good a shape as necessary to complete your no doubt very clever work."

THE TUNNEL never felt so cold as it did on the way to the king. Part of that coldness was probably the fact that my blood wasn't quite flowing properly again yet—some of it could have been the poison from the brawlers' knives—but it was likely that the awful dread sitting in my stomach was from the very simple fact that I didn't know if I really could trust Athelas, despite what I'd said to him.

I glanced across at him, seeing shadow and blood mingling in his eyes as the water reflected in them, and even though I'd said otherwise, I felt the coldest fear I yet remembered suffering. Because there was no way to know for sure that he would actually help me—no way to know for sure that he would give up his final chess piece and trust and wait—no way to be sure that what I thought of him was the truth this time when it hadn't been last time.

Athelas was right; he knew all the best ways to manipulate me, all the most effective ways to appeal to my judgement and my trust. He knew enough to be capable of showing up here with the sole intention of turning me in to the king for real—and my friends along with me now that he knew where they were. If that was the case, I'd given up myself and my friends for absolutely no benefit, and everything we'd done here in the tunnels was for nothing. Chelsea and Chantelle—and possibly Jin Yeong—had died for nothing.

Colder and colder it became, until I was shivering with every step, lead in my stomach and fear in my heart. There was still time to choose differently, said a small, terrified voice. I could make a different decision.

I would have given a great deal not to have to make that decision at all, in fact. But I had to choose, and if there was only one choice to make, I was going to choose to hope. To hope that I could see clearly enough. To hope that I was right in my estimation of Athelas. To hope that in all the darkness and twistedness of his heart, there was still a part of him that was as righteous and justice-seeking as the original desire he'd had to bring down Lord Sero, the king, and the entire order of the world Behind. To hope that he wasn't so far gone after the execution of that plan as to make him part of the system that needed excising.

The brawlers all stood back and let us pass through as we went. I hadn't expected anything else, and I don't think Athelas had, either. They didn't just stand back, either; they actively avoided Athelas, though they looked as though they wanted to hiss at me. And when we reached the crack in the wall once again that led to a bigger, more concrete version of itself further Between, they didn't follow us through.

"Here we go," I said, and I was happy I could say it without my teeth chattering. "He'll know we're here now. You better be flamin' convincing."

"Tell me that you have a plan, at least!" he said softly, pushing me along as the ground seemed to move beneath my feet.

"I wouldn't go right to *plan*," I said, a curious coil of laughter curling in my stomach as we drew closer to the king's side of the cracked concrete. "It's more of an idea."

Athelas closed his eyes for the briefest moment. "Enough. I am not going to save your friends while you martyr yourself. They can join us with the king and do their job of distracting him so that you can work your plan in peace. Self-sabotage was not a part of my plan, nor ever will be."

"You don't have to tell me that!" I snapped at him. "No one is too precious to sacrifice when it comes to getting your revenge, are they?"

"You're yet alive," he said. "And will be for quite some time, if you'll only listen to reason."

"If reason is letting my friends get slaughtered one by one so that I can use the time to undermine the king's magic, you can bet your boots I'm not going to listen to reason," I said fiercely.

Athelas had no right to insinuate that I was precious to him—not after he'd killed my parents and my friends. Not when he had lied to me and played games with me as though I were just a chess piece ever since he'd known me. Especially not when I wanted desperately to believe it was true.

"I utterly refuse to leave you here while I save your ragtag group of heroes," Athelas said. "We will—"

"You're gunna have to," I said. "'Cos I reckon that's the king coming now, and I'm pretty sure your revenge doesn't go as far as being killed by him—especially when it wouldn't do any good. You can't back out of this in time—you know you can't. You're gunna have to sacrifice me instead."

I saw him hesitate; saw the regret that clouded his grey eyes, the way his lips thinned. But I also knew he wouldn't hesitate long. He was used to sacrificing everything except himself to get what he needed, and he still hadn't got what he needed. In one way, I could understand it: if Athelas lived, he had another chance to win. In quite another way, it hurt to see the moment acceptance came into his eyes, even though I knew it had to happen—needed it to happen.

"I think you'll find yourself regretting this moment," he said. "I think you'll have to sacrifice more than you expect."

"Wish you'd flamin' stop talking to me," I said, trying not to breathe too quickly. "The sooner you get on to pulling my friends out of the hole they're in, the better. You can have a snark at me about sacrifices and regrets later on. We'll compare wounds or something. Get your flamin' game face on."

"I warned you," he said, and for an instant he could nearly have been Jin Yeong, all snarl and furious heat. "I *warned* you, Pet. I am not your chess piece."

"I know," I said. "I'm yours. But I'm the flamin' queen, and you better not forget it."

That was how the king found us when he stepped lightly from the concrete wall: me glaring at Athelas and Athelas fairly snarling at me.

"I see that the Pet doesn't endear itself to everyone," he said.

He looks so innocuous when you see him up close; he's a tall, scruffy, golden-retriever of a man, his limbs a bit too long and his expression a bit too hopeful to be human. He turns his head slightly to the side when he talks with you so that you have the feeling he's really listening to you—considering you.

And he probably is, but probably not for the reasons you might think.

He said pleasantly to Athelas, "I suppose it bit you?"

"Funny how we're back to *it* now," I muttered to myself. The king was one of the few fae who had called me *she* and *her* from the start—and, contrary to the rest of the world Behind, he had been one of the few I had met who now usually still did it.

"I managed to avoid that particular irritation," said Athelas, bowing. "My liege, I trust that you'll accept this human as a show of regret for not being able to warn you of its intentions in advance? As you'll see, I came here myself to assist—it really was not possible to get the intelligence of it to you earlier."

"As usual, you are unexpected but thorough," the king said.

"See if you can add to your usefulness by finding out where the pet's motley group were concealing themselves from me last night —I gather that there are still one or two more of the party to find, and I'd think they're hiding together. There were fewer this morning than there were last night."

"I will do my best to find the errant members," said Athelas, his shadowed eyes passing from the king to me.

I couldn't read them—couldn't do anything even if I did know whether he really was on my side or not. So, as Athelas bowed to the king and left me in the tight grip of two brawlers, all I could do was hope that I was right to trust him this time.

CHAPTER ELEVEN

There are things you know but don't really realise until you're plonked down into the middle of a circle of iron filings and salt.

"Oi," I said, falling onto my backside in the middle of the dusty circle as the king carefully shook iron filings from a paper bag into the hole he'd left in the circle. "That's my trick. Flamin' derivative, that's what you are."

"I've no desire to have you running around and getting up to mischief while my back is turned," he said.

"If you're gunna turn your back on me, you're dumber than I thought," I said.

"You're always so yappy," he said. "Just like a little dog. No wonder the steward was able to read you so well—all he had to do was prompt you and you'd bleat out everything he needed."

I mean, it wasn't as if it wasn't true, but it was flamin' rude.

"Whose filings are you using, anyway?" I asked him.

"Your werewolves should have been more careful about where they left their stash," he said.

"They're lycanthropes. Exactly what are you planning on doing with me? I figured you'd want to kill me pretty quick."

"That's nothing you need to know about," he said. "I'm not going to help you become a thorn in my side by an unwise word, so you'd best get used to being imprisoned for as long as I choose to keep you."

"Fair enough," I said. "That's a bit insulting, though: I figured I was already a thorn in your side."

"People who can't remove themselves from circles of iron and salt shouldn't complain about how unimportant they are. They should look on every passing moment still alive as a boon."

I shrugged one shoulder. "True."

I mean, it would have been true except for one thing.

There aren't a lot of advantages to being human when compared with being fae, or behindkind, or whatever. Behindkind in general are faster, stronger, and able to heal more quickly. They're harder to kill.

But that's not to say that there aren't any advantages. There aren't many—but there are a couple.

That's what I mean when I say that there are things you know but don't fully realise—stuff like me knowing I'm fully human but not really getting the point of it until a fae king, who thinks that as an heirling you must have a bit of fae as well as a bit of human in you, chucks you into a circle of iron filings and salt.

Didn't know how he'd managed to find our stash of filings. Didn't know where he'd gotten the paper bag he was carefully storing them in.

Definitely wasn't going to tell him that the iron filings didn't burn, stop, or impede me in any way except for being annoyingly gritty underneath my palms when I reached out to catch myself after he threw me into the circle.

That's called strategy.

And it was a little piece of knowledge that I was going to use to my advantage, even if that advantage was only to run away if I found that I couldn't do what I needed to do. So when the king left me alone—but not, if I was correct, unwatched—I worked desperately hard to think about exactly what advantages I had, what they could do for me, and how best to use them.

That's what the front of my brain did, anyway; at the back, all that existed was a froth of despair and worry and awful regret. All I could think about in that part of my brain was the memory of Jin Yeong's limp, bloody body being carried into the temporary safety of a Between-laced utility cupboard. The safety of that cupboard relied on the door being the only way in and out: behindkind couldn't get in, but neither could my friends get out without someone breaking through the lines of behindkind for long enough for them to make a run for it to the bridge.

Were they out yet? Had Athelas rescued them or decided against helping them, only to turn his mind to the problem of slaughtering the king? I knew he wouldn't just leave—even if that had been possible—but I knew him well enough to be sure he had at least three or four plans revolving in his head, and here I was trapped with the king and unable to make sure he did what I'd told him to do.

Unable to make him do the right thing.

Unable to know if I'd made the right decision to trust him again.

I didn't have my phone—it probably would have been smashed to pieces before now, anyway—and there was no way of knowing exactly how long passed while I waited in the darkness with a fast-beating heart, trying to calculate exactly how long Athelas would need to fight his way through the king's brawlers, convince my friends that he was there to help, not hinder, and get them back to the bridge before more of the king's brawlers—or worse, the king—found them.

I did know that the king hadn't gone further than the outside of the maintenance cupboard he'd dragged me into, which was a relief. He still didn't seem to understand how much of a connection I had with Between: he seemed to think that since he apparently had my magic in check, I was powerless and blind.

Unfortunately for him, I was very well aware of where every-thing was when it came to my immediate surroundings.

I was even, faintly, aware that some of my friends were still alive—though not how many of them were. The echo of the group of them danced through the rivulet and made a nonsense of left and right, up and down, as it bounced off the human magic-laced brickwork.

I would have given a lot to know how many were still alive. If Jin Yeong was still alive.

I would have given a lot to know if they were already on their way to the safety of the bridge.

Unfortunately for me, the king didn't stay outside for very long. That was what I'd planned on; it was what I needed to happen. I needed the king to stay away and unaware of where my friends were so that he couldn't use them as leverage again. I needed him to stay close so that I could work on tying up his magic while he thought he had me contained.

But I also knew that it was when his attention was focused on me that things would get more dangerous for me, and I couldn't afford to die just yet. I had to get to work as soon as possible, with as little fuss as possible, and live as long as possible in order for everything to go well.

So when the king came back into the chamber alone and made a big show of getting himself a chair, pulling it along the floor and setting it up with deliberate precision just to sit down with folded arms and one leg crossed over the other, I used every skerrick of that time to slip the delicate needle of Between into the brawl of power that was his magic. And as he took the time to gaze at me consideringly, drawing out the unsettling silence, I used the thread of Between, gossamer and desperately fine, to draw in the rope of his magic and began to weave it back over and into itself.

It wouldn't do any good to do the working with my own magic: it would never be strong enough to contain all of his magic, let alone stop it doing whatever he wanted it to do. No, like the brownies who had woven an enchantment over themselves that was so comprehensive that even when I knew what they were I couldn't *see* what they were, I was going to use Between to make the king's own magic weave a spell around itself. A spell that said *no magic here, bucko.*

I think the king was waiting for me to say something; from his perspective, I was just sitting there, glowering at him and maybe doing tricky things with Between. I couldn't do much of that, of course, but I had to do something. I had to do it clumsily enough that he'd notice, too, which was good; the spell took up too much of my attention to be doing fancy things with Between.

From now on, I just had to focus on making sure the working kept going, and that the king stayed close enough to prevent my connection either breaking or becoming obvious to him. To do that, I let the call I was sending through Between get a bit too strong—strong enough for him to sense it.

The king leaned forward as I did so and said pleasantly, "Stop trying to call things Between. They won't come to you—they're my subjects."

"Didn't think you did much work Between," I said. That's it. Lure him into thinking I don't know much about Between apart from how to walk through it.

"Enough to spot silly tricks like that," he said. "There's no King Behind who wouldn't."

"Oh well," I said. "It was worth a shot."

"Now," he said, without acknowledging that. "Let's get right down to business, shall we?"

"D'rather not do business with you," I said. Another forty seconds of work done. "Don't reckon our business styles match— and I'm flamin' sure our goals don't align."

"We can come to some sort of agreement, I'm sure," he said. "And it would be ridiculous to refuse to hear me out when you have nothing but time."

That was true, even if he didn't know *how* true.

"Not sure why you're not just killing me," I said. That was true, too; I'd expected to have to do a lot more fighting by this stage, and now that I knew how hard it was to keep hold of my hybrid Between-and-king's-magic weaving spell, I was very glad I hadn't had to. "So I'm gunna take a stab in the dark and say that I'm probably not gunna like whatever you want me to do."

"It's simple enough," he said. "Your friends are an irritant to me right now: I want that irritation gone. All you need do is tell me where they are, and we'll both be spared a very unpleasant hour or so."

It was so unexpected that my mind went blank for a moment or two; I had never expected to be asked something like this. My friends weren't important to the king in the way I was, so *why did he want them?*

Maybe if I'd been thinking a bit straighter I wouldn't have said so baldly, "Go jump in the lake, mate. Why would I tell you where they are?"

"Because if you don't, I'll cut off one of your fingers for every time you refuse to answer the question," he said, as if it was a perfectly normal thing to say.

I went cold from my ears to my toes. I don't think I moved for a good thirty seconds, and the worst thing was that he *knew* how badly he'd affected me. He just smiled at me in that friendly, shaggy dog kind of way and waited.

"Well, that flamin' sucks," I said, my heart racing.

My mind raced too, because there was no way I was losing fingers—or an arm—and there was no way I was giving up my friends. Which meant that it was time to fight—and hope that I could hold off the king for long enough to do what needed to be done to his magic.

A fight would definitely distract him enough.

It would also distract me, and the working I was doing had never felt so tenuous and fragile. I could feel it threading, weaving, joining, but like knitting, it could all be undone in a moment with a tug on the wrong thread.

"There's no need for things to get as nasty as that," he said gently. "I don't have any reason to be kind to you, but I still remember the child you were—bright and inquisitive, glittering with magic. If you tell me where your friends are, you can keep your fingers."

"What do you want with my friends, anyway?" I asked.

He was open and unguarded in a way he wouldn't have been if I'd been outside an iron-and-salt circle, and if I could just get him to talk long enough, I might be able to do all that I needed to do before he realised I wasn't as helpless as he thought.

Just fifteen minutes more. That was all I needed.

"You've got me," I added. "You could just kill me and go home. I don't get why you're trying to grab them as well."

"This is why you'll never be king," he said to me, as I concentrated just a bit more on the Between needle that was weaving its way through his magic and tangling it in itself. "You, I can execute at my own pace—even keep you alive, if I should wish it."

Liar, said a part of my brain. As if I didn't know the rules of the arena after calling him here! But instead of saying that, I just looked at him and let the filigree of his own magic grow up and over itself, knitting away to form a façade of magiclessness so utterly believable that even his own magic didn't know it was magic.

"Brownies are really flamin' useful," I said vaguely instead, then added, "You saying that you're crushing every sign of rebellion, even if it isn't rebellion that can really harm you?"

"All rebellion harms me," he said. "I am king. To rebel against me is treason and I reserve the right to punish traitors. Not one of them will live. I have no way of knowing if another of them is an heirling, after all."

"If you're trying to convince me to give up my friends by telling me you're just gunna kill them—"

"No," he said, laughing. It was the kind of laugh you give when a kid does something unreasonable but cute. "We've passed that point—we passed it a long time ago. You can consider it a punishment."

"I'm surprised you think I'll fall for the *I might not kill you after all* line, then," I said, unimpressed.

"There are many things I'm capable of giving to those people who are loyal to me," he said. "The very least of those is their life."

"Yeah, well, my life doesn't belong to you, and you can't take it or give it as you like," I said.

It wasn't exactly true, but if my life was in the balance here, I was going to sell it for as much pain, trouble, and nuisance as flamin' possible. Mind you, it wasn't like he couldn't just open the circle and drag me out—or bring in a couple of brawlers to do it— and that wouldn't leave me in a very good position. I would rather be free to fight and waste a bit more time than already be in his clutches.

Might as well see how well surprise did as a weapon then, I decided. I strode forward and right out of the iron-and-salt circle, suppressing the instinct to run out. I hadn't finished the job of tying up his magic yet, and the further away I got from him—the more my thread of Between had to strain—the easier it would be for him to discover what I was doing.

So I drew my two swords from Between, the weight of them familiar but somehow insufficient in my hands. If I was going to die today, I'd better make sure I finished up the job of binding his magic. At least then Zero would have an easier time finishing him off—and I had no doubt that Athelas would be there to make sure Zero *did* finish off the king, whether or not he had done as I asked him to do.

"You," said the king, sharp and slightly savage, "are a constant surprise. You're mistaken if you think you'll confuse me with your ridiculous tricks, however—I suppose you left a doctored stash of filings for me to find so that you could stage your little surprise.”

“That’d mean I was here deliberately,” I said, grinning at him humourlessly with a sick feeling in my stomach. “And that would mean I’ve got bigger mental problems than an urge to be king.”

The king drew his own weapon; it was belted on and very pretty—and very deadly. The one thing it *wasn’t* was Between-drawn. That wouldn’t stop it killing me, but it was further confirmation of my ideas about the king and his abilities when it came to Between.

“I see you’re determined to bait me to kill you,” he said, and strode forward. “Perhaps I’ll oblige.”

I fought bitterly, savagely. I fought like my life was on the line, because it was. I fought to stay alive for as long as it took to finish off the binding that still moved *so slowly* because if it moved quickly he would sense it.

And in the end, it was the working that was my downfall. I could either fight or work with Between, and it didn’t seem as if I could do both at once. I retreated a bit too fast—probably retreated exactly where the king meant me to retreat—and tripped over an uneven bit of the brickwork that felt almost as though it reached out and grabbed my heel.

I lost one sword on impact; the king was on me in another moment with a knife at my throat and his knee on my solar plexus, his other hand reaching out to wrench my second sword away from me.

He tossed it into the darkness, breathing heavily, and said, “It’s a shame you chose to sell yourself to the Sero family. You would have been a good pet.”

I would have said that I hadn’t sold myself to anyone, but the truth was that I kind of had sold myself—at least at first.

Gasping a bit, I said, “You behindkind fae are all the flamin’ same, you know that?”

"You really are indomitable. I won't play with you any longer—where are your friends?"

His magic, so close and so unaware, threaded itself together more swiftly, following the lead of my needle of Between. Bright with hope and prickling with dread, I knew that it would take at least another five minutes for the spell to complete itself.

How many fingers was I going to lose? Could I lose two and still use my hand? What if he started out with my entire hand? Would I lose too much blood and die before I could complete the working?

No use trying to distract him with anything else Between or Behind—I had to concentrate on my working. I wheezed at him until he got the idea that I couldn't really breathe with his knee where it was, but he only moved it to pin down my right arm at the shoulder instead.

Another twenty seconds gained.

I tried to feel good about that, but I was already sweating, cold and dizzy with fear and awful anticipation. He could see it, and he enjoyed that too; he took his time leaning forward over my hand—touched each one of my fingers lightly as if he was trying to decide which one to start with.

Twenty more seconds. One minute. Only four minutes to go. Could I even put up with the pain of losing a finger?

The king cut off my thumb first, the mongrel. I think I closed my eyes, but I felt the coldness, and then the deep, dull pain that swept up my entire arm and forced a small scream from my throat. My body tried to curl in protectively, but the king's knee pressed down harder, and something shifted out of place in a movement that was more noise than pain. Pain throbbed in my shoulder, huge and hot.

"Where are your friends?" he asked coolly. "There are still four more fingers here—yours to keep or still to lose, just as you choose."

"Look at Athelas being right," I said, trying not to throw up.

The king probably wouldn't let me choke on my vomit, but I didn't want to throw up anyway. "Reckon he knew you'd do something like this."

The king gave a small, derisive smile. "No doubt he wanted to have his fun with you before he brought you—I prefer knives to words. Now; your friends."

"Nope," I said. It was all I could say without throwing up. All I could say without losing hold of his magic and my sanity all at once, because I knew he was going to cut off my forefinger next and he was moving the knife and it was dripping with my blood and there was no hesitation and then pain and burning in my throat and more screaming...

There was a white space for a little while where he cut off more fingers and blood flowed, warm and sticky, while I shook my head with my teeth ground together every time he asked, "Your friends?"

The third and fourth fingers didn't seem to hurt but when he cut off my smallest finger I screamed again.

I'd been crying for a while, but I didn't remember starting. The pain was somehow mind-numbing, but the real horror was not being able to look away; seeing the mess he'd made of my hand and the blood just...pumping its way out of my butchered arm as if it didn't belong to me.

And by the faintest thread I still held my sanity and the working. It glittered and wove itself within the complicated movement of the king's body, and for an instant I thought I saw the whorls and sinews that made him up as he said impatiently to himself, "I'll have to slow the blood. We don't want to lose you yet, little pet. *Where*. Are your friends?"

Were they out? Were they safe?

I didn't know because I still didn't even know if Athelas could be trusted. I knew he couldn't be trusted, but there had to be a way he could be trusted, too.

And then I screamed because there was no hand and no arm,

just deep, cold pain and the stump of an arm below my armpit where the king's knee pressed down.

I screamed and writhed, and the spell writhed and drew itself together, complete. I saw the world Between, bright and knife-edged and sharply in focus with the king at its centre, a blank spot without magic or the ability to use Between.

I shoved him away with the air itself—air sparkling with Between that made itself firm for me—and sent the king tumbling backward across the brickwork. Then I dragged myself to my feet, swaying.

The king caught himself and leapt to his feet, eyes hard and still uncomprehending.

"Been a change of plans," I panted, and retched.

I sent a crawling surge of Between down my shoulder and toward the stump of my arm that was draining the blood from me, and it closed over the bare, severed flesh and skin. It might not hold, but hopefully it'd hold for long enough.

When the blood had slowed to a trickle instead of a surge, I said thickly, "Heck. Time for me to have my say."

"Ridiculous," he said, with a small, contemptuous huff of air.

"This bloke is getting on my last flamin' nerve," I said to myself, still swaying. I had to keep talking or I'd start throwing up or falling down, and I couldn't do that right now because I was finally where I needed to be.

Not dead. Not surrounded by behindkind.

Alone with the king.

Only Between around us to play with.

"Sit down," he said to me. "You'll fall down anyway. You're not going to leave this room, so sit down and rest until we begin again. If you tell me what I need to know, I'll give you a quick death at least—there's nothing left for you now."

"That's the thing about you blokes," I said, with the sweat rolling down into my eyes and stinging them. It hurt so much just to stand there that the whole world was moving around me. "You keep on acting like things that are weaker don't have any value. Look at you! You're standing there alone and wasting time playing with me instead of calling for help because you think a human with only one arm left is the same thing as a dead human."

"Are you not?" he asked, tilting his head enquiringly at me. "Do you think you have enough strength in your other arm to do anything against me? Even if you do have some strength there, do you think you have the skill for combat in your off-arm? Had you such skill, would it help you against anyone but another human?"

I laughed, because if it was still possible to trust Athelas, all of my friends must by now be safe—and because if I couldn't trust him, everything was over anyway. At the very least, I had bound up the king's magic so tightly within itself that he would never again use it, no matter whether or not I was the one who killed him. At least now I could fight to the death properly.

"That's flamin' typical of behindkind, too," I said. "You think everything is important only because of how it relates to you."

"Tell me what isn't true," he said.

There was a crease between his brows, and I could almost have sworn that he was trying to understand me. Why I was the way I was, how I worked—why I did and said the things I did and said. It was probably that quality in him that had kept him alive for so long: the quality that had made him seem so human and friendly.

"I mean, that might almost have been true if I was right-handed," I said. "But I'm left-handed, so I hate to break it to you, but you chopped off the wrong arm. And stop trying to ruin my point —you asked me what I could do against you with just one arm? Dunno about you, but it's never taken much strength to do *this*."

I reached Between, without sight, without medium, without anything solid to reach for, and drew the heirling sword into my physical reality in one smooth, certain sweep. It came to me without hesitation, as if it had been waiting for exactly this moment, and in that moment it glowed, rich and warm, entirely yellow.

The king stared at the sword—forgetting me completely, if I was any judge—and there was a terrifying hunger in his eyes. I knew that hunger; I'd seen a similar hunger in Athelas' eyes what seemed like a lifetime ago, when I offered him the dryad I'd gone on to give to Detective Tuatu instead. In that case, it had been a chance for safety and security that Athelas hadn't ever had, and he had wanted it *so badly*. The king badly wanted the sword because it represented safety to him—but instead of safety merely to live and exist for himself, it was safety in his position as king that he coveted.

And that told me everything I needed to know.

"You've never pulled it out from Between, have you?" I said. "You've never been able to pull the sword out of anything, let alone raw Between. You ever even touched it?"

"Still," he said below his breath, his chest rising and falling just a touch too quickly. "Left-handed or not, heirling sword or not, it's only a human with a missing limb. A few minutes' fight ought to end it all. I'll deal with your friends later."

"Maybe," I said. "Maybe not."

With how carefully and completely I'd tied up his magic while he was torturing me, he would *have* to use his strength. He had nothing left.

Me, on the other hand? I had magic, I could use Between, and I still had three limbs, which was more than enough to make trouble with. My life wasn't about to end because I'd lost an arm —though it might end sooner than I wanted if I didn't wrap up things here and get to a certain vampire pretty quickly. A certain vampire who, said a cold thought, may or may not be too healthy himself.

"Oi," I said, grinning savagely while the sweat rolled into my eyes. "Try to use your magic. Dare you."

He stared at me, at first uncomprehending, then disbelieving, then blazing with anger as he reached for the one constant power he had always had access to and found that it didn't exist.

I saw the rise and fall of his chest as his heartbeat sped up, and that was wearyingly satisfying.

"What did you do?" he demanded.

"One arm for a king's magic," I said. "A bit expensive for what it's worth, but at least you can't use it. How long do you reckon you'll survive out there with Zero after you, no magic, and no sword?"

"That won't matter to you," he said through his teeth. "Because you'll be dead."

"Maybe," I said, but I couldn't help grinning, because I could see something moving in the darkness behind him.

Athelas hadn't been the only one to sneak into the arena before I sealed it by calling on the king: he hadn't been the only one I was hoping for either. I had a deep, sparkling sort of feeling that things were starting to pull together exactly as I'd hoped—or maybe that was just the blood loss talking.

Because despite the help from vampire spit, I'd lost too much blood. I could barely stand, let alone fight, but behind the king was Les, all shadowed eyes and carefully quiet feet. And even if his methods were unorthodox and his pockets stuffed with my best forks, Les knew how to fight—and how to stay alive.

I should have expected it: he always had been there. Every time I looked around—every time I played with Between or wandered where I shouldn't.

Every time there was danger to heirlings in general and me in particular, he had been around. I laughed, gasping and gripping the sword tight, because I understood exactly how things had fallen together—and what I needed to do.

"Oi, Les," I said to the shadow. "Got something for ya."

And then I threw the heirling sword to him, up and over the king's head.

The king tried to grab it, but it wafted straight through his fingers as though it was insubstantial—no, as if *he* was unsubstantial. It sailed over his head and smacked satisfyingly 'into Les' palm, pommel first, the blade continuing its arc for a brief moment before he brought it under control. The blade flickered blue.

Bright and whole and more functionally insane than I had ever seen him, Les seemed to connect with the sword—or maybe he just felt safe and weighed down for the first time in his life. He sank a bit at the knees as though familiar with a sword. Maybe he was, for all I knew. He definitely lifted the sword as if he knew what to do with it, and as he settled into a guard position I saw the reflected blue glow of the sword on his face, oddly peaceful in such a context.

Something inside me broke a bit with unexpected relief and the sensation of letting go.

"You know what the funny thing is?" I asked the king, as he turned at bay to face Les, who still stood as firm and solid as I'd ever seen him with the heirling sword now again blazing yellow in his hand. "Not even the sword thinks you're worth touching. You've been so busy trying to kill everyone that you haven't even been looking after your world—and I don't reckon it likes you too much right now."

"Who are you?" the king demanded, his stance shifting into a fighting one. He didn't exactly say it through his teeth, but it sounded as though he said it through a throat full of bile, and that made a small burr of happy spite at the back of my own throat.

"This is Les," I told him. "It's not his real name, but it's the only one you're getting. You tried to kill him about a hundred years ago, and he's been skipping in and out of Behind ever since, getting twistier and harder to kill with every year. And every cycle that has tried to start, he's still been there, still not dying."

"I will kill that steward," said the king, pale and furious. "He *swore* he'd dealt with that!"

"Good luck," I said. "Athelas is about as hard to get rid of as Les is. If he's clever, he's somewhere far away from here by now."

"I warn you, harbinger," the king said to Les. "If you should choose to throw in your lot with the heirling instead of me, it will be your last mistake! Consider carefully!"

"That's another funny thing," I said, with a heady hilarity building up in me. I leaned against the dark wall, cold everywhere, but especially where my right arm wasn't. "He's not the harbinger."

"Hullo, hullo!" said Les happily to the king. "Not the harbinger!"

The king, still wary and furious but not frightened yet, said coldly, "Of course you're the harbinger! Who else would be?"

"G'day," I said, laughing at the shadows that danced around me. "My name's Pet. I'm your resident harbinger. That over there? He's the last heirling. Or maybe he's the first one, I dunno. He's not dead, not as daft as he looks, and he's been out killing other heirlings with my best stainless steel over the last week, so you'd better get ready to fight. He doesn't play fair, either."

CHAPTER TWELVE

It's funny how things fall into place when you use the right tools for the job—or maybe just when you put the pieces in the right places and stop shuffling stuff around in a mad panic trying to sort it out and do everything on your own.

All that to say that as I stood there with the wall holding me up, and still trickling blood through my Between bandage, everything suddenly seemed a lot easier, even if normal stuff like standing and breathing was getting hard. All the heavy things—the expectations of Between, the old king, the new king, the Order of Life, and whatever else you call what was basically a self-fulfilling Ragnarök—suddenly got lighter and took themselves out of my hands.

All I was left with was the business of staying alive for just a bit longer and making sure the wall kept holding me up.

I don't know who taught Les to fight. It definitely wasn't someone like Zero, and it *showed*. It made a difference, too; the king had been trained in real sword fighting, where every move had a counter move and every thrust had a parry. Les had been trained through several lifetimes of living through certain death and trying desperately not to give in and die. He fought wildly and unpredictably, his bare feet alternately gripping and moving with stunning speed, ducking beneath slashes that should have killed him and somehow avoiding thrusts that should have skewered him.

The king fought desperately too, and as time passed, he grew more and more frustrated, blue blood leaking from wounds over his arms and legs. I grinned to myself, because I knew what was likely to happen at this point—and whichever way things went, there was going to be an end pretty soon.

I wasn't prepared for it to be exactly the way it happened, though. The king was so frustrated that I expected a mistake—and there was a mistake, but it wasn't from him. Les didn't back away quickly enough from a vicious slash from the king, and the heirling sword spun away and clattered along the bricks.

The king pressed in without a second thought, swift and deadly, and I pushed myself away from the wall, wearily aware that I was going to have to fight again...just as the king stumbled back again with a fork sticking out of each shoulder.

"Oi," I said, rocking on my heels. "Those are my best forks!"

They were pretty close to poison for a fae king without quite enough human in him, too: he staggered back another step and dropped to his knees, then, helped on by another four swiftly-thrown forks to the chest, tumbled over onto his back on the cold bricks.

"Flamin' heck," I said.

It's hard to think of someone as the Big Evil when your troppo old childhood playmate has them pinned to the floor with pretty much every fork out of your cutlery drawer. In his life, the king had been all supreme and beyond reach of the very power that kept him in authority—free to kill, preserve, or imprison as he saw fit.

Now, pinned to the floor with stainless steel forks, his magic tied up and unreachable, the power he should have been able to access so utterly out of reach, all he could do was roar his rage, pain, and frustration at the rocky ceiling.

I said, "Ow", but had neither the hands nor the energy to try and cover my ears, so I just waited until he stopped yelling. And as I waited, I saw Les pick up the heirling sword again.

"Traitor!" snarled the king. "Don't you dare to try and kill me with the powers that made me king!"

"Not your power anymore," pointed out Les, still moving toward him.

"You, Pet—"

"You know what?"

He stared at me in helpless rage, and then, as if he thought it might do some good to humour me, snapped, "What?"

"You look flamin' ridiculous," I said, dripping blood on the wall as I leaned into it again.

I only had a moment to see the sheer rage and impotence in his eyes before Les cut off his head.

"Didn't even get a chance to monologue," I muttered. I supposed I should say something about the banality of evil, but I just didn't have the energy. Instead, I added vaguely, "Lots of blood."

"Yes," said Les, with satisfaction. The blood ran around and beneath his feet, soaking the skin and making blue rivulets all around the body. "He is very dead."

"Oh well," I said. "Reckon it's good to make sure."

Les prodded the body with his bloody toe, then took another fork out of his pocket and considered it.

"Okay, I didn't mean you have to stab the bloke again," I complained. I knew I should push myself away from the wall again, but it was *hard*.

"Isn't moving," Les said, in a soothing sort of way.

"What am I supposed to do for forks now?" I asked him, when I managed to make it over to the king's body. It took me longer than was probably healthy to stumble over there, but even if his head was cut off, I wanted to be sure the old king wasn't going to get up again. "Not sure that was sportsmanlike."

"It's always sport to them, lady," he said.

He looked a bit more tethered than he had looked a few moments before—not so much as if the act of killing had solidified him, but that contact with the sword might have.

"How long have you known?" I asked him. I didn't reach for the heirling sword even though my fingers itched to do so, because it wasn't mine anymore. I'd only ever been a guardian of it. "That you're an heirling, I mean?"

"Lady," he countered, "how long did you know that you're the harbinger?"

"Not flamin' long enough, and don't change the subject. I threw you the sword because I knew you could kill the king and I've got a pretty good idea that you'll be a half-way decent king, if you're still sane enough to do it. How long have you been out and about in the world? I guessed at the 1920s, but that was only based on how much trouble there's been from Behind over the last hundred years."

"Days and nights," he said. "Years and months, they don't sit still for me. I remember the dancing and the drink, but I was hiding in the glitter and trying to avoid the blood."

"Yep, sounds like the twenties," I said, leaning against the damp bricks and trying to breathe a bit more deeply. It didn't seem as though I was getting enough oxygen, and I was tired of the world spinning around me. Any vampire spit I'd taken in that morning had long since vanished, eaten away with trying to heal me as my blood slowly but surely drained from my severed arm. "Oi. At the start, when we first met again, and you skipped out on me and the detective after leaving us all twined up in vines—did you know then? That I was the harbinger?"

"Always knew, lady," he said. "It was a wrong thing to do, but I thought if I could live just a little bit longer—"

"You were going to leave us there to be fed on?"

"You wouldn't have died," he said, though he still wouldn't look at me. "But you would have been nice and quiet and still alive when I got you out. I thought if I had the harbinger with me —but then your big friend came, and it was all up."

Maybe it was stupid to trust him, but he hadn't *had* to tell me. For anything I knew, back then it had just been an unexpected attack followed by a quick escape because he saw Zero coming and knew we'd be safe but didn't want to be seen by any fae. He hadn't had to admit that he'd done anything wrong.

"All right," I said, trying to catch a breath that would *stay* caught. "That was messed up, but you saved me a few times too, so let's call it even."

He looked at me quickly, and I wasn't sure if it was relief or calculation that flashed in his eyes for a moment, so I reached into Between and pulled out the heirling sword once again, leaving him staring at his empty hand.

"You can't kill me," I said, resting the point of the blade on the uneven floor. I was panting, but that didn't diminish the look of cold realisation on his face. "Not with this, anyway. I'm pretty sure I can kill you with it, though. That's what the harbinger is there for, I reckon—to keep some sort of balance around the place. No king gets too powerful, no heirling gets too dangerous. You get what I'm saying?"

"Yes," he said, as sober as I'd ever seen him look.

"You need to understand," I said, "that me forgiving you isn't a weakness you can exploit. The past is in the past, but if you try to hurt me or my friends—if you start doing the same sort of things as the last king, I'll come and put this sword through your heart myself, and there won't be anything you can do to stop me."

"That isn't written in the laws, lady," he said, wary and very, very still.

"Written, no," I agreed. "But it's right at the heart of the law, or we wouldn't be standing here today. I'm not behindkind, and

I'm not going to argue about all the minutia until I've been argued out of the spirit of the law. You can do that between yourselves."

"I'm not behindkind either, lady."

"Yeah? You sure about that? Because from where I sit, you've done a lot of wriggling and careful talk to get where you are. I don't know how much of you is human, but you've played their game, and you're pretty nearly one of them."

His eyes met mine and then dropped. "I had to live, lady."

"I know," I said. "That's why I threw the sword to you. I reckon you're worth taking a chance on. I just want to make sure you know that there are gunna be consequences if you forget where you came from."

This time when Les' eyes met mine, they held. "I won't forget. I'll do what I can to be just and fair, and I'll do what I can not to make you think you made the wrong choice."

"It'll be worth it just to see their faces, anyway," I said, grinning suddenly although there was cold sweat on my brow. "What do you reckon all the toffy-nosed fae out there are going to do when they realise that they have a human king and a human harbinger?"

A faint shadow came across his face but cleared a moment later. "Make trouble."

"Yeah, I reckon you're right," I said. "If I were you, I'd head on out before the trouble comes down here looking for you. I need to get back up to the bridge to find out if—if—"

I found that I couldn't say it. I couldn't bring myself to put out into the sparkling mix of Between and magic the doubt that Jin Yeong was alive.

I caught a breath that was nearly a sob and asked instead, "We can leave the body here, right? It's already mostly gone."

"Corruption should stay underground where it belongs, lady," he said, one side of his mouth lifting in brief disgust.

Wary of any brawlers who might have outlasted the old king's demise, I walked with him as far as his exit—right up until I saw the shadows reaching deeply into the tunnel from the direction of the sun and the hospital. Those shadows were behindkind—or, to be exact, fae. I'm not sure the new king noticed me dropping behind, because as he walked forward to meet them his stride grew longer and more certain. There was still a slightly off kilter gait to it that reminded me of his days dancing around after me and leading me on chases through the streets and alleys, but now Les walked as though the ground was firm beneath him.

I, on the other hand, couldn't seem to find my feet beneath me properly. I breathed, but it didn't seem to help; my right side, wet with blood where my arm had once been, set my walk at an odd angle that I couldn't seem to correct now that the ground seemed to move beneath me. I heard the faint mumble of conversation that said *The Pet? Where is it?* and felt the curious probe of fae magic that was too clumsy to find me and my copy of brownie magic that told it I was just part of the running rivulet.

I half expected the new king to send someone after me. He probably would have been able to catch me if he had: I was slow, dizzy, and still losing more blood than I could really stand to lose. He didn't do it, and I found myself giggling in relief as I staggered back through the darkness toward the bridge that was somewhere in the fuzzy distance, at once close and too far away.

I'd made the right choice. Well, somewhere in the morass of bad and worse choices, it *looked* as though I'd made the right choice. Time would tell—if I still had time after this long, tiring walk—but I felt hopeful, even as the world grew dimmer and my feet slipped in my own blood.

"Where's that flamin' vampire when I need him?" I muttered to myself.

Then I fell over a body.

The body huffed as I hit the ground but barely moved, and as I lay on the hard bricks with my legs caught up in someone else's, it occurred to me vaguely that whoever it was I had fallen over was in a worse state than I was.

It took me a while to sort out my own legs, and by the time I finally did get them untangled and found myself sitting against the tunnel wall, it was very nearly a surprise to find out all over again that someone else was sitting there too.

"Flamin' heck," I mumbled, waking up a bit again. "I know you. You're that flamin' twisty old tea drinker."

He laughed with his head tilted back against the stonework. "Here we are once again, my dear. I fancy you've been bleeding just a little too much."

He tried to reach out for me but couldn't do it; the hand shook as he tried to move it and fell short despite the lack of space between us.

"Keep your magic for yourself," I said, trying to catch my breath. "Reckon you're gunna need it more than me."

"Not for too much longer, I believe," he said.

"Shut up," I said flatly. "You're not allowed to die until you get a flamin' good look at the mess you caused."

"It was beautiful chaos, wasn't it?" he said, laughing and coughing up blood. "I knew if I could keep it secret just long enough, that chaos would be enough to take over and turn the clock onto the next change. I just had to cover it for long enough. That's why the parents had to die: there had to be a nice, tidy cover over everything until it was big enough to turn the tide."

The sound that choked in my throat could have been a sob, or it might have been an incredulous laugh. I turned my head to look into his bloody face. "You killed my parents to keep things *tidy*?"

"Yes," Athelas said. He didn't look away, and that was unnerving. It was like he was punishing himself by not allowing himself to look away from me. "No. It was the only way I could stay alive: follow orders without quite following them until things caught fire on their own. I gave your parents the same choice I gave to the little zombie's parents: die for your child, or allow your child to die and go on uninterrupted in your own house."

"Saw how that happened for Morgana," I said.

My head reeled, but I wasn't sure if it was from the shock, or because it was hard to breathe. Maybe it was hard to breathe because of the shock. There was enough blood around the place, but it was all on the outside where it didn't do much good.

I said faintly, "Didn't work out too well."

"Her parents chose to let her die," said Athelas. A smile, twisted and dark, contorted his lips. "They usually do, after all."

"No, they flamin' don't!" I said savagely. "And just because yours were like that—"

"A great many were like that, in fact," he said.

"That why you kept this?" I asked, showing my remaining hand with the citrine band bloody but present on my ring finger. I couldn't hold it up for long; like Athelas, I lacked the strength to do what I wouldn't normally have to think about.

"Ah, that," he said, and he closed his eyes again. "I rather fancied it might help to unravel things once I was gone. A matter of having enough but not too much evidence on me. It fits you well."

"You and your flamin' secrets and plans!" I snapped. "I'm surprised you're not intent on dragging them into the grave with you!"

"Oh, if one is to die, one might as well make sure that one's story is well told, after all! I rather fancy dying a hero."

"You better not!" I said fiercely. "You better flamin' *live* and be sorry for what you've done! I'm not having you die like a hero when you haven't lived like one."

"There's very little chance of that," he said. "Should I survive today, I'll die a traitor's death in the king's court regardless."

"Yeah?" I had my own, bitter thoughts about that. While I didn't think Les was a fan of Athelas, I wasn't sure he would really try to kill Athelas if it wasn't necessary. Not when Athelas was largely responsible for bringing down his predecessor. "You reckon the new king is gunna be too worried about you taking out the old one and clearing a space for him? Even if he does, it won't make up for all the people you killed."

"The king was the one who perpetuated it all. There was once a soupçon of justice in the world Behind—but when your king clings to the throne and murders his way through the worlds to keep his power, that rottenness seeps through the entire world. Until he was gone, there was no chance for justice."

"That's flamin' garbage," I said, my head sinking against the wall in weariness. "You just want to give yourself a big enough reason to make all the killings seem worth it. You would have been happy to just take down Lord Sero, wouldn't you? You just couldn't do it without the king and the Heirling Trials, and you couldn't take down the king without Lord Sero. If one fell, they both would. It was two for one, so don't pretend you were being noble and trying to bring about the end of a reign of terror instead of just wanting to get revenge."

"Perhaps so," he said, his voice grey and tired. "I seem to remember that it all hung together at one time; reason and will and righteous possibility. Perhaps it never did; perhaps I imagined it."

"Was it worth it?" I asked him through my teeth, sick with pain and blood loss. "Killing all those people just to make sure you were the one who brought down Lord Sero and the king?"

"The sacrifice had to be made," he said. He nodded at my arm —or at least, where it would have been if it was still there. "You of all people should understand that."

"It was *my* arm," I said. "I get to sacrifice my arm if I think it's the right thing to do. You don't get to sacrifice other people—it stops being sacrifice if it's not you. After that it's just a massacre."

"After all," he said, and his voice was bitter, "I was a murderer from the start. How else would I bring about my revenge?"

I could have replied, but I didn't have the strength or even the words. I didn't have the means to express the depths of my disagreement, or the strength to cry them aloud. All I could do was breathe in air that didn't seem to give me any function or freshness, while my heart thundered but didn't seem to move blood about like it should.

I was going to die here in the tunnel beside the fae who had murdered my parents, without even being able to see Jin Yeong—or perhaps, said a cold thought, the body of Jin Yeong—one last time.

Even worse, I was pretty sure that the fae I would dearly love to hate was weeping, silently and tiredly, too old and tired to be able to continue believing the lies he'd always told himself.

I let out a shaky breath that was just short of a sob, and fancied I could see it dancing in front of my eyes. Darkness that moved with two pinpoints of savage life, and the brief flash of white teeth.

"Jin Yeong," I said, staring into the darkness with the breath catching in my throat. "Jin Yeong!"

He materialised from the moving shadow and dropped down beside me, bloody and dishevelled, his shirt in ribbons and a tear in his trousers from just below the pocket to the knee. He caught me as I fell back into the wall and pulled me into his arms, too tight to be able to breathe.

I couldn't hit him, so I bit him on the shoulder instead. I choked, "You flamin' promised me you wouldn't die!"

And then I cried. I cried while he pulled me into his lap and carefully rearranged the stump of my right arm. I cried while he drew me close and bit me gently below the ear to set vampire spit coursing around my body to do something to keep off the death that was circling. I cried until what breath I had left was gone and there was a huge hollowness in my chest.

And I cried as he tucked his head into my neck and left the wetness of his own tears there while his chest shook with sobs.

And when all the tears were gone and the breaths I took in seemed to bring me oxygen instead of heaviness, I wiped the blood and tears from his face and kissed him until he pulled away.

"*Choshimhae*," he said, his breath a bit too quick. "If you have too much—if it mixes with my blood—Ruth—"

"Right," I said laughing unsteadily. "Slow down on the vampire spit."

"For now," JinYeong said, and I saw the bright, mischievous glitter to his eyes. "There will be time later."

I don't know how long we spent there against the wall, not a hundred metres away from the exit but without the strength to make it out. While we took the doses of vampire spit slowly, JinYeong told me that the others had gone to take the bodies of the lycanthropes above ground to keep them from being lost to the world Between while he came in search of me.

"Good," I said hazily. The world was becoming less dark bit by bit, but I had a feeling it was going to take longer than usual to recover this time. "Reckon they'll be just in time to meet up with Zero and the others."

I didn't know if I was imagining it, but it seemed as though I could almost feel Zero's presence. Somewhere up there in the sunlight, I was sure he and Morgana were getting closer.

"What about him?" I asked, my eyes flicking toward Athelas.

"I am alive, thank you, Pet."

"No, I mean did you come back for Athelas, too?"

"*Ani*," JinYeong said, shifting a little to move me closer for another gentle bite, this one lower down on my shoulder. "More of them came on us as we escaped; the old man stayed back to defend the tunnel. He would not let us help him—he threw *magic* at us."

Athelas laughed, a faint, breathless sound. "Still stopped by the weakest magic! Fighting the king with the North Wind, two humans, a few lycanthropes, and a leprechaun! Foolishness!"

"We thought he was dead," said JinYeong. "This is a problem."

"Not for long if we don't get him out of here," I said, trying to sit up.

Jin Yeong curled his arms around me more tightly. "No. You must sit still for a little while longer. The old man will live."

"Oh, no need to think so despondently," murmured Athelas, and fell silent.

I might have fallen asleep, or perhaps I fainted, because the next thing I remembered was the sound of footsteps—lots of footsteps, both heavy and light. Magic approaching, Between moving.

North's voice said dispassionately, "Is he dead?"

"No," said Morgana's voice before I could answer, with a very faint sniff. "He's still fresh."

"That's one way to put it," I said, my eyes cracking open. I was so glad to see her that my chest hurt, but all I could do was grin at her like an idiot. "Thought you blokes were never coming."

There was a pretty awful silence before Morgana asked, "What happened to you?"

"Weight loss," I said. "Figured this was the quickest way to get it done."

"You shouldn't joke about it," she said quietly. "We were really worried."

"Can't you tell?" I asked, still light-headed and inclined to slur a bit. "I'm not all here. Can't make appropriate responses when I'm not all here."

Ralph, staring at me from between the twin shield of Sarah and North, asked, "Can you grow it back?"

"Be quiet," said Zero, skirting around them all. He crouched in front of me, pulling me briefly away from Jin Yeong—who leaned forward alongside me with a reflexive snarl—and did something brief and perfunctory with magic. "Did Jin Yeong already bite you?"

"Yeah, no need to worry," I told him, waking up a bit more. I was pretty sure his little magical check-up had told him the same thing. I smiled reassuringly at Morgana over Zero's shoulder and said for her as much as for him, "It's just taking a little while to sink in. I lost a fair bit of blood, and we had to make sure the bite wouldn't do anything we didn't want it to do."

"You've killed the king, then?"

"Let's just say it was a cooperative effort," I said. "But I'm not the one who did the deed. You'll have to thank Les for that."

Zero sat back on his heels with a complete lack of expression that I was pretty sure was him being stunned, while Five gave vent to a rude cackle of laughter.

"We've got a madman for a king?" he chortled. "The one we had before wasn't the sanest, but I would have preferred you, kid."

"Thanks for the vote of confidence," I said.

"Did he do that to you?" asked Morgana, still looking at the bloody stump that was all that remained of my right arm. "Or was it Athelas?"

"The old king did," I said, shuddering just a little bit as a sliver of memory flashed through my mind, all heat and chill and pain. "He was trying to persuade me to do something I didn't really want to do."

"You'll have to tell me about how that happened later," Zero said, his blue eyes narrow and hard.

"Yeah, 'course," I said, perfectly well aware that I would never tell him that, now or later. There was no reason for everyone to know that I'd lost an arm to make sure they were safe—I would have hated knowing that someone had done it for me.

"The pet gave her arm to buy time for me to secure the safety of the rest of the rabble," said Athelas, his thread of a voice startlingly carrying.

I looked over at him and found that he was watching me mockingly through heavy-lidded eyes, though from the tension in the vampire energy beside me, I was pretty sure he'd been looking at Jin Yeong when he said *rabble*.

"We'll discuss this later," Zero said, his eyes going from Athelas and then to me.

"Yes," said Morgana, her lips very narrow and dark. "*All* of us."

"Heck," I mumbled, settling back against JinYeong. "Reckon I'd better just run away from home."

He didn't reply—didn't even give me a reproachful look—but he did nuzzle his face into my shoulder, his arm tightening around my waist, and I couldn't help feeling guilty.

"Where is the new king?" asked Zero, his gaze flicking around and then down the tunnel. "We'll all have to present ourselves to swear loyalty, and—"

He let the sentence drop, a slight frown creasing between his brows, and I heard the whisper of a laugh from Athelas.

"Yes, much wiser not to present yourself to the king before you're certain you can report comfortably to him."

"I have no reason to fear appearing before the king," Zero said coldly to him.

"Reckon he's got kingly stuff to do," I said, though wasn't sure why I did. Maybe I was trying to distract Zero from hurting Athelas, which would have been stupid. "He seemed to know what he was doing, and as soon as he got out there was a flamin' search party waiting for him, so..."

"I see," said Zero. "Did they see you?"

"Don't think so; I ducked back into the rivulet as soon as I saw 'em. Don't reckon the king was expecting that, because he didn't try to stop me."

"He has enough to attend to," North said, shrugging. "The dance has only just begun for him. And I think he might be frightened of you."

"Yeah," I said, gratified. "I reckon so. I made sure of it."

"You've got a cheek," Tuatu said directly to Athelas. "Telling people that they need a bit of breathing time before they meet up with the king."

"I was not referring to you."

Zero was brief and concise. "I'm not trying to hide anything."

"Oh, I'm sure you have things that need to be...tidied up... before you meet with the king," Athelas said, his eyes still closed.

"Be quiet, Athelas!" Zero said in exasperation.

"What are we going to do with him?" That was Morgana, but I could just see Ralph watching from behind Sarah, eyes burning.

"We'll take him home until we can hand him over," said Tuatu. "What else? You lot have your legal system, don't you?"

Morgana's eyes narrowed. "I don't know about that. I don't think it's a good idea to take him along with us."

"Ah," said Athelas, smiling at her. "You'll avenge your parents, then?"

I aimed a weak kick at his leg that only glancingly connected with the toe of his scratched up brown shoe. "Stop trying to egg people on to kill you," I told him crankily. "We're taking you home with us."

Athelas' eyes opened a bare crack. "Just as you like," he said, and fainted.

"Flamin' typical," I said. "I'm the one with the missing arm and blood loss. *I'm* the one who should be fainting heroically."

"You're looking better already," Morgana said. She hesitated, and added, "You smell better than before, too."

"That a new thing you can do?" I asked her. "Smell test for freshness?"

Her eyes didn't shadow so much as grow deeper. "I've been getting a lot to eat lately, so I'm feeling pretty sensitive."

"You okay?"

"Better than ever," she said, but I could see the same kind of regret in her eyes that I felt pulling at me from the stump where my arm had been.

Morgana was regretting something new and extra; I regretted the loss of something. Neither of us could do anything about it, and I was pretty sure neither of us would decide differently if we could go back again.

"Glad you're alive," I said to her.

I saw the brief glow of tears in her eyes. She sniffed them away and said, tilting her chin at Zero, "I told him you'd still be alive. I knew you would be."

"That's pets for ya; always turning up alive and well," I said. I couldn't see all of the lycanthropes, so I asked, "Everyone else get out all right?"

"We lost Kyle on the way as well," Daniel said, his hands shoved deep into his pockets. "I've sent him and the girls back to the house—which is where we should all be going if we don't want to be caught up in whatever the king sends back here to clean up."

The tone of voice dared me to say anything—dared me to try and comfort him. Morgana already had her hand around his, nearly as tall as he was in platform shoes that were stained dark in patches, so I didn't try.

I just nodded and asked Zero, "You reckon he'll clean up here?"

"I would," he said. "If only to make sure there was nothing incriminating left. Let's go home."

He knelt again to pick up Athelas' bloody and battered body, rising as easily and swiftly as if he'd been picking me up.

"We're really taking that with us?" North's voice was unimpressed. "We ought to kill him here and now. The king won't blame us for it, and it'll be safer."

"I'm not killing him," Zero said shortly.

"I'm not going to kill him, either," said Daniel. "He took on everything the king threw at us to get us out alive. Saved Dylan and got Tuatu out before it was too late."

"He's not a hero," Sarah said sharply. "He was just with you for today. We don't know who he'll be with tomorrow."

"He'll have to be taken to be judged," Zero said. "It doesn't matter what we think."

"If we leave him here, the slugs will finish him off," Morgana said prosaically. "Enough people have died today."

"Not flamin' likely," I said, at the same time that Jin Yeong sniffed a small laugh and said, "He would not die. He would be gone as soon as we turned around."

"Anyway," I added, "we won't have to worry about it for a little while. Not until the new king settles in and Palomena reports to him. Reckon he'll send her to us in the next couple of days."

"Good," said Sarah. "Then we have more time to decide whether we're going to kill him ourselves."

"Can you stand?" Zero asked me.

"Still got both me legs," I said, but when I stood up with Jin Yeong's help, I was still listing sideways. "Heck. Gunna have to get used to this."

"Want us to go in there for your arm?" asked Daniel. "It wouldn't take long to find it."

"It's not like you can stick it back on," I said, keeping my voice light. There was no way I wanted them finding the bits and pieces of what was left of it—no way I wanted them to know the extent of the horror that had happened there. "Leave it there. The slugs probably already ate it, anyway."

There was a deep sadness sitting deep in my stomach; I'd told the old king that I wasn't less of a person or any less of a threat with only one arm, but that arm had been *mine* and now it was gone. I wouldn't ever be able to hug Jin Yeong properly again, and I would only ever be able to fight one-armed.

More presently, I didn't seem to be able to stand straight, and that bothered me.

I grinned at Jin Yeong to try and banish the hollow feeling, and he slipped his arm around my waist, a warm and steadying force.

"Let's go home," I said. "But someone else is making the coffee."

CHAPTER THIRTEEN

It's pretty flamin' rude when the murderous fae you made sure to free two nights ago *still* hasn't escaped by the second morning.

I brought Athelas his breakfast that morning as usual—even if I was expecting him to be gone, it had to look good for when Palomena arrived—and he had the flaming cheek to still be there, still in his chair, as if the steel-lined cuffs around his wrists weren't open and the spell that supposedly kept him in the room hadn't been defunct since three days past.

It was already bad enough that I was basically lying to most of my friends about what the plans were for Athelas: I'd only discussed the real plans with Morgana and Ralph—and only because I knew they needed to have a say in the decision. They'd agreed with me, and for Athelas to still be hanging around and just waiting to be taken into custody was the final, irritating straw for my camel's back.

I banged down the breakfast tray on the dresser-top harder than intended.

Athelas' eyes met mine inquiringly. "Something wrong, Pet?"

"Why are you still here?"

The inquiring look seemed to edge toward sardonic. Athelas displayed his steel-bound wrists and said, "No doubt you forgot that I'm bound and spelled."

"I didn't forget anything," I said shortly. "Don't pretend you didn't notice that the cuffs have been unlocked for the last two nights."

He lifted one shoulder for a brief moment. "Should I escape, no doubt my lord would be after me in a moment."

"That's flamin' rich when you *know* he disabled the confinement spell three nights ago," I said bluntly. I hadn't told Zero what I was up to, and he hadn't told me what he was up to either, but I was pretty sure we both already knew what the other had done. "There isn't anything you can do with Between or magic around me or my house that I'm not going to know about. Even if the cuffs hadn't been undone you would have been able to winkle your way out of them."

Athelas seemed to settle more deeply into his chair. "There are some things that require punishment, after all," he said. "And why should I live any longer as a fugitive when I can end it in one moment?"

"Funny thing, isn't it?" I said, and I heard the coldness in my own voice. "You got what you wanted—you still even try to tell yourself you did the right thing. But you're determined to die, anyway. Reckon you're not so sure about everything you've done to dethrone the king and kill Lord Sero."

"I gave you," he said unsteadily, "the best chance I could to survive."

I had so little breath left to sigh with, but as small as it was, the sigh felt as though it pierced right through my chest. "You didn't give me anything—you *took* it."

"If I had not taken it, someone else would have."

"Maybe, maybe not," I said. "But we won't know, will we? Because you did do it. It happened because you just followed orders. You're clever enough to have found a way around it—you could have hidden the people you were supposed to kill, for a start."

He shook his head. "Too many loose ends that could come free to sweep my feet from beneath me. I kept alive as many as I could through the Bargains."

"You could have said no to Lord Sero."

"I would have died had I done so, and someone else would have taken my place."

"It's not like there are many people as good at killing as you are," I said. "That's not an excuse."

Athelas huffed a small laugh down at his chest and hesitated for only a moment before he said impatiently, "Oh, there are no good excuses for what I did, Pet! At first, I killed for my lord's father because I couldn't bear to die; before long I killed for him because I wanted to burn down the world, and it was the only way I could do it. If I'd stopped then, it would have been an end to every plan I'd put in motion, and the sacrifices would have been meaningless indeed. I thought it better to burn it all down than to stop short of the goal."

"You did that, all right," I murmured. "The world burned, then went full phoenix on us."

"It couldn't have happened without you," he said. "I knew you were special when I first saw you, but I didn't know how special—you even left the house when none of the others could. I thought from the start that you'd either be king or enough of a distraction to make my lord king while everyone was trying to contain you. If I'd thought further, I would have realised that you must be the harbinger."

"Good thing you didn't," I said. "If you had, Lord Sero and the king would have, too; things would have been a lot dicier. And it wouldn't have changed anything back then, either. Lord Sero would have killed my parents just to get his hands on me as an ally for Zero."

"Your parents," he said, and hesitated. "They were one of only two sets of parents that didn't hesitate when they made the decision. I didn't—I didn't make them suffer, Pet."

"Yeah?" I said, though I couldn't seem to breathe. "Didn't much look like it when I found them."

"They were dead long before that process," he said quietly. "A mere breath of time severed soul from body—everything that happened afterward was as much for show as it was for warning. My lord's father wanted to send a message to anyone else that competing heirlings would not be borne, and it was necessary to hide the fact that there only two bodies."

It should have been a relief that he hadn't lied in the memory I'd seen—that my parents really hadn't suffered. It should have been a breath of life and liberation. Instead, it was a heavy, achingly breathless feeling of *uselessness*.

"Got something for you," I said, and since he hadn't moved at all—not even his hands, although the cuffs were unlocked—it was easy for me to step forward, pulling Mum's citrine ring out of my pocket, and push it onto his pinky. "I want you to flamin' remember."

"Never fear, my dear," he said tiredly. "I'll not forget them for a moment."

"You should go now," I said. I found that I couldn't quite look at him. If I did, I might just try to kill him after all. Kill him, or forgive him outright, and I wasn't sure which one was worse. "Palomena will be back at dinner time to fetch you: king's orders. I wouldn't hang around, if I were you."

There was the faintest of impatient movements from him. "Better to have me put to death and have done with it. What will you tell your allies?"

"I've already spoken with Morgana and Ralph," I said coldly. "I told you: you don't get to just die like that. You have to live and struggle and learn how to feel sorry for what you've done."

His head lifted, as if hearing a sound he understood at last.

"Shall I take my orders from you, then? Reform? What shall I do first?"

"No!" I said fiercely. "You need to learn to take responsibility for your own actions! You don't belong to anyone anymore. Make your own choices! I'm just saying that you don't get to take the easy road out. Live and do some good in the world to try and repair some of the damage you did."

"Some things can only be paid for in blood."

"I'm not telling you to pay for them. I'm telling you you're not going to pay for them, even if you want to. You *couldn't* if you wanted to—you can't give back anything in exchange for all of the people you killed. I want you to live in the world and try to repair it as if you really did die and come back as a different person."

"So you're giving me orders, after all?"

"Nope," I said. "Once you're out of here, that's up to you. I'm just telling you how you can turn into something other than an empty husk now that you don't have anything to live for. Who knows, you might even be able to do some good. Just...just don't try to come back here. I won't see you."

I'm not sure why I said it: it wasn't as though he would have done so anyway—wasn't as though it was exactly true. Perhaps it was the desire to hurt him as much as possible. If it was, it was only because I knew it *could* hurt him. But perhaps it was because I knew how dangerous it would be for Athelas to be forgiven straight away, without even acknowledging the full extent of what he'd done wrong.

Athelas smiled, and the bitterly amused understanding of it would have been heart-breaking if my chest didn't already feel as though it had been thoroughly carved out. "Never fear, Pet," he said. "My lord was very clear on what would happen if I presented myself before you again. You will live long and happily, I should think."

He said that mildly, but it sounded like a benediction—a benediction from the fae who had murdered my parents.

"Breakfast time," I said abruptly, and left the room.

I nearly fell over Jin Yeong outside the door. I'd known he was there, but I'd been too much occupied with the confusion and rage and sorrow of my parents' room that I'd all but forgotten about him.

He uncrossed his ankles and pushed away from the wall. "That will cause trouble, I think," he said, his eyes flicking briefly toward the door.

"Yeah," I said. I still half regretted what I'd done. Because of me, Morgana and Ralph wouldn't get the justice they deserved for their parents, nor would any of the other people that Athelas had killed. "But I can't help feeling like it's the right thing to do."

Athelas' world was already dust and ashes—it had been since the start, or very nearly, I suspected. In a very dim way, I understood that he'd done the best he could with what he had, and he'd had so very little. If there was a chance for him to change and grow, I wanted him to have it. He couldn't have it here with us— not yet, at any rate.

My eyes felt hot again. I said unsteadily, "I don't really want to talk about it right now. I'm pretty sure it was the right thing to do, but it also feels wrong, and if I think about it for too long, I might go mad."

"There is no need to talk," Jin Yeong said, slipping his arms around me, warm and comforting. "This is nice, too."

I let myself laugh shakily into his chest and didn't pull away. A very small part of me tried to warn me that it wasn't clever to get used to being comforted by someone else—a small part of me that was a bit too much like Zero—and I wrapped my one good arm around Jin Yeong's waist, ignoring it.

"We better not stand here too long," I said, though I didn't much feel like moving. "Don't wanna undo all the good work I just did."

"You mean the old man can't leave until we go? He can wait."

"Yeah," I said. "But I reckon if I give him too long to think, he'll just decide to stay out of sheer stubbornness. C'mon, I'll make you some of the really good coffee for breakfast."

THERE SEEMED to be a conspiracy in the house these days. For the last two mornings, I hadn't been allowed into the kitchen—Tuatu had cooked very badly the first morning and Morgana had cooked quite well, the next—and this morning was no exception.

"I can still cook with only one arm!" I yelled at Daniel that morning as Jin Yeong led me down into the living room, grinning.

"Never said you couldn't!" he yelled back, politely refraining from pointing out the fact that I probably actually *couldn't* cook with one arm. "Sit down and shut up! I'm cooking today!"

"No one invited you, either," I called back. He was spikier than usual, but he'd had to bury three of his pack this week, and I knew him well enough to know that he wanted the distraction. I would have. "Dunno why the lot of you can't go home."

Jin Yeong, still grinning, said, "Ah, sit down, Ruth. Let them do this; we will have steak for breakfast, and I will bite you—"

"I'm starting to think you only appreciate me as a blood bag," I told him, even though I knew exactly why he was suggesting it.

I'd been having some trouble healing properly from my brush with the old king—Morgana seemed to think that the knife he'd used either hadn't been clean or had been deliberately poisoned—and a gentle dose of vampire spit each day had been pushing back the infection that tried to creep in through my blood.

That, and the fact that after a bite I was more inclined to settle with Jin Yeong on the couch for the next few hours while the bite did its work. For somebody who bit as a sign of affection, Jin Yeong was also surprisingly dependent on soft, slow hugs and shared warmth. Catlike, he would happily sit beside me in an elegant sort of sprawl until I was ready to get up again, then rearrange himself to be even more elegant to entice me back again.

This morning he sniffed my neck gently and said, "*Johah, johah. It is getting better. I will bite you anyway.*"

Morgana came past from the bathroom on her way to the kitchen, a spiked collar around the neck, and said, "You smell better this morning."

"That's what my mosquito says," I said, as Jin Yeong's lips closed around my shoulder, and I felt a faint, piercing pain. "You got a new necklace?"

"The pack gave it to me," she said, touching a finger to one of the silver spikes there. "They think it's funny that I like to wear collars."

"It's not a collar," said Daniel, from the kitchen. "It's a necklace."

"Try and tell them that," Morgana retorted.

"You look taller these days," I said, a bit hazily, leaning back against Jin Yeong as the vampire spit started to take effect.

"That's my shoes," she said. "They're a bit harder to wear than I thought: it was easier when I didn't have to think about how I'm supposed to walk in them."

"At least someone's getting out of the house, even if it's only to grab their clothes," I said.

I hadn't gotten out of the house, but that was mostly from a combination of frustration that Athelas hadn't gotten away yet and concern from Jin Yeong and Zero about the way I wasn't recovering as quickly as I should.

Nobody else seemed to want to leave and go home either, and I couldn't really blame them. It was hard to settle to anything, hard to sit down and rest, especially when we were all waiting for the knock on the linen closet door that would mean Palomena was here to escort Zero and Athelas to the new king.

Especially when we were all waiting to see how the entirety of Hobart Between and Behind were going to take the overturning of the old king and the reign of the new—not to mention the rest of Australia and the world beyond that.

At least life seemed quiet on the outside lately, according to what Tuatu had told us yesterday. No more sudden murders in the streets, or kids dancing off the tops of buildings.

"No more brownies outside either," I said in realisation, tilting my head up a bit to gaze at Jin Yeong. "Or are they just hidden better than I thought?"

"They are gone," he said, idly playing with the tail of my braid. I saw the instinctive, almost imperceptible little biting motion he made before he said, "*Hyeong* and I went to...talk to them."

"Yeah?" I gazed at the ceiling for a while, feeling almost content and sleepy with his warmth at my side and the fizz of vampire magic wafting through my blood. "They still alive?"

"Yes," he said regretfully.

"Don't worry, someone will probably attack us by the end of the week," I said comfortingly, patting his chest. "You can get some fresh blood then—or whatever it is they're running on. We can go out and get you more sap if you want?"

He narrowed his eyes at me. "No sap."

I snickered contentedly into his ribs and settled down to enjoy the pleasantness of having my person next to me and no one trying to kill me. Even the little tickle that was a constant wondering if Athelas was getting away, or had already gotten away, confined itself to the back of my mind, and by the time I heard the sound of someone knocking, I was almost half-asleep.

I jerked forward but knew in the same instant that it came from the front door and not the linen closet, and relaxed again. I heard claws tapping along the kitchen floor, then the soft padding of paws along the hall and scratching at the door.

"You'll need hands to open it!" I called out, turning a little on the couch.

Tuatu's voice said impatiently from outside, "All right, all right, just move out of the way; I'll open it myself."

North was with him when he did open the door, of course, dancing lightly down the hall and into the living room to settle in Athelas' chair with a waft of fabric and the faint scent of meadow flowers in the sun. Tuatu strolled into the kitchen with a brief nod in my direction, to help himself to a cup of tea around the three assembled lycanthropes, who sat up and panted at him.

"They better not be salivating for my blood," he said to Daniel.

"They're just messing with you," Daniel said. "Or they want you to throw a ball out in the back yard. Could be either."

"Don't throw balls in my house," I said mildly, curling my feet up onto the couch with me and watching Tuatu migrate to the living room with a cup of tea for himself and one for North.

"How's the blood?" he asked. "Is the vampire spit killing off the bugs?"

"Seems to be," I said. "I'm feeling better today, anyway."

"Pity it hasn't fixed your face," said one of the lycanthropes in passing, more flesh than fur and in the middle of his change.

I roused myself enough to kick the back of his knee and sent him tumbling over backward with a face-full of tea, much to the amusement of Daniel, who skirted around him and sat down next to Morgana.

"Told you," I said to Jin Yeong, while the lycanthrope was still spluttering on tea. "You should have gone for a beautiful fae or something while you could—now you're stuck with a one-armed feral human who kicks people."

"I do not wish to be with a beautiful fae," said Jin Yeong. "I do not wish to be with a beautiful human, either."

Daniel and Tuatu exchanged unimpressed looks, while North said coldly, "You should think your girlfriend is beautiful."

"He doesn't mean that I'm ugly," I said to North, sleepily amused.

"I do not like beautiful people," Jin Yeong said, matching the coldness of North's tone. "Beautiful people are sneaky and bothersome."

I caught his eyes, and said before he could say anything else, "You're the one who said it, not me!"

"Yes, but I am *beautiful*," he said. "It can be forgiven."

"Yeah? Depends on what *it* is."

Tuatu said stubbornly, "All boyfriends find their girlfriends attractive—and they certainly don't go telling them they're not beautiful!"

JinYeong's eyes began to glitter dangerously. "If you wished to say attractive, you should have said it. Attractive and beautiful are not the same."

"Told you," I said, trying not to grin. Unlike North, I had no trouble understanding the subtext of JinYeong, nor was I in any danger of feeling as though he didn't find me attractive enough.

After all, JinYeong was beautiful, but it wasn't his beauty that had attracted me to him—what had attracted me was the part of him that had once murmured times-tables in my ear to help me sleep after being killed in my sleep. The part of him that deliberately made himself warm for me when I needed comfort, and still caught his breath when I kissed him. The least I could do was believe he felt the same way about me.

"You understand," JinYeong said, turning his gaze down on me. "Your face is warm and changing. I love warmth and change because I am cold and motionless beauty. Why would I want more of it?"

"I understand," I said, uncurling myself so that I could sit up and swing my legs over JinYeong's to give the tea-soaked lycanthrope space to sit down too. I slipped my left arm around JinYeong and said directly to North, "Would you rather have a marble statue of Tuatu with all the imperfections smoothed out, or the real thing?"

"Marble statues are no use to me," she said. "And they don't breathe, either."

"Yeah, but the marble statue would be more beautiful," I said. "If you just want beauty."

"All right, all right," said Tuatu. "I give up. Has Zero given him the 'hurt my kid and I'll hurt you' talk yet?"

JinYeong sent a long-suffering look down at me, and I glared at everyone across the coffee table. "What is this? An intervention? Since when is everyone so interested in my love life?"

"Since you're dating a vampire," Morgana said. "Especially when the vampire is him."

"You must have been listening to Zero," I said. "What, are you gunna threaten him too, now?"

"I just want him to know that I'm happy eating vampire brains," Morgana said, with a dark smile. "In case he forgets you've got friends."

"And I," said JinYeong in outrage, "am verrry happy to drink zombie blood."

"You're both flamin' liars," I muttered. "*You* were complaining about sap! And *you* had to eat brains without looking at them first! Why is everyone being so flamin' protective today?"

"Because someone came back from the fight without an arm," Daniel said. He didn't say that three someones hadn't come back at all, but it was there in the shadow of his eyes. "We've had enough of people dying and losing limbs."

I couldn't help glancing over at the lone wolf-form lycanthrope in the room: Kevin was back in his wolf form. I assumed, rather than knew, that it was because the death of his brother hurt less as a wolf than it did as a boy—I'd seen him change back to human to heal the last of his injuries, so at least we didn't have to worry about losing him, too.

I'd watched the lycanthropes leaving the house the other night to do what Morgana later told me was a "howling"; a time to go back to the scene of their packmates' deaths and howl over it —something like a lycanthrope funeral. Since then, the others had been human as much as they'd been wolf, as if the howling had torn something painful and sharp-edged from them and given them some sort of peace. Kevin hadn't done the same, but that was understandable. His brother was gone and wouldn't be back; even the rough and tumble attentions of Darren and Dylan hadn't done more than waken him temporarily from his sadness.

That would come in time. In the meantime, there was nothing I could do but make sure there were always good steaks in the fridge and let the living lycanthropes be as noisy and boisterous as they wanted to be.

"Fair enough," I said. "But no drinking zombie blood or eating vampire brain. The house is messy enough as it is."

I also didn't think I'd be able to break up a fight if one started. My missing arm might not have been my dominant one, but it was still throwing off my balance more than I liked—not to mention somehow making me more hungry than I'd ever been with two arms. Until I learned how to rebalance myself properly, peace was the best option.

And we had a nice bit of peace, too. We had peace for another hour or two until Dylan and Darren went upstairs to take some lunch to Athelas—then tumbled back down the stairs in a mess of fur and feet and turned just human enough to say, "Boss! The old tea-drinker is gone!"

Zero, who had been propped up against one of the support beams to drink coffee for the last few minutes, didn't say a word, but I felt North's gaze sweep over me. She looked amused and not at all surprised. "When did you let him out?" she asked.

Tuatu's eyes closed briefly, then opened again. "Ruth, did you let the serial killer go?"

"I mean *technically* speaking—"

"He helped us," Morgana said, leaning back in her chair with a very faint shrug. "And he nearly died while he was doing it. He could have run away instead—we'd never have had the chance to catch him again."

"He killed your parents," Daniel said quietly. "Is that something you can live with?"

"I was raised with wolves from the start," she told him,

sparking a soft glint of laughter in Daniel's brown eyes that surprised me.

He isn't the softly laughing kind—he's the angsty, teenaged wolf-boy-with-a-family-he-inherited-far-too-early type. It was nice to see that there was another side to him coming out.

"If you can live with it, I've got nothing to say," he said. "He saved my life a couple times at least: I didn't want to see him dead."

"I don't care," said North. "He didn't try to kill me."

The frustration visible on Tuatu's face sharpened his voice. "It's not justice!"

"No," I said quietly. "It's mercy. And it's going to eat Athelas alive until it's a kind of justice anyway—unless he learns to deal with it."

"You think he's got enough of a soul for that?" the detective asked sceptically.

"Yeah," I said. "Otherwise he would have escaped two days ago. The cuffs have been unlocked that long, and the spells have been down for longer."

Tuatu swallowed. "I was in there yesterday! He could have killed me!"

"Yeah," I said again.

"You might have warned me!"

"I didn't know you were going to go in there!" I said indignantly. "If you're going to go see fae serial killers without letting anyone know, you don't get to complain that I didn't warn you not to do it!"

"You knew he was going to use me to get free the first time, though, didn't you?" he asked grimly.

"It was the only way I could figure to get him out of here and thinking he'd done it by himself," I explained. "Sorry. I knew you could bargain to make sure that this was your last favour like I told you, and I needed to know for sure which side he was really on."

He hesitated. "I didn't have to tell him it was my last favour," he said, finally. "He said it before I could. *One last favour and you are out of my debt.* And I couldn't say no or stop myself helping him."

It wasn't as though I hadn't had doubts about letting Athelas go, but I had been sure it was the best thing to do. And now as I stared at Tuatu, a few icy edges of doubt around my heart melted.

"Good for you," I said. "Things might have been a bit dicey for you otherwise."

"I'm aware of that," he said pointedly. "I felt *so guilty* for having been the one to let him go!"

"Sorry," I said again. "I really am. But it was the only way I could think of to make sure that everyone got out of the king's Challenge alive and that everyone else kept thinking what I needed them to think for just long enough to sort everything out."

"All's well...?" he said, and let it linger.

"No," I said quietly. Because there were still three dead lycanthropes and a missing arm to account for, and those were all consequences I was going to have to deal with.

I was also going to have to deal with another one: Tuatu might have a bit of trouble trusting me for a while—or at least still have a bit of resentment—and I couldn't blame him for it. I would have done the same thing over again, so it wasn't fair to ask him to forgive me straight away.

"Funny that everyone's concerned about my love life," I said, by way of changing the subject as North wandered off to the kitchen. I heard her opening the fridge like some sort of teenaged forager, and that meant that she was feeling pretty human today—for whatever reason. "When there's *that* to worry about."

The detective sent a sour look in my direction. "What?" he asked.

"*That*," I said again, tilting my chin at North. "She knows you're a human, but she still wants to be near you. She's gotta know you're gunna die years before she does."

"She must also know that the closer she gets, the more human she will become," Zero said, breaking his silence at last.

Tuatu's lips tightened. "Yes. I noticed that."

"You say that like it's a bad thing," Morgana said, with a dangerously red gleam to her eyes.

"It's a dangerous thing," Tuatu said. "It makes her more vulnerable, and my grandmother always said that things in flux are—"

"Yeah," I said, as he stopped to think about what he'd just said. "We've got to have a bit of a word about your grandma some time, Tuatu. Reckon there's a few things that might make a bit more sense once we do."

"Not today," he said.

I might have pushed a bit more, but that was when I heard it: a knock on what was definitely the linen closet door this time.

"Showtime," I said, glancing across at Zero.

His eyes grew faintly bluer, which made me very happy. Happy because he could still laugh. Happy because I had the feeling he was looking forward to this particular visitor—and maybe messing with her a bit.

JinYeong, who had gone to open the door for Palomena— because of course it was Palomena—gave her his most annoying smirk and sauntered back across the room to sit next to me.

"I'll take that as a bad sign," she said, in the general direction of me and Zero. This time definitely to me, she said, "I'm sorry about your arm. I was glad to hear you're alive."

"You know what us pets are like," I said, grinning. "Always popping up just when you least expect us."

"There is tea," JinYeong said, pointing at the teapot that someone had brought out.

Palomena's brows rose. She turned an enquiring look on Zero, who seemed to be struggling with amusement once again.

"He doesn't usually offer food or drink to people," he said. "You might as well accept it."

"Then I'm honoured, I suppose," she said, which Jin Yeong accepted with a small tilt of his nose, as if to say, *Of course you are*.

"No food, though," I said. "This lot haven't let me in the kitchen for days."

"I suppose they expect you to rest after throwing off the old world and putting on the new," she said, and this time it was me she was looking at—in something like wonder, I thought. "I trust you have been resting."

"Worried about me?"

"Perhaps slightly concerned."

I beamed at her. "I knew you loved me."

"Let's say I'm fond of you," she said, amusement lightening her eyes.

"We love you, too," I said, beaming even more brightly.

That made her gaze at me a bit longer, and I wasn't sure if she knew I was just playing for time, or if her thoughts had inevitably gone to Zero.

"I almost hesitate to ask if the steward is ready to go?" she said, and there was a delicate uptick to her voice that made the statement into a question.

Well, that answered *that* question.

Zero said emotionlessly, "The steward is gone. He escaped earlier today."

"His timing certainly doesn't seem to get any worse," Palomena said. "But then, I doubt the king will be too worried about it, considering the...circumstances."

"Figured," I said.

"Yes, I thought you would," she said, and her gaze lingered on me once again. "Can you live with it?"

"Better than I could live with the alternative," I said, shrugging. "Will you be safe to tell the king yourself, or—"

"I'll go with her, of course," said Zero.

"Will you?" I said, grinning wickedly at him.

"Don't smirk at me."

"If you're coming, we'd probably best leave as soon as we can," Palomena said.

Zero's brows went up. "You're in a hurry?"

Was he trying to give Athelas more time to get away safe? It was hard to tell, but I liked to think so.

"No, but everyone is a bit excited at court, and they want to get things moving," she said. "Ah. One more thing before we go."

She reached into an inner pocket somewhere around rib level and brought out a golden envelope. You probably think I mean it was gold coloured, but it wasn't: it was pure gold, threaded with lines of Between to keep it supple and useful without breaking.

She presented the envelope to Zero, and the way he hesitated so long before he took it left me with no doubt as to what it was.

"They want you back in the Enforcers, do they?" I said, making sure my voice was cheerful enough to show that I was happy for him and thought he should accept the offer.

"We're still having a bit too much trouble with Upper Management to rest on our laurels," said Palomena, as if it was an answer. "And the new king seems to be of the opinion that our policies regarding humans need to be looked at again. This particular position became vacant in the light of those two realisations."

"Too flamin' right they need to be looked at again," I muttered, my stomach sinking despite the fact that I knew how good of a thing this was.

I'd known that Zero would be off again at some stage—whether by himself or with the Enforcers—but I'd expected a bit longer to come to grips with it. A few weeks. Maybe a month, or a year. Some time in the future, anyway.

Mind you, there was always the possibility of hanging around in Jin Yeong's prospective clothing shop just to annoy him and mess with his ties, so my future wasn't looking too bad despite everything. Maybe the two of us would even have a chance for a real date—or maybe just one where we didn't both end up covered in blood, guts, or debris.

That hope didn't take away the deep sense of sadness that had settled over me so suddenly, though. We'd only been a family for a little while, and I couldn't help the deep, faraway ache that sank into my stomach at the thought of Zero going off again, never to come back.

"What's the deal?" I asked, somehow unable to stop the words tumbling out.

"I'll be based on the human side," he said, reading the notice without looking at me. "And I'll be a liaison. I'll need to find somewhere to stay that gives me good access to Between as well as being well established in the human world."

"Good grief!" I said, relief flooding through me. I didn't have to lose him, either. "Just ask if you can stay with me in the house and get it over with, will you?"

Zero said in a pained sort of way, "I don't think you understand how invasive it will be, Ruth."

"Oh yeah, it's not like I had Between and Behind encroaching on my house and my life since I was a kid or anything."

"I will be here, too," said JinYeong, cocking an eyebrow at Zero.

Zero's blue eyes became ice. "We haven't discussed that."

"I'm not kicking him out, and I'm not letting you go sulk in another house around here. You're gunna have to live with each other for the foreseeable future, so you better get used to it again, starting from now."

JinYeong fairly exuded smugness; Zero didn't try to argue, but there was a look to his eyes that said the conversation wasn't over, even if he *was* going to be staying in my house. I couldn't help grinning a bit, because I suppose that's what family does—they look out for you and argue with you and try to do what's best for you, even if you don't always agree on what *best* is. It was just nice to have family again—especially when that family was Zero.

. . .

I WENT UPSTAIRS LATER, more by instinct than anything else. Maybe I felt as though I really should clean out Mum and Dad's room now that their killer was out of it—open the windows and door, air it out and see if it couldn't get back some of that peace and quietness it had once had to it.

Maybe I expected to see exactly what I saw when I stepped into the room—some version of it, at least.

The bed was made and clean, the room empty of anything that had once been Athelas'. Well, except for the fact that there on the chair we had confined him to was Athelas' phone, right in the middle of the seat.

There was no reason to think that he'd left it for any purpose except that everything Athelas did *was* with a purpose. I almost didn't pick it up anyway. I didn't want to see any message that he'd left for me. I didn't want a last benediction or a promise that he'd change, or return—or worse, a threat. I wanted a bit more time to think—or better yet, *not* think—before I started poking at too many of my recent memories.

Of course, I ended up looking anyway. What else could I do? I've always been too curious for my own good. And when I unlocked the screen, a single message was there: a notification, actually. It had been there for a few weeks, by the looks of the date. An unknown number that started with the Australian country code, as if it had actually come from another country.

Did they have phones Behind? I couldn't even think of anyone from the human world who wasn't currently in the house, who would be in contact with Athelas. I tapped the notification and the screen whisked me away to the message centre.

The message said, *Yes, I was made aware; I've been working on the issue since then. If you provide the parts, the merman will provide the receptacle, and I'll manage the transfer. A part from each will assure continuity of the scene, and I'll leave the disposal of the scene to you. Three days are all we need. If you can guarantee safety until then, I guarantee that no loose ends will be left to disrupt your plans.*

I frowned *A part from each?* Each what? Had Marazul been mixed up in whatever Athelas was doing? He was pretty risk-adverse, and I didn't think he would have volunteered for the job. And if they were talking about a transfer with Marazul, who knew how to fuse human and behindkind tech and who knew how to transfer—

Wait.

Fingers. Ears. Toes. Ezri saying that her finger being gone was all in a good cause. The echoes I had heard in Marazul's closed network through the badge I still had—those echoes I had thought were echoes of the day my friends died, but that hadn't quite matched the memories I had seen in Athelas' mind of that day.

The date—

I drew in a shuddering breath, because I finally understood the memory I had experienced of Athelas going over to the human headquarters.

He hadn't been thinking about my death with any sense of emotion or interest because it *hadn't occurred yet*. He hadn't made the attempt on me yet. The memory I had seen of his meeting with the human group had been days before he made his carefully calculated and knowingly abortive attempt at killing me. He had gone there to kill them and had instead been persuaded to leave them alive with the promise that they would be out of sight and out of reach of anyone who could possibly want to see them dead or use them against me.

He must have known exactly what I was about, and he had known I would leave the memory at exactly the right time if not before. He had been happy to be captive in his memories for a little while if it would mean that I would see enough to figure out all the different parts of his plan. Even though he had resigned himself to dying, he hadn't been able to stop trying to justify himself to me.

Which meant, I thought, hot and cold at once, that my friends were almost certainly still alive. No one knew better than I did that Marazul was about the only person who could possibly do the kind of *transfer* that the message was probably talking about—a message, I was now convinced, that had come from Blackpoint. Blackpoint was probably the only person who had ever coded himself into a computer game. If I added those two behindkind together, Marazul and Blackpoint, I was left with answer that made a faint, wondering hope flicker ablaze in my chest.

Between the two of them, they could definitely have figured out a way not only to transfer the humans safely out of the human world but to store them somewhere safe—and Athelas was the only one who would have been able to figure out how to make it look like they had all died.

A lot of small, seemingly disconnected things suddenly made so much sense.

All the new gear I'd seen the humans installing in the depths of their headquarters.

The missing ears, fingers, toes—the wry jokes about parts not growing back—there was no way it didn't add up to exactly and *only* one thing.

I had messaged Blackpoint just before it happened. I'd warned him that life was getting dangerous, and that if he wanted the humans to be safe, he should probably do something about it. I'd thought he'd ignored me—or that he'd just been too late to do anything about it.

What if he hadn't been too late? What if he and the humans had cooked up something with Marazul that was so new and dangerous that no one else—not even behindkind—knew about it yet? What if Athelas, tired of death and destruction and wanting to make as big of a mess as possible, had agreed to let the humans live?

I couldn't help the grin that spread over my face. Couldn't help the tears that were already gliding down my cheeks and into my mouth. I let them alone for a moment of two, then carefully wiped them away and hurried downstairs.

"Oi, Tuatu," I said, overbalancing by the bannister as I tried to grab it with my missing arm. I steadied myself and asked, "You still got that phone of yours?"

His eyes rested on me thoughtfully. "It's basically a brick at this point, Ruth. It doesn't make calls out, doesn't take calls—it won't even let me use the browser. The books that are supposed to be in there only open after dark, too."

"But you kept it, right?" I said impatiently.

"Of course," he said, and a huge weight left my chest. "They asked me to look after their records, so I'm going to look after them for as long as they hang around. Is that what you're crying about? What's going on?"

"Nothing much," I said, still grinning and with tears leaking from my eyes again. "C'mmon, Tuatu!"

I darted across the room and up the hall toward the front door with JinYeong close behind, and broke out into a sunshine that was as physically warm as the sunshine in my heart.

JinYeong caught up with me in the sunshine, and I saw that he was grinning, eyes bright with mischief. "Life is becoming fun again," he said.

"What's happening?" demanded Tuatu, catching up with us at the front gate. "Where are you going? Why is the vampire grinning at me? I'm not open to making donations."

"You mean where are *we* going?"

"All right, where are we going?"

"We're gunna go see a merman about getting some people out of your phone," I said triumphantly. "He's pretty good at emailing humans, so I reckon he'll have an idea about how to get them out safely."

"We're seeing a merman about *what?*"

"Getting people outta your phone!" I said, with a gurgle of laughter deep in my throat. "Keep up, Tuatu! You gotta get with the new world!"

EPILOGUE

This is it. The end. What are you doing back here, anyway?

My arm hasn't grown back, if that's what you came to find out. Arms don't—not human ones, anyway. I've got my balance back, though, and Zero's been teaching me some footwork to help speed me up again, even if I can only work with one blade now. The vampire spit helps with that, too; these days I'm getting a fair bit more of it than any of my other human friends are comfortable with. They're gunna have to deal with that, because vampire spit aside, I don't seem to be able to do without the vampire himself these days.

If it's closure you want—well, I suppose I can give a bit of that, at least. I can tell you that all of us who came out of the underground alive are still alive, which means that the new king hasn't tried to have us killed. He hasn't caught Athelas yet, either. I don't think he ever will: not sure he even wants to.

It's not much, I know, and if you're feeling like there's no real closure, well, welcome to the party. Some days I still don't know if I did the right thing by letting Athelas go. Sometimes, when I'm sitting next to a warm, soft Jin Yeong, I feel as though I might one day be able to see him again. I don't seem to be able to make up my mind, and maybe that's all right for now.

Maybe right now it's just time to let all the weird, uncomfortable feelings out to untangle themselves. Apart from Athelas, most of it's a matter of trying to figure out who and what I am now that I'm no longer a pet who's nearly dying every day.

But if you just came here for a real introduction, well, here it is.

G'day. My name's Ruthanne, but everyone calls me Ruth. It's safer that way. I'm not supposed to tell you stuff like this, but I've never really followed the rules anyway. Sometimes following the rules is dangerous—sometimes it just makes you predictable. Sometimes it stops you from seeing what the rules are really there for.

You'll learn all of that sorta stuff in time, I suppose. If you live long enough.

But if you run into trouble in the meantime, just come and see us. If you know the right way to see, you can find us in a little boutique clothing store somewhere along Elizabeth Street. We help with stuff that the police can't deal with—stuff that goes bump in the night.

Heck, a few of us here *are* the things that go bump in the night.

Thank you for coming along for the ride! The *City Between* series is complete at 11 books (10 main series, and one of collected short stories). When you're done, you can go onto the 5-book *Worlds Behind* spinoff series (but not until you're finished the *City Between* series—spoilers, sweetie!) or you can take a detour from Hobart to Melbourne and dig into the *Shattered World* series (very few spoilers for the *City Between* series, and can be read either before or after!)

Please do me a favour and drop a review where you purchased this ebook (or on Goodreads) to help spread the word and also the Aussie vernacular! With the help of Bluey, we're going to take over the world one day!

9 781923 125063